## Also by Nicole Helm

BIG SKY COWBOYS

*Rebel Cowboy*

*Outlaw Cowboy*

*True-Blue Cowboy Christmas*

NAVY SEAL COWBOYS

*Cowboy SEAL Homecoming*

*Cowboy SEAL Redemption* (coming summer 2018)

# Cowboy SEAL Homecoming

# NICOLE HELM

sourcebooks
casablanca

Published by Sourcebooks Casablanca, an imprint of Sourcebooks, Inc.
P.O. Box 4410, Naperville, Illinois 60567-4410
(630) 961-3900
Fax: (630) 961-2168
sourcebooks.com

Printed and bound in United States of America.
OPM 10 9 8 7 6 5 4 3 2 1

# Chapter 1

"I CAN'T BELIEVE YOU TALKED ME INTO THIS," JACK SAID.

Alex Maguire smiled at his friend's utter disgust. The big Montana sky, famous for its size and unending vastness, stretched out blue and bright. Mountains lined the distance, and if he squinted, he could almost forget he was in the parking lot of the Bozeman airport.

It was a strange thing to be back in Montana and know it was probably for good, even though in the back of his mind, he'd known he couldn't be a Navy SEAL forever. There'd been the vague idea that, when he was old, he'd probably make it back to Blue Valley and the ranch he'd grown up on.

He hadn't expected that to happen at the age of thirty-four, and he certainly hadn't expected...well, any of what lay before him.

"So, what does this woman look like?" Gabe asked, scanning the parking lot.

Truth be told, Alex had only fuzzy recollections of his stepsister, Becca. His visits to Blue Valley had been quick and infrequent since his father's second marriage.

Alex hadn't been conscious of how purposeful that had been until news of his father's sudden death had reached him. He'd been in the rehabilitation center, recovering from his injuries. There, he'd had to come to terms with his father's death, and he'd had to face the fact that he'd avoided home over the years because he had never quite grown comfortable with the idea of someone taking his mother's place. He'd never wanted to witness it.

That meant that, including his father's funeral, he'd only met Becca a handful of times. She was almost ten years younger than him, so each time he saw her, she looked completely different. He had no idea what kind of changes she could have gone through since the last time he'd been home.

Still, he was the leader of this trio of men come to Blue Valley to build something for soldiers like them—soldiers who'd lost their purpose long before they were ready to do so. He couldn't let them think he was leading them into this blind.

Uncomfortable with that line of thinking, Alex scanned the parking lot again. "Short. Brown hair. Woman."

"How very descriptive of you," Gabe returned dryly.

"I told you I don't know her that well."

"But you trust her enough to do this?" Jack demanded. Though he sounded surly, Alex much preferred Jack surly to quiet and moody. The youngest of them—and the one who'd suffered the most—he'd had the longest recovery and seemed to be the worst for the wear.

This would fix it though. Alex was sure of it.

"My dad trusted her with half his ranch. He wouldn't do that for just anybody." Which was as true as it could possibly be. Though Becca and her mother had lived on the ranch for much of the time Alex had been away, Alex had been shocked to find his dad had left half the place to Becca, instead of leaving it all to him.

Alex glanced at the two men who had become first his brothers in combat, then his friends, then his fellow wounded veterans. They'd had their plans and dreams ripped away from them in the same instant. Over and over in the past year, Alex had vowed to himself to fix this. To give them all some hope again.

He could tell, standing in front of this vast landscape, Gabe and Jack had their doubts, but Alex would make sure no matter what it took, they would find something new to sustain them here.

"That her?"

Alex looked to where Gabe was gesturing. A small brunette was walking toward them. She had her hands shoved into her jeans pockets and a baseball cap low on her head, covering most of her face. The height and build was about right, he thought, but he couldn't see her face to be certain. Then again, he wasn't certain he would recognize her face if he could see it.

But she was walking straight for them, and that was proof enough. This was the woman he was going to share his ranch with—his stepsister. Technically. Or she had been when his father had been alive. Whatever the case, she was a part of this whole puzzle, and he had to deal with it. Accept it. Find a way to make a partnership work.

Alex liked having goals like that. The purpose. So as she approached, he did his best to smile welcomingly.

"You never mentioned she was hot," Gabe said with a mischievous grin.

Alex gave him a hard elbow to the ribs that had Gabe sucking in a breath. "You'll be respectful." He shifted on his feet as she looked both ways before crossing the road between the airport exit and the parking lot. "Besides, you can't see her face," Alex muttered.

"Her face wasn't what I was looking at."

Alex knew it was good-natured, but he also knew this was a damn perilous partnership. "You're an ass to her, you answer to me."

"Yes, sir."

Gabe offered a mock salute and Alex considered elbowing him again, but the woman was watching. When she got close enough to speak, she pushed the hat up on her forehead.

The first thought he had—one he wanted to erase immediately—was that Gabe was right. She was hot.

And she was his stepsister or whatever, so that was completely inappropriate. Besides that, she was his partner now. If he hadn't had time for women in the past few years, he certainly didn't have time for one now.

"Hi, Alex," she greeted. Her voice was soft, maybe a little…intimidated. He was used to reading people to gauge a situation, but he couldn't read Becca. Not quite nervous, definitely not confident, but none of the words he had in his arsenal adequately labeled her demeanor.

She smiled, something small and definitely timid. Fleeting. "Welcome home," she offered with a nod.

The word hit hard. *Home*. He'd never dreamed of coming home to a ranch his father wasn't running.

"Thanks, Becca. Allow me to introduce my colleagues. Gabe Cortez. Jack Armstrong. Guys, this is…" Alex realized too late he didn't remember her last name. Unless she'd taken Dad's which would have been… weird. Very weird.

"Denton. Becca Denton." She held out a hand and shook both Gabe's and Jack's outstretched ones. "It's good to have you all here. I'm sure this will be a really interesting experience for all of us."

Alex didn't miss how forced the words sounded, but he supposed a young woman inviting three former military men into her home wouldn't be easy. Even if the home was technically his.

He really had to stop thinking that way. Their home. Their ranch. Dad had left it to both of them. That was the reality, and Alex had accepted it. Just like he'd accepted his injuries and not being a SEAL anymore. He was an expert at accepting things.

"Let's get you guys to the ranch. It's a bit of a drive. Do you have any bags?"

All three of them pointed to the bags at their feet—small but all they had. If Becca was at all surprised by that, she didn't show it.

"All right. Follow me then."

They shouldered their duffel bags and followed her to the parking lot. If she noticed all three of them limped to varying degrees, she didn't comment on that either.

It was a good start, all in all. A very good start.

———

Becca thought she was doing a pretty good job of not appearing nervous even though that was exactly what jangled through her like an electrical shock. She'd been nervous about this for she didn't know how long. Probably from the very moment Alex had called her up, out of the blue, and said he was coming home.

This man she'd exchanged a handful of words with in the entire time her mother had been married to his father. After a year of letting her run the ranch as she saw fit, he'd decided he was coming home.

Coming home at the exact time Mom had finally

decided to move off the ranch. Coming home at the time she'd finally scraped out some independence and confidence in herself. Now three big, muscled military men were moving into her house—at least until they could get the bunkhouse hospitable.

She drove, focusing on the road and her breathing and trying to corral her thoughts into a sensible path. She had some issues with Alex that were neither fair nor at all his fault, and she'd hoped to never have to work through them.

She should have known life didn't work that way.

It wasn't fair to think of Alex as an enemy or as an outsider. Though she'd only met him a few times, she knew how much Burt had loved him. Burt would be overjoyed his son was coming home to build a life.

Even knowing that, telling herself that, she couldn't tap into any of that joy. She wasn't happy at all. She felt invaded. She couldn't help but wish Burt had left her the entire ranch.

*Not fair, Becca. That is not fair.*

She blew out a breath which sounded exceptionally loud in the cab of her truck. The three men were not chatting, not fidgeting. They were silent walls of *presence*.

She drove down Main Street, which cut through the valley the town had been named for. The town itself was surrounded by ranches of varying sizes, products, and degrees of success. The Maguire ranch was situated on the north side of town and dealt primarily with cattle. Quite successfully too.

No matter how many times she drove past the northern limits of Blue Valley and up the rough, curving road toward the Maguire ranch, she always remembered the first day she'd seen it. Her mom had dated Burt for a long time before she'd allowed him to meet Becca, or maybe it was vice versa. Back then, Becca had always assumed it was for the same reason Mom kept everything from her: to protect her fragile health.

It was only later she'd learned her mother hadn't wanted Becca under the influence of Burt's teenage son.

She flicked a glance at Alex.

He was exactly as she remembered him. Tall and broad and serious. He had one of those faces that looked like it was carved from granite, all intense cheekbones and strong jaw. There was a sharpness to him she'd always found fascinating and scary at the same time.

Truth be told, everything about Alex had always been a little fascinating and a little scary. He was Burt's biological son, so she'd always felt a kind of competition between him and herself, though she knew Alex felt no such thing. He was...

Well, he *was*. He was attractive. Strong and determined. Tall and solid. And his arms...

Where were her thoughts going? This was ridiculous. He was technically her stepbrother and she'd always felt weird thinking he was hot. But there he was, being all hot.

*Stop thinking about him being hot.* All three of them could have been Captain America and it wouldn't have mattered. They were going to be partners in this business endeavor she was totally, one hundred percent committed to above all else.

She'd wanted to start a therapeutic horsemanship arm of the ranch long before Burt had suffered his stroke. She'd originally planned on focusing on kids going through illnesses, but after Alex's injuries, she hadn't been able to get him out of her head. It was better than wallowing in her grief over Burt. So she'd started thinking of her dreams in a different light.

When Alex had called to talk about taking his half of the ranch, she'd had an idea ready for him. He'd jumped on it with an enthusiasm that had surprised her.

Now, they were here. On the Maguire ranch, barely knowing each other, ready to start a business together. A nonprofit. It filled her with so much joy and hope and bone-numbing fear.

"Well, here it is—your new home. Well, your old home. Home. It's…home." She pushed the truck into park and hopped out. She knew she sounded like a bumbling idiot, and she didn't plan on seeing how they reacted to it.

Ranger and Star came running from the porch, yipping and barking in happy welcome.

"Stop. Stay." The dogs wiggled into a sitting position, barely containing their excitement over new people. They wagged their tails and panted happily at the three men who assembled next to her.

Becca took a step next to the dogs, resting her hands on their silky heads. She let out a steadying breath.

"Where's Clark?" Alex asked.

It was amazing the way waves of grief could hit out of the blue. Burt's dog dying so close to Burt had intertwined the two deaths in her heart. "I'm so sorry," she croaked. "I guess…no one told you. A few days after the funeral, Clark passed too."

If Alex had a reaction to the information, he didn't show it. Not in his face, not in his dark eyes. He was completely and utterly blank.

But maybe that was a reaction in and of itself.

"We have Star and Ranger here," she offered, point-ing to each dog in turn. "We have a lot of random ani-mals around these days. I should show you around the house. I mean, I know you know the house. But I have a room, and you have... Well, I didn't know what room you would want and—"

"Becca?"

She blinked up at him, trying to get a handle on her fraying nerves. This was all so weird, and she was alone. She'd convinced her mom she could handle this, so she had to. Didn't make it particularly *easy*. "Yeah?"

"You don't have to fuss."

"Right. Right. I just... You... I can just get out of your way, and you can explore and do whatever you want, and I'll just go to the stable. I have chores and horses and..." They were looking at her like she was insane, and she probably sounded like it, babbling non-sense. But she didn't know what to do when they were all staring at her. Alex knew stuff about the ranch, but she didn't know what her role was, what he expected.

She backed away and eventually turned and tried not to run for the stable, but her pace was quite fast.

Ranger followed her, but Star stayed behind with the guys. Which was fine. Good. Great. This was all half Alex's. Why wouldn't he get half the dogs too?

Becca paced the middle pathway of the stables trying to get a handle on her breathing. There were no pressing chores, but on a ranch with cattle and horses, there was always something to do.

She'd wanted to send Hick to pick up Alex and the other men instead of going herself, but this was all part of being an adult. Proving to her mother she could handle real life. Proving it to herself. She could handle her business, handle having partners she shared a property with. She could handle being a woman.

She wasn't the sickly little girl anymore who needed all the protection in the world.

"Becca?"

Becca jumped and whirled to find Alex and only Alex in the stable doorway. "Is everything okay?" he asked.

"It's great," she said with far too much false enthusiasm. "Why wouldn't it be?"

"You're acting…a little off."

She felt defeated. Not like the strong, capable woman she was supposed to be. "Well, that's something you'd better settle in and get used to."

His mouth curved—not a smile exactly, but something soft. "This is going to be awkward at first."

She wanted to say *no shit, Sherlock*, but she was trying very hard not to be any more off-putting.

"We'll work through it. We have a common goal."

Becca nodded, but she didn't say anything. They did have a common goal, but that didn't mean things were going to get any less awkward or any less hard.

That was a lesson she'd learned a long time ago.

# Chapter 2

THE STABLES WERE EXACTLY LIKE HE REMEMBERED. IT WAS as if sixteen years hadn't passed since he'd lived here. Instead of stepping into a new location, he was stepping back in time.

The high rafters, the smell of hay and horseshit, the tools lined up haphazardly on a pegboard along the south entrance. The sounds of horses moving about and the filtered daylight.

He'd never allowed himself to wallow in homesickness while he'd been away, but it hit him now—how many years he'd missed this. Home. Belonging. The smells, the air, the freedom.

Except Becca was standing in the middle of the stables like a skittish bird. Fluttering and radiating nerves. That was nothing like the home he remembered.

He couldn't get a read on her, which was odd. He'd always been good at figuring people out, and this was just life, no added stress of, say, war to mess with his judgment.

"I don't have a key to the house," he said as gently as he could manage.

"Oh. Right."

"You know, growing up I don't know that we ever locked the doors."

She laughed, something genuine mixed with all the discomfort. "Yes, and you should have heard the arguments Burt and my mom had about *that*."

Alex tried to smile in an effort to put her at ease, but he didn't like being reminded his father had had this... whole other life. A life Alex hadn't been a part of. All of that had been Alex's own doing, but...

Well, that old melancholy was for another day. A day when he didn't have things to do and goals to reach.

*So, hopefully never.*

Becca handed a key ring out to him. "The one with a three on it. There are extras in the house, and I'll make sure to get you each one. I mean, I have them for you. I just have to hand them to..." She blinked profusely.

He couldn't even begin to figure out what was going on in that head of hers. He understood her being a little uncomfortable, a little awkward. But this was so much more than that, and Alex was at a loss for the first time since...

Well, for the first time since he'd accepted his injuries were the end of his SEAL career. It was not a feeling he enjoyed or welcomed, and he ungraciously was irritated at her for prompting it.

"I'm not used to having anyone here," she said. "I'm not used to being around a lot of people."

"We're only three."

She looked up at him through the fringe of bangs that hid her eyes enough for him to continue to have trouble reading her. "You don't really know much about me, do you?"

What the hell did *that* mean? Before he could find a gentle to way to ask, she powered on.

"Anyway, when Mom and I moved here, it was just us and Burt. Your dad hired Hick back a few years ago," she said, referencing the ranch foreman who'd worked for his dad throughout Alex's childhood. "I'm used to having the run of the place. I'm used to being alone, or very close to it. Have been most of my life. So this is weird for me, and when things are weird for me, I'm a little weird. Looking at me like I've lost it doesn't help matters."

"I'm not looking at you like that."

She shrugged, wrapping her arms around herself and squinting at the rear stable door. She still held the keys and her eyebrows drew together. Her profile was surprisingly strong for as clearly timid as she was. The midafternoon light from outside glowed against the elegant slope of her neck, the wisps of dark hair falling out of her braid. She had a strong, rounded jaw and a sharp nose. Dark, long eyelashes framed big eyes, and she had the lightest dusting of freckles on the apples of her cheeks.

Why was he noticing shit like that?

"I don't want you here," she said on something that was no more than a whisper.

But it hit him hard, like a sharp slap. He even stepped back. She'd been the one to plant the seed of this whole foundation. She'd been the one to—

"But you *should* be here, and we have something really important to build together." She looked at him then, and it almost seemed like a forced movement, like she had to fight to meet his eyes. "Just don't expect me to be Ms. Welcome Wagon or Chatty Cathy. Even if I wanted to be, I wouldn't have a clue as to how."

"So you really did learn a thing or two from my father."

She laughed, a surprisingly potent smile lightening up her pinched expression, relaxing it. "He was not an effusive man, that's true. Probably why I liked him so much." The smile died, quick as it had come. "I loved him like a father." She blew out a breath and looked away again. "He was a good man."

"Was." Alex had spent a year getting used to the fact that his father was gone, but there was something about being here, using words like *was*, that fanned the spark of grief into something bigger. "Yes, he very much was."

He rubbed at the pain in his chest. *Was.* Yeah, he didn't want to think about that. "I think you'll find three former SEALs don't need you to be chatty or welcoming. We'll focus on the ranch, and we'll try to stay out of your way. It was never my intention to come back here and make you uncomfortable."

Her lips moved, but he wouldn't have classified it as a smile, not after seeing what a real one looked like. "Oh, I seem to do a good enough job of that all on my own," she muttered. She looked down at her hands, seemed to realize she was still holding the key chain, and then thrust it toward him.

He took it, and when their fingers brushed, she jerked away. She rubbed her palms on the sides of her pants as though she needed to wipe his touch off of her. Then she clenched her hands into fists.

"Got work to do," she muttered, turning on a heel and walking toward the back of the stables.

He watched her march away, her words ringing in his head. *You really don't know much about me.* No, he didn't, and he'd never thought to find out. If he examined that too closely, he might have to admit he hadn't wanted to find out.

These were feelings he most definitely didn't want to examine. So he turned and headed for the house, ready to settle his crew in.

---

Becca worked herself to the bone that afternoon. It soothed her the way it always did, working with the animals, accomplishing routine tasks and knowing everything she did was an important cog in the machinery of the ranch.

But now she had to go in and rustle up some supper before she passed out from hunger. Except there were three men there. In her house.

She'd known this was going to happen and prepared for it the best she could, but the reality of it shook her. An embarrassing amount.

She couldn't believe she'd told Alex she didn't want him here. What on earth had possessed her? Not only was it *mean*, but it also wasn't fair. Two things she hated to be.

*She* had invited them to stay at the house until the bunkhouse was redone. *She* had suggested they meld their two dreams together. *She* had been the one to initiate this.

Why couldn't she be normal?

She glanced at her horse and rubbed its muzzle. "I'm learning. Can't be a drama queen about things being a little difficult, can I?" Pal nickered and stamped, and the calmness that came from working with the animals worked its way through her.

It was why she was doing this in the first place. She believed in what they were doing. She believed in

the healing that could be found in the life of working
a ranch.

Those men had faced far scarier situations than she
could even dream of. It was time to find the courage
she'd lost sometime in the walk from the airport parking
lot to the line of three broad-shouldered soldiers waiting
for her approach.

She'd known it would take more courage and backbone than she'd displayed in her entire life put together.
Which wasn't saying much except that it would be
incredibly challenging, and Becca was used to backing
away from a challenge.

*Not anymore. Not anymore.*

Right. She was standing up and stepping out. She
could do this. Stand on her own two feet, trust her own
decisions, interact with people.

She just needed to think of them like animals. It
wouldn't be hard. Alex already reminded her of the
quarter horses kept on the ranch. Sturdy and solid, sure
and calm. Once she spent a little more time with the
other men, she'd figure out what kind of animals they
were, and then she'd know how to deal with them.

Or so she'd tell herself anyway.

Giving the horse one last pet, Becca stepped away.
She had to face the music of her own making and inhabit
the same house as three strange men. It would be like...
college, if she'd gone. A dorm experience. Whatever
rationalizations worked.

She closed up the stables and trudged through a cold
spring evening toward the warm glow of the ranch. She
wasn't sure what Alex and his men had spent the afternoon doing. She'd kept herself scarce and out of their

way, but it appeared they'd all gathered back at home base for the evening.

Which was fine and as it should be—and *temporary*, she reminded herself. They just had to get the bunkhouse livable and then Alex said they'd live out there.

She tried not to worry too much about if that was fair or not. Alex had grown up in the ranch house, but then again, so had she. It was more a home than anything that had come before. Her first home, her first sense of freedom after years of hospital rooms and doctors' offices.

She deserved to be here as much as Alex did. Half this ranch was hers. Legally. Rightfully. Centering herself on that knowledge was important.

She walked up the wooden porch steps, avoiding the loose floorboard she kept forgetting to fix. She wiped the caked-on mud off her boots with the scraper next to the door as she looked out at the ranch.

A half-snow, half-brown landscape stretched before her until it reached the mountains in the distance. Dark, dusky peaks against a quickly graying sky. It was a salve to all the insecurities of the day, this beautiful eyeful. She'd never in her life seen anything near as beautiful as the Maguire ranch.

On a deep breath and fortified by the beauty in front of her, Becca turned and stepped into the house. She closed and locked the door behind her out of pure habit.

The entryway was as it had always been: the first line of defense against the mud and muck of ranch existence. She tugged off her boots and hung up all her muddy outerwear on the appropriate pegs.

Pegs that had been empty save her own things and Mom's minimal ranch gear, for a full year. Now they were lined with coats she didn't recognize. Masculine coats. It was difficult in a lot of ways—not just new people being in her space, but the reminder that Burt was gone.

*For good.* It wasn't the same as her mother moving into town. It wasn't even the same as Alex being deployed overseas. Burt was dead. Gone forever.

She swallowed the lump in her throat and wondered if any amount of time would ever make the grief disappear. She supposed it had lessened to an extent. She could get through hours without thinking of how much she missed her stepfather.

But when she thought of him, it still hurt with surprising force. He was the first person she'd loved and lost, and even a year later, all she could think was she had not been ready.

But life didn't wait until you were ready for things. It never had, and it likely never would.

Her outerwear having been shed, Becca stepped into the living room. The rest of the lower floor was a fairly open living space. Cozy living room with soft furniture and a stone hearth, a large kitchen that had enough room for cooking and a table to eat at.

Burt's office was off to the left, along with another mudroom for the particularly bad winter days. She hadn't been back there much the past year, and she didn't plan to start.

Luckily, her attention was drawn to the men in the kitchen. All three were gathered around the small table she had eaten almost all of her meals at for the past decade. They were chatting easily, as she supposed old friends did.

She wouldn't know. She didn't have old friends. She had Mom and Burt and the animals.

Now she had…them.

"We fixed supper," Alex offered, standing. He gestured toward a casserole dish at the center of the table. "We dug into the freezer stash. Hope that's all right."

"It's your house too. Food comes out of the collective ranch funds." She'd thought about all of this before they'd arrived, how to divvy up money and chores and all manner of things.

She wished that made it easy.

"Did you make all those casseroles in the freezer?" Alex asked, and Becca knew an attempt at conversation when she saw one, even if she usually killed any and all attempts accidentally.

"No, that was my mother. She was worried I wouldn't feed myself without her living here." It was one of the many concessions she'd had to make in order to convince her mother she could do this alone. Happily, safely.

"She's a fantastic cook. You'll have to give her our compliments."

Finally Alex sat down and Becca hesitantly made her way into the kitchen. While she'd overthought every part of what working with Alex and his Navy SEAL brothers might entail, she had never thought to envision this—Alex and his friends eating with her. Sharing a table and meals. She figured she'd still take hers alone. Be alone.

That had probably been a foolish thought, but she could do this. In fact, dinner was a great idea. She could sit down and talk to them and figure out what animals they were.

*Such a normal way of dealing with people, Becca,* she chided herself. But as long as she didn't share it with them, she supposed it didn't matter. Especially if it put her at ease.

Alex was the strong, certain leader. The quarter horse. Gabe… She had to think for a few seconds to remember who was who. Gabe was the dark-haired one, a darker complexion compared to Alex and Jack. Jack was fair. Blond hair and blue eyes. Gabe tended to smile reassuringly. Jack seemed to have a perpetual scowl on his face.

So perhaps Jack was a cat. Always unhappy and not afraid to let you know it. Gabe was easygoing, cheerful. Happy to see you, happy to go with the flow, a good ranch dog. All animals were protective of their home turf and their own. She imagined men who had been Navy SEALs would be the protective type. Courageous. Each of the three animals could demonstrate those characteristics.

There. She'd figured that out. Of course, even then, ease and comfort didn't magically settle into her. She wanted to go to her room and hide. But Alex gestured her toward the empty seat and she felt like she had to take it. She had to eat with them. She had to make an effort to be friendly.

Never mind the fact that she'd never learned how.

"Empty plate for you." He nudged it, then nodded toward the casserole dish. "Help yourself. What can I get you to drink?"

"You don't have to get me anything to drink. I can get it myself." *It's my house. Mine.* But it wasn't. Not anymore.

"All right," he returned, eyeing her carefully. She didn't like that stare. It was so analytical and sharp, like he could see right through her. But he never *stopped* the analyzing, so she doubted he did actually see.

An awkward silence settled over the kitchen and Becca knew it was her fault. She should have accepted the gesture. Why couldn't she relax?

Maybe she could drink whiskey. She would definitely relax then. The thought made her smile. Mom would have had a cow at the idea of Becca drinking alcohol with dinner. Or drinking it period.

They were all staring at her, as well they should have been considering she hadn't made a move to take the seat Alex had offered. Which was the next step then. Move her feet forward. Slide into the chair that was Burt's usual spot.

Right. Fun times. She forced herself to do it though. She was learning to apply *force* to herself, and courage. She sat and scooped herself some dinner, bound and determined to get through this thing.

"So…" She had to start a conversation. She'd killed the last one. "What are your plans for the bunkhouse?"

"That eager to be rid of us?"

She blinked at Gabe, her stomach swooping down in an embarrassed roll. "Oh, no, that's not what I meant at all. I was just—"

"Hey, no worries." Gabe flashed her one of those reassuring smiles. "It was just a joke. Teasing, that's all."

"Oh. Right. Joking." The heat of embarrassment washed over her and she knew it was obvious on her face. A red, blotchy beacon.

"He thinks he's funny, which takes some getting used to. Feel free to ignore him completely. It's what Jack and I do."

She tried to smile at Alex because she knew he was trying to make her feel at ease. He was trying to help. She was probably the only person in the world who would sit there thinking Gabe wasn't joking.

"I think this will take some getting used to for all of us," Alex said, and he really did remind her of Burt. Not so much in appearance, but in that quiet ease he led people with. A certainty he was right and knew what was best.

It was an odd comfort and a reminder that Burt had impressed upon her that she *was* capable—of running a ranch, of starting a business, of finding out who Becca Denton was beyond her old health problems and her mother's heavy-handed protectiveness.

Not only could she do this, but she would. No matter how many awkward meals she had to live through.

# Chapter 3

AFTER DINNER BECCA INSISTED ON CLEANING UP. SHE'D shooed the three of them out of the kitchen, and now Alex stood in the living room of his youth at a loss.

It was an incredibly surreal thing to have eaten dinner at the kitchen table of his childhood and not have his father there. It was beyond awkward to have a woman he barely knew doing their dinner dishes in the place his mother had once stood.

Even after dinner, he didn't have a better read on Becca. She was skittish, that was for sure, and maybe that was reasonable, but it seemed…over the top. He stared at her back, trying to work through the puzzle as she washed.

But no matter that his mother had once done the same thing in the same place—he only saw Becca. She had a slim frame and her hair was a riot of different shades of brown and red all braided together. She had her shoulders hunched over the sink as if she could block out the world.

If only he could figure out why.

He blew out a breath and turned his attention to Gabe and Jack. They were sprawled out in the living room, Jack flipping through the channels on the TV and Gabe scrolling through something on his phone. The dogs curled up on the rugs on the floor, seemingly happy with a little company.

Alex had enough responsibility to deal with before he figured Becca out, so that's what he needed to focus on.

He strode back to the entryway where he'd left his bag. Though he'd instructed Gabe and Jack on what rooms to take, he hadn't ventured to his own room yet. He'd needed some time to gear up to stepping foot into his childhood bedroom. He needed time to brace himself for the onslaught of memories that would be found there.

Alex grabbed his binder that kept his meticulously organized business notes and returned to the living room. The room was different than he remembered. He had memories of clean, gleaming dark woods and furniture and blankets in shades of tan and brown.

Now, it was colorful and cluttered, two things his father had never cared for. Even when his mother had been alive, there hadn't been knickknacks or stained glass or vases littering every surface.

Which meant this was likely Becca's mother's influence on the house, or maybe even Becca's.

He'd have been lying if he'd pretended it didn't bother him a little bit. It shouldn't have—he *knew* it shouldn't have. Still, it grated along his nerves.

Another thing to shove away for the time being. He had a foundation to get off the ground.

Alex plopped himself onto the couch and the binder onto the coffee table in front of him.

"Please, God, no," Gabe said, pretending to recoil from the sight.

"Tomorrow is the first day of this new venture. We need to go over the plan."

"Isn't the plan to figure out what the hell we need

to do to get the bunkhouse hospitable? That's hardly binder worthy."

Alex flipped to the schedules tab. "I've created a five-step plan for determining our next course of action with the bunkhouse."

"Christ," Jack muttered. "You've lost it, Maguire."

Alex ignored the bubbling urge to refute Jack's claim. An argument would hardly prove his point. He was fine. Being organized and prepared for each next step was hardly a reason for censure or concern.

"Alex. Just this one time—*one time*—couldn't we play it by ear?"

Alex hated when Gabe used that reasonable, careful tone with him. Alex had been the first one to heal, which meant he was the one most removed from the accident and the lingering effects of it. Gabe didn't have a right to be careful with *him*.

"You know as well as I do what playing it by ear gets you."

"Hardly going to die here," Jack returned, an edge to his voice Alex recognized. It was half of why Alex and Gabe had worked so hard to get Jack on board with their venture. Jack needed an extra dose of healing, but he was never going to take it.

Not unless it was under the guise of work.

"I think we need a plan." Alex glanced back toward the kitchen. "Becca? When you're done in there, can you come in here?"

There was a long pause before she offered an okay.

"She's a jumpy little thing, isn't she?" Gabe murmured. "What's the story there?"

"Hell if I know," Alex returned, his voice just as low

so Becca couldn't hear it in the kitchen. Alex focused on his binder. He'd spent the past year collecting information, making timetables, estimating cost and labor. Gabe and Jack had both been irritated with him for doing it in such detail, and for being so high-handed as to do it all himself.

But Gabe and Jack didn't seem to understand the necessity of a full, detailed plan of attack, and Alex was most comfortable with a situation when he was in charge. Being in charge had kept everyone under his care safe and unharmed.

Except for that one time. Which reminded him of the time when he'd been a boy. In a car. Powerless...

He shook it away. Neither accident was his fault. He'd been through all the required therapy. He had no guilt and no blame. None.

How could he have known some guy was going to throw a grenade into their vehicle? How could he have planned for that eventuality in enough detail that he could have kept from crashing the DPV? He couldn't. He couldn't.

His mind screamed one million possibilities, and he ignored them all. It tried to prod him with memories of his mom's accident. He pushed it all to the back. Because that's what he was supposed to do. Ignore the guilt, ignore the pain, ignore the lives that had been lost.

"You okay?"

Alex glanced at Jack, who was eyeing him with an all-too-shrewd gaze.

"I'm fantastic." He would make sure of it.

Becca stepped into the living room, hands shoved into her pockets, shoulders still hunched as if that might protect her from them.

"What's up?" she asked, her eyes darting around the room and never staying on any one thing for long.

"I had some questions if you've got a few minutes to spare?"

She glanced back at the kitchen almost wistfully, but she nodded. "Sure, I've got time."

He knew he'd done nothing to make her afraid. Clearly she had some issues, and they were all her own, but that didn't mean he wasn't responsible for putting her at ease and making sure she understood they were all on the same team here.

"I was about to go over my plans with the guys, but I definitely want your input. I had a chance to walk through the bunkhouse this afternoon while the guys were settling in, but you might know something that I didn't notice."

"Okay."

"Here. Have a seat." He gestured next to him.

If she tried to hide the grimace, she failed, but she didn't bolt. She moved around the back of the couch and sat down with a very large and safe distance between them.

"Here's my schedule for tomorrow. I want you to take a look and see if anything seems off."

She blinked down at the binder. "You already have a schedule for tomorrow?"

"I have a schedule for the next six months."

Her eyes widened and she looked up at him. It was the first time she'd done that without looking like she was working very hard to meet his gaze. Her eyes were a dark, pretty green that reminded him of summer.

"If we want to open by winter, we need a solid plan. A detailed plan. I know you probably have plans of your own. We can compare and contrast, compromise when necessary."

"I don't have anything like this. I just kind of go with the flow. Address problems as they crop up. Figure out what I'm going to do in the morning based on what happened the day before."

Alex glared at Jack and Gabe as they made choking sounds in an attempt to swallow down laughter. Well, Gabe was trying to hide the laughter; Jack made no bones about it.

Becca looked around the room at all of them. "Did I say something wrong?"

"Not at all. You just uplifted Jack's and my spirits beyond belief," Gabe said with a grin.

Her face scrunched into confusion. "I did?"

"We are constantly telling Alex to play it by ear, take it day by day. Mr. Six-Month Schedule doesn't listen."

"Just because you schedule something, it doesn't mean you're not flexible," Alex returned. He wasn't going to let Gabe or Jack give the wrong impression of him. "If something changes or something happens and we need to alter this, we can do it. I have it all saved on my computer."

Jack snorted.

"Did you do this before?" Becca asked, poking at the binder much like Gabe and Jack did. As though it were some foreign object brought from outer space.

"Before?" he grumbled, trying and failing to keep the irritation out of his tone.

"Before you went into the military? Burt and I ran the ranch in a much more…laid-back way."

Alex scowled and then forced himself to relax. "This

is slightly different. We're starting an entirely new venture. It's going to require some organization if we want it to run smoothly."

She cocked her head and studied him. It was the first time he felt like she was really looking at him. She wasn't hunched into her own world—she was trying to figure him out.

He couldn't say he liked it. "What?" he demanded.

She shook her head and smiled. Not something nervous or timid, but the kind of smile nurses gave a guy when he asked about getting the hell out of the hospital. Kind but with a little bit of pity laced in there to undercut that kindness.

No, he didn't like that at all.

"Nothing. Let me take a look at your schedule. I'll see if I have any thoughts."

She pulled the binder toward her, and Alex had to resist the urge to yank it back. He didn't particularly want an outsider's judgment, but that was going to be part and parcel with all this. Even when he didn't like it, even when she gave him that pityingly *kind* smile, he had to deal with it.

She was now his partner, which meant treating her like he'd treated his men. Gentler, maybe, since she was not a Navy SEAL or even a soldier, but with some trust.

So he linked his fingers together and tried to get over the roiling frustration bubbling through him.

⌐∞⌐

It was the first time Becca felt like she wasn't…less. Her nerves had settled, her shyness receded. Because with shocking clarity she suddenly understood Alex. Maybe not completely, but a big component of his character. It was quite familiar.

In the aftermath of her childhood illness, her mom had employed that same fervor. She'd begun to think she could plan everything out, schedule everything, protect Becca from every possible threat. Her mom had thought that, with enough control, she could ensure Becca never got hurt or sick again.

Clearly Alex had different motivations, but Becca was willing to wager he thought that, if he planned out everything, he could control his life instead of having it unexpectedly changed for him.

It was the first time since he'd arrived that she felt some empathy for him.

She looked over his schedule for tomorrow. It was meticulous to the point of…she didn't even know what. She'd never seen anything like it. Burt had certainly never been the kind of man to type things out, let alone print and organize within an inch of their lives.

Alex was a guy who seemed like he was on top of it all and had everything under control. He had that calmness that radiated off of him and made her all the more nervous.

But this… It pointed to something far different underneath that facade. It was an incredible comfort to Becca that he wasn't as with it as he appeared.

"This is a good start," she said. "I think you're going to want to bring in a professional to inspect the bunkhouse. I'm sure you can do a lot of the repairs yourselves, but you want to know the roof and foundation are going to stand up to any plans you make."

"Can you get me a list of people who'd be able to do that?" Alex returned.

"Sure. I think Connor Black is probably the only one in town. Of course, you could have someone from Bozeman come out too."

"Connor Black." Alex rubbed his large hand across his jaw. "I know Connor."

"I'm sure you know a lot of people. Not exactly a lot of outsiders in the valley. Even after being gone as long as you have." She gestured at the rest of the binder pages. "May I?"

Alex nodded his assent and she began to flip through his detailed plans. It would be good to work with someone like Alex because this was so beyond her scope. Becca had learned not to make plans. Not too far into the future anyway. Goals, yes. Plans with timelines? No.

Life could be unpredictable and she'd decided to embrace it rather than fight it. One day at a time. She'd had so many setbacks as a kid recovering from meningitis. Autoimmune problems. Minor sicknesses hitting her harder than everyone else. It had taken years to get her health under control, and then more years to convince Mom it really was.

Plans like this were great in theory, but maybe it would be good for Alex to have someone like her who knew how to change ideas on a dime. Who knew life enjoyed sweeping in and knocking your feet out from under you.

After all, hadn't she been feeling settled and happy and sinking into planning things when Burt had died?

She flipped back to Alex's plan for tomorrow. Tomorrow was all she was going to focus on. She'd leave the meticulous planning to Alex.

"Tomorrow's plan looks good. I'll get Connor's

number for you, so you can call him first thing. I have a meeting with a possible therapist tomorrow afternoon."

"Therapist?"

The sharp demand came from Jack. She had to look away from his intense and slightly angry glare.

"I have the horsemanship background, not the therapeutic part. We'll need someone who's trained. No one in Blue Valley is licensed in what I need to get my mentorship hours, so we'll have to hire someone who can do that. I've had some phone conversations with a few candidates, but this woman seems the most interested and the most qualified. I'm going to conduct a formal one-on-one interview to make sure she's what we need."

"We don't need a therapist," Gabe said, clear and flat.

"Especially a civilian," Jack agreed.

Jack's little comment had her spine straightening. "What kind of problem do you have with a *civilian*? *I'm* a civilian."

Jack didn't say anything, though he held her gaze, not once blinking his unflinching, blue eyes.

"We're bringing military men here to work and find purpose," Alex said, clearly trying to play peacemaker. "I'm not sure I agree with Gabe and Jack that we don't need a therapist on staff, but I do think it should be former military. Add to the fact that she's a woman—"

Becca whirled on Alex. "What problem do you have with her being a woman?"

"We don't have the facilities to house a woman. You can't have us and her living in the same bunkhouse as anyone who comes here. It wouldn't be comfortable for her or them. We need to focus on men. At least as we start."

"Bullshit," Becca retorted. Every single one of them raised their eyebrows at her and she was mad enough that she could only think, *Good*. Good she had surprised them and good they learned she could be...a bit nervy at times, but she had a backbone too.

"A therapist licensed in therapeutic horsemanship and counseling who has studied PTSD extensively has exactly the background necessary regardless of her military experience. Not to mention, this isn't for *men* only—there are plenty of women who've been deployed and deserve to find purpose here if they choose to."

"That would be complicated, Becca. Right now we're creating a single bunkhouse. That's not about excluding women—it's about what we can reasonably do."

"My ass," she retorted. "If we have an interested *female* veteran, we'll find arrangements for her as well. I'm not going to be the only woman here just because you guys are afraid of some breasts."

Again, she enjoyed the shocked looks on all of their faces. At least until they exchanged glances. It irritated her they could communicate with each other like that, excluding her.

At least when she was irritated with them, her fear and nerves tended to dissipate. Maybe she should just be irritated with them all the time.

"This is a group effort, I know, but the therapeutic horsemanship is mine," Becca said fiercely. "That's my baby. We agreed on that. You guys are going to be in charge of all the stuff with the cattle and bringing the veterans in. I'll handle hiring the staff I need."

"Don't you think we should have a consensus, being partners and all?" Alex asked coolly.

She glared at Alex. "No. Certainly not if you're really going to sit there and say a *licensed* therapist isn't qualified to be part of your oh-so-manly endeavor just because she's a civilian."

"That's not what we're saying. That's not what Jack meant," Alex said all too carefully, and while Jack didn't look pleased to be spoken for, he didn't say anything further.

"We never talked about having therapists wandering around. It's going to make a lot of the guys uncomfortable," Gabe said, and Becca figured it would make *Gabe* uncomfortable, but she didn't say that aloud. "At least former military adds some common bond."

"A guy who's been through what we've been through wants somewhere to have a purpose. We need work. Hard work. Value. *That's* the point of what we're doing," Alex said, his voice still so calm and even that it stoked her irritation higher.

"I think it's important we have a licensed therapist on staff," she returned with none of Alex's stoicism. "If that's going to scare you and the other men off, regardless of their military background, then you and they are not ready. You cannot heal someone who doesn't want to be healed. There has to be some desire, a desire that isn't wrapped up in whether you can be military buddies with the therapist. We haven't figured out how the program will go on the day to day, which a therapist will help us with, by the way. That being said, therapeutic horsemanship can be optional, but I'm not giving this part up. And I'm not compromising on this *necessity*. Even if it makes you lot uncomfortable."

"Why is this so important to you?" Alex asked, his voice quiet and concerned.

Which made her nerves flutter. She had a lot of reasons for doing this and she wasn't comfortable sharing them. They were personal and somewhat embarrassing.

She swallowed. "I was planning on having a therapeutic horsemanship arm of the ranch before you called and told me that you wanted to move home. Before Burt died." She took a deep breath and tried to calm her rioting nerves. She focused on finding the right combination of words to give them enough so they didn't argue with her, without giving so much of the truth she made herself uncomfortable.

"My focus was going to be kids with terminal illness, but this is pretty rugged terrain. We're isolated. It would have been difficult for families like that to get here with the health risks involved. Expensive to create the kind of facilities and doctors needed."

No one seemed particularly impressed, which meant she had to give a little bit more. She looked down at her clasped hands.

"I don't know you very well, Alex, but I thought a lot about how hard it must have been to be injured and lose your father all in one fell swoop. I couldn't help but think about how many people go through really hard things after their deployment and how they'd be the perfect candidates for hard work as healing. When you were talking about your idea to bring some soldiers home to find some purpose, I couldn't think of a better new focus for my horses than wounded veterans."

That seemed to reach them a little deeper, but still they said nothing. They didn't exchange glances or look at her—they all had a certain military blankness about their expressions. Becca wondered if it was a choice to respond that way or simply habit.

"Maybe you guys are perfectly healed emotionally." She didn't believe that, because if they were healed, they wouldn't be concerned about having a therapist on the grounds, but she'd give them their space on that right now. "But there will be men and women who come here who will need someone to talk to. Someone who can help them work through their conflicting feelings. You should all know that. Even if *you* don't need it, you should know some people will."

Alex glanced at the two stoic men he'd brought to their ranch. Becca still couldn't tell what those looks meant, but clearly they were communicating.

"All right. I think if we all agree, it's fair that Becca handles the therapeutic horsemanship without our inter-ference. We'll set it up as she had planned, allowing her to hire who she wants. If you do hire a woman, you'll also be in charge of securing housing for her."

Becca softened a little. She'd voiced her opinion, and Alex and the men had listened. Maybe she didn't need to be so sensitive, so knee-jerk in asserting her indepen-dence. They weren't her mother. "Of course."

"I'll look at the schedule and determine a good point to reconvene after we've got some guys here and see if it's working."

The warm glow of compromise faded. "What do you mean 'if it's working'?"

"If we're carrying a therapist on staff and paying her, but she's not doing anything because no one wants to talk to her, then we'll have to dissolve that part."

Becca bit back a nasty retort. She breathed. She counted to ten. She focused on the fact that she knew the soldiers would need this. They still had a lot of work to go before they got there, so she needed to hold her tongue and her ideas would prove themselves.

If they didn't, she'd fight all three men. Nerves and timidity be damned.

# Chapter 4

ALEX WOKE UP WITH A START. HE WASN'T SURE WHAT HAD knocked him out of sleep, but he looked around the darkened room and tried to calm his uneven breathing.

He was home, so to speak. The home of his childhood. The only home he'd ever really had. Otherwise, it was bases—flung all over the world. His entire adult life had been homeless in a way. He'd almost always had shelter—except for the few missions when he hadn't even had that—but never a home.

He wasn't sure he liked the idea of home. Being one place forever. Of sinking your heart and soul into something the way his father had into this ranch. It was too much, too overwhelming of a thought.

He glanced at his watch. Five in the morning. It wouldn't be the worst time to wake up. There would be chores to do and he wanted to call Connor as soon as his office opened. He wanted to look through the bunkhouse a little bit more himself and develop his own theories before the "expert" came in.

Alex rolled off the twin bed. It wasn't the most uncomfortable place he'd ever slept, but the mattress might have actually been from his childhood. He didn't know whether that was funny or not.

Last night he'd unpacked his duffel bag and placed everything in the dresser. Though this was temporary until the bunkhouse was ready, and he didn't want to get too comfortable here, where memories clouded the air like dust, he wasn't going to live out of a bag anymore.

So he'd meticulously unpacked the duffel into the ancient dresser, and this morning he pulled out a T-shirt and a pair of jeans. He gave a fleeting thought to a shower, but they needed to discuss some ground rules with Becca first.

Although she had overtaken the master bedroom with the en suite bathroom, and he and the guys were going to share the hallway bathroom, there was still a hot water issue to be worked out before someone ended up with a frigid shower.

But before any of that, he needed coffee. A nice, strong pot. He pulled on the clothes and exited his bedroom. He was immediately greeted with a little shriek that caused him to instinctively crouch.

He looked at the source. Becca. Ignoring the fact that he'd immediately gone into military mode, Alex straightened to his full height.

Becca had plastered herself to the side of the hallway wall. He tried not to notice the fact that she was wearing shorts and a tank top, clearly her pajamas.

Despite her height, she had pretty, long legs. Pretty, long, bare arms. Pale skin, freckled at the shoulders.

No bra.

Alex looked up at the ceiling. "Sorry. I didn't mean to startle you." His voice sounded oddly strangled in his own ears.

"No, it's my fault. I kind of didn't expect you guys to be walking around yet. I usually go start coffee before I get dressed." She made an odd sound, something like a throat clearing and a groan. "Not a good idea," she muttered. "I'm going to go get dressed."

Alex nodded, eyes still on the ceiling. He meant to keep his gaze focused there until Becca's footsteps receded, but somehow his eyes drifted down to her backside as she scurried away.

He most definitely did not look at her ass, because that would have been weird. And he was not weird. Everything was fine.

On a heavy sigh, Alex trudged downstairs. He measured enough coffee for ten people because he was going to need to drink enough for four if his brain was going to be this muddled.

He stood there waiting for it to brew, willing his mind blank. He heard footsteps, but they were too heavy to be Becca's. He glanced back at Gabe, who stepped into the kitchen with a yawn.

"Coffee," he said on a grunt.

"Slept well I see," Alex returned.

"You know, we've slept in a lot of shitty places. I think that's why I can't sleep in a nice one." Gabe collapsed into a chair at the table.

"We'll get used to it. You on breakfast duty?"

"Coffee first. Chore talk second."

Alex nodded and waited impatiently for the rest of the coffee to brew. When another footfall sounded, it was clearly Becca's. Soft, a little hesitant. He stared hard at the coffeepot instead of turning to face her. Not because he could clearly picture her legs or her ass in shorts or her...

He closed his eyes and counted to five. He was not attracted to his stepsister. That would be weird.

"Morning, Becca," Gabe greeted.

"Good morning. Thanks for starting coffee, Alex."

"Any day."

"How about I make breakfast?" Becca asked.

"We should probably come up with some sort of chore schedule," Alex offered. Of course, he'd already made one, but he didn't think it'd do him any good to mention that.

When Alex glanced over his shoulder, he caught Gabe and Becca exchanging a look. Which didn't irritate him. He was not irritated they could share a look already. He was glad. Glad everyone was getting along. It was great. *Great*.

"I'll take breakfast today and that's how we'll start. You guys did dinner last night. It makes sense," Becca said, moving to the fridge. She was wearing heavy jeans and a thick thermal, and she was bent over the fridge and her ass was pretty much *right there*. Which was something he didn't even notice.

He flicked a glance to Gabe, who was looking at the exact same place. Alex glared, but when Gabe looked at him, Gabe only grinned.

Alex jerked the coffeepot out of the coffeemaker. He opened the cabinet door, but where coffee mugs had been his entire childhood, there was now an assortment of colored vases, colorful bowls too big for single servings, and place mats.

Place mats.

"Coffee mugs are in the left one."

"Thanks." Alex took Becca's instruction and found the mugs. He was certain the pressure banding in his chest was a need for caffeine. Not discomfort.

He didn't care if things had changed. Of course things had changed. That was what things did. They changed. Things could look exactly the same on the outside and be completely different on the inside.

Which was a metaphor for jack shit. And it didn't bother him in the least.

He filled three mugs, leaving the fourth empty for when Jack appeared. He set one on the counter next to where Becca was scrambling eggs and then took his and Gabe's to the table.

"You, uh, said something about Dad rehiring Hick, right? Does he do the morning chores?" Alex asked.

"He handles most of the stuff with the cattle. I see to the horses. I'm sure Hick'll be glad to have help though. He's been hiring some seasonal staff, but it's hard when we don't have a place for them to stay."

"Obviously…" Alex trailed off at the sound of a—actually, he didn't know what that sound was. Gabe was looking around the kitchen trying to find the source of it too.

Becca cursed and wiped her hands on a towel before tossing it onto the counter. "Damn it, Ron Swanson."

Alex exchanged confused glances with Gabe. Gabe shrugged. Becca hurried out of the kitchen and Alex followed her. She went straight toward Dad's office, which caused Alex to pause.

Before she could get to the hallway that led to the office and the mudroom, an animal clopped forward.

Becca fisted her hands on her hips. "You know you're not supposed to do this," she scolded.

The animal was not a dog or a cat or any normal inside, domesticated pet. It was a goat. And it bleated at her as if in answer.

*What the fuck?*

Becca glanced over her shoulder at him. "Ron Swanson here figured out how to use the doggie door. When he's feeling particularly mischievous, he tends to try and sneak in."

"Why…" So many whys. "Why do you have a goat who sneaks in through a dog door?"

"Long story. Will you finish with the eggs while I get him back outside where he belongs?"

"Yeah. You grab the goat, and I'll fix the eggs. This is totally normal."

She laughed. Such a pretty sound. Oddly comforting. Strange to realize it was something he hadn't had enough of in the past ten years—pretty women laughing.

"If you came here looking for normal, boy, you came to the wrong place," she said, sounding mostly amused.

She lunged for the goat then, and Alex watched with morbid fascination. She got her arms around its neck, but it bleated and kicked and Becca swore.

"You're feisty today, Ron. I really don't like it when you're feisty," she muttered to the goat.

To. The. Goat.

The goat bucked again and Becca lost her grip as she dodged the kick. The goat took off toward the kitchen. Without thinking the action through, Alex made a move to block the hallway, but the *goat* was a tiny, little thing and darted right between his legs.

"The hell?"

"Goats are very smart," Becca replied, hurrying past him. "We better get him before he eats everything."

"Again, *how* do you have a goat that goes through the doggie door?"

"It's a—"

"Long story, right." He followed her to the kitchen, his long strides easily matching Becca's jog.

Back in the kitchen, Gabe was standing in the corner by the stove looking wide-eyed and horrified. Alex could hardly blame him. The damn animal was now standing *on top of* the kitchen table.

"Why the fuck is there a goat on the kitchen table?" Gabe asked, all but pressing himself into the corner of the counter.

"You're more afraid of a goat than a sniper?" Alex asked, grinning.

"Damn straight. I know what the hell to do with a sniper."

"He's mostly harmless, just desperate to be human," Becca said, calmly studying the goat.

Alex didn't know how to feel about this except baffled and entertained all at the same time. "With a name like Ron Swanson, I can't say I blame him."

"Do they bite?" Gabe demanded.

Becca laughed again, and Alex didn't fail to notice Gabe had much of the same reaction he did—a startled look at Becca. Then a little bit of a smile at the sound.

It was a strange moment, all in all, to feel with a true, bone-deep certainty he'd done the right thing and come to the right place. He didn't often let himself doubt it, but they needed this—laughter and home. Even if it meant a goat on the kitchen table.

"All right. Who's going to help me grab him?" Becca asked.

Alex felt a certain lightness that had definitely been missing for a while. "Since Gabe's a coward, I think it'll be me."

She pressed her lips together like she was trying not to smile as she stood next to one corner of the table. Alex situated himself across from her. Her gaze met his over the body of the miniature goat.

She grinned, a full-on grin he would never have expected from her.

"Welcome home, Alex," she said, green eyes dancing with humor.

He could only laugh.

---

Becca was running late, which wasn't that odd. She tended to get a little sidetracked by the animals and her own thoughts and inevitably lost track of time. Thank goodness for cell phones and alarms.

The potential therapist would be here in a few minutes and Becca was sweaty and covered in dirt and probably smelled like horseshit.

All in all, those were a few of her favorite things, but Becca didn't think the therapist would appreciate it. Maybe she should get used to it though. If Ms. Finley took this job, she would be spending a significant amount of time here.

Before last night, Becca wouldn't have cared if it didn't work out. She would've been happy to have conducted an interview on her own even if it had gone poorly. An adult experience that intimidated her checked off the list.

But after the men's skepticism that a therapist

wouldn't be of help, Becca was *determined* to make this work.

The morning of goat wrestling with Alex had helped her confidence a lot. He had a good sense of humor about the whole thing, and she felt more at ease around all three men. She just needed to give herself some time to get used to everything. It had been silly to think she wouldn't be nervous at first.

Of course, there was still the moment from this morning ringing through her head. When Alex had stepped out of his room and she'd been in her pajamas and... She didn't think she'd been mistaken that he looked at her breasts.

She stomped up the front porch and crossed her arms over her chest, feeling oddly self-conscious even now.

It wasn't necessarily a bad feeling, which was the weird part. There'd been a jittery sort of excitement shivering through her when she'd realized that a guy might be interested in what she looked like.

She didn't exactly hate the idea of any of them finding her attractive. She just hadn't been around enough men to know if she *was* that kind of attractive.

*You are one sick puppy.*

She pulled her boots over the scraper and then swore under her breath as a car appeared on the rise.

No time to clean herself up then. She took a deep breath to settle her nerves. If she thought of Jack's and Gabe's obvious disapproval, she could focus on proving them wrong instead of being nervous. Maybe it was messed up that she needed someone's disapproval to calm her and offer some confidence, but if that's what she needed, she'd take it.

The shiny sedan that stopped next to her truck appeared to be a rental of some kind. She needed to remember to give Alex and the guys keys to Burt's truck. If they wanted more than one vehicle between the three of them, they'd have to work that out themselves. But they could certainly have Burt's.

Even if it might kill her to see someone else behind the wheel of the old Ford.

She ignored that unwelcome thought and smiled as a blond woman got out of the car. Becca pulled off her gloves and shoved them into her back pocket as she walked toward the woman. "Afternoon. You must be Ms. Finley."

"Monica." The woman smiled and held out a hand for Becca to shake. "And you must be Becca. You have a beautiful place here."

"Thank you," Becca returned, shaking the woman's hand quickly. "We like it. I didn't have a chance to clean up, but if you'd like to come inside, we can sit down and discuss the position." Becca was so impressed with herself at how adult and in control she sounded.

She turned to the house and walked inside, ushering Monica with her. As she was gesturing her into the living room, Alex appeared at the bottom of the stairs.

Becca frowned at him. He was wearing nice clothes. Khaki pants and a button-down shirt. His hair was a little wet, like he'd just taken a shower.

"Where are you off to?" she asked before she could think better of it.

He cocked his head. "The meeting with the therapist is now, correct?"

"Yes. This is Monica Finley. Monica, this is one of my business partners, Alex Maguire."

Alex held out a hand and shook Monica's with an easy, charming smile. "It's good to meet you. What can I get you to drink? A pop? Water? Coffee?"

"I'll take some coffee, if you're offering."

"Absolutely. Why don't you take a seat on the couch? Becca, would you help me with the drinks?"

Becca trailed after Alex trying to figure out what the hell he thought he was doing. This was her deal. They'd agreed on that.

She followed him into the kitchen, lowering her voice. "Why are you here?"

"The meeting with the therapist," he said as though her question were a stupid one. "Why are you dressed like that?"

She didn't want to admit to her lack of time management, especially when she was already nervous. "It's called work. I still have to do it, even if I have to also do this. Which is my arm of the business. We agreed on that."

"Just because it's your arm and it's your decision whether you hire her doesn't mean I'm not going to be part of the meeting."

"I can't believe you're trying to take this over," she muttered while he made the coffee. She should have seen it coming. He wasn't all that different from her mother.

"I'm not taking anything over. I'm just participating," he replied calmly.

She wanted to pinch him. Instead, she would match his calm with a serenity of her own. She strode over to the cabinet and got out three mugs and then went to the cabinet where her mother kept all sorts of decorative serving ware. Even though they'd never served much of anyone, her mom had loved to collect the stuff.

Going through the array of trays and large bowls calmed her down though. It reminded her of all the things her mother had sacrificed in trying to keep Becca healthy. It was a good reminder when her head was about to explode. Sometimes people did obnoxious things from a really good place.

Alex was trying to do the right thing. He just wasn't very good at knowing how to let someone else lead. Still, he was sacrificing things for other people and she had to appreciate that.

"Do you have questions prepared? Do you have—"

And then he had to say shit like that. "You will sit there, and you will be silent as I talk to her. You offer nothing unless I directly address you. Do you understand?" It was the most forceful she'd ever been with anyone, including her mother. Who was usually the only one she ever stood up to.

But this was important, and she had to draw on that well of determination and certainty and, yes, forcefulness. She had to be a woman she'd never been before. This wasn't about Alex; it was about *her*.

"I'm not going to agree to those terms," he said, leveling her with a stare that surely worked on Navy SEAL subordinates.

"Then you are not invited," she returned, crossing her arms over her chest.

"I don't need to be invited. This is *our* business."

"The therapeutic horsemanship is mine. I won't tell you how to raise the cattle. You don't tell me how to do this. Deal?"

"No deal." He poured the coffee calmly and she wanted to scream, but she didn't. She took a deep breath.

She counted inwardly to herself until she was calm—an oasis of ease and happiness and light.

An oasis that wanted to punch him in the junk.

She opened her mouth as Alex filled the tray with three mugs full of coffee, but before she could speak, Alex did. "But I will give you one concession."

"Oh, and what's that?"

"I'll let you lead."

*Whoopdifuckingdoo.*

# Chapter 5

ALEX WAS QUICKLY LEARNING THE DOWNFALLS OF WORKING with someone you didn't know.

She didn't at all seem to appreciate he was letting her lead as she stormed back to the living room where Ms. Finley was waiting.

The potential therapist had settled herself into a chair and looked serene and at ease. That was the thing about psychologists and the like—they always looked so damn *calm* and *pleased* and it did nothing but make Alex edgy.

Luckily, he knew how to hide that, just like those people had to be hiding their own shit.

Alex passed around the coffees with his own serene smile in place while Becca asked the woman about her experience.

Oddly enough, Becca seemed at ease. He figured she'd be as skittish as she'd been with him and the guys yesterday. It was why he'd wanted to be a part of the interview. To help, to smooth over any issues. He was used to being in a place of authority. Becca clearly wasn't, but she appeared to be totally in control and comfortable.

The therapist asked some questions of her own about the position. She and Becca discussed therapeutic horsemanship mentoring, developing programs, horse care, but nothing they discussed put Alex at ease.

What he didn't know about Ms. Finley was why a young woman would want to move from Denver to the middle of nowhere Montana and try to help a handful of soldiers who meant nothing to her.

"You've given me a lot to consider," Becca said with a smile. Something about that soft, easygoing smile made him think of this morning and smooth, long legs and—nope, he wasn't going there.

"I have a question," he blurted with no finesse whatsoever.

Becca scowled at him but he ignored her.

"Absolutely," Monica replied with a nod. "Fire away."

"Why is military PTSD and recovery of interest to you?"

"My father was in the army during Desert Storm. He struggled when he returned, mentally and physically, and I was inspired to look into fields that might allow me to be of some help. Aside from that, my husband was a helicopter pilot in the army, and he was killed in Afghanistan. If you're looking for understanding, Mr. Maguire, I have it."

*Shit*. "Ms. Finley—"

She lifted a hand to cut him off. "I know how men like you think, to an extent. There's a distrust of mental health professionals and a distrust of anyone who hasn't been through what you've been through. That's understandable, but I have a unique perspective. I have observed a variety of responses to the stresses of war as a daughter, as a wife, and as a professional. I'm very, very invested in your idea and I hope you'll seriously consider hiring me."

"We'll do more than consider it, Monica. I think you'd be perfect for the position," Becca said, her tone brooking no argument.

Except Alex had some argument. They needed time to discuss this, but Becca sent him a killing glare.

"Thank you, Becca," Ms. Finley said warmly. "I do feel like it's pertinent to let you know I have a son. If you hire me, we would need to make the move before the school year starts. If you wouldn't be paying me until the men are brought on, I may need to make some alternate arrangements. And it'd be incredibly important to me that Colin be allowed to spend time here and not feel unwelcome or underfoot."

"Oh. Well, I don't see why that'd be a problem. Do you, Alex?"

Alex tried not to think too hard on it. A kid who'd lost his dad to war. He'd known those dads, who'd left behind entire families. "No," he said, surprised to find his voice sounding a little too scratchy. "We'd have no problems with that."

"Good."

"And we'll work something out about getting you guys up here before the school year starts," Becca added. "I think you'll be such an asset."

Becca and Monica stood, so Alex followed suit. While he agreed with Becca that Monica would be an excellent choice for an on-site therapist, the idea of all of it left him…itchy.

Becca and Monica shook hands, and then Monica turned to him. She offered a genial smile that put him on edge, which probably wasn't fair. He just…

He just…

Damn if he had an ending for that thought. He shook Monica's hand and tried to force a smile of his own.

She placed her hand over their clasped ones and

looked him directly in the eye. "Thank you for your service," she said emphatically.

It took every ounce of willpower not to jerk his hand away, and something about her expression gave him the more-than-uncomfortable feeling she knew that.

Becca showed Monica out and Alex stood in the living room trying to breathe through whatever the hell was working through him. He felt shaken and his breathing wasn't even, but surely it was just…hunger. Too much coffee. Why would the woman's thanks affect him in any way?

He didn't hear Becca come back inside until she spoke. He very nearly jumped.

"She's perfect. Admit it."

"She is perfect for the role," he agreed, but that discomfort in his gut wouldn't allow him to leave it at that. "I remain unconvinced we need the role."

Becca rolled her eyes and began collecting the half-full coffee mugs. Alex ignored the fact that he'd only had a few sips of his.

"What? Are you afraid she's going to find out you're not the paragon of mental health you'd like to think you are?"

He tried to refute that, opened his mouth to explain just what his thought process on the matter was, but he couldn't seem to get those all-important words out.

She glanced at him with too-soft eyes and a cocked head, her expression making him tense. "That's actually it, isn't it? You're afraid she's going to tell you you're messed up in the head."

"Hogwash."

She snorted. "Hogwash. Who says *hogwash*? Hick is like eighty and even he doesn't say that."

It had been his mother's favorite word, but he didn't want to think about that. "Hick says *fiddlesticks* instead of *fuck*."

Again Becca paused her tidying, but this time she smiled at him. Soft, sweet, tempting.

No. Wrong word. Something else.

"Yeah, he does," she murmured before walking into the kitchen.

Alex watched her disappear. It felt like things were spiraling out of his control, but he needed to stick to what they'd decided last night. Give Becca the space to do this, and reevaluate if it wasn't working.

*And the kid?*

Alex pushed the thought of the kid away. He tried to push the thought of an on-site therapist away. Jack, Gabe, and he were fine. They didn't need to get messed up in worrying about any of that.

They'd been discharged honorably and with all the debriefing required by the Navy SEALs. They were *fine*.

Let Becca worry about the therapist. She hadn't needed his help in the interview, so things were great. He needed to focus on the cattle. His plans for teaching Gabe and Jack—and the men who would come—how to be cattle ranchers.

Admittedly, back in the hospital in Texas, he'd thought ranching would be like riding a bike. He'd get back and remember all the different aspects to it, but everything was proving to be a bit more difficult than he'd imagined.

Which meant he needed to go have a good couple hours' conversation with Hick and really settle himself in for what his end of the bargain would require.

Some therapist thanking him for his service…or all the ways he hadn't done his job…weren't worth a second thought. He was fine.

No one was going to convince him otherwise.

---

Becca rode her horse through the north pasture. It wasn't part of any of her chores for the day, but as the sun set on this beautiful spring afternoon, she'd wanted some alone time. Time to breathe. Some time to ride in the cool but vibrant air.

She was going to have to explain to the guys that her mother was coming for dinner tomorrow. She was going to have to warn them about the way her mom would fuss and say all sorts of things that would make everyone uncomfortable.

Becca could ask Mom not to go on and on about how the men needed to take care of Becca. She could beg her mother not to badger them with directives on how Becca needed someone to make sure she was healthy and safe, but if Becca told her not to do it, she was almost certain Mom would do it all the more.

It was going to suck, but Becca couldn't dwell on that. She was still just happy her mom had given her some independence by moving off the ranch. Something Becca couldn't have dreamed possible in the direct aftermath of Burt's death.

Becca drew her horse to a stop at the top of a swell of land and looked out over the mountains in the distance. It was the most beautiful sight in the world. Awe inspiring. Every time she looked out at those mountains, she knew she had a place here. Felt it deep in her bones and her soul. She belonged to this ranch and she was doing some good with it.

Moments like this filled her with a renewed sense of purpose. Every time she'd gotten so worried about Alex and his friends coming that she'd been ready to call him up and call it off, she'd ridden out here and found her strength again. Her courage.

Becca watched the blaze of gold fall deeper behind the mountains. Bitter cold swept in fast, but she could feel spring in the air, the way the snow melted throughout the day. No more had fallen for a week. A good late-winter storm could swing through and bury them again, but spring was getting there. Rebirth and renewal were everywhere.

She'd needed that reminder last year, repeatedly. That new things and lives could come from death and grief and cold. She needed the reminder again this year as she started this new venture. And found her strength. The strength in herself.

She'd done a great job yesterday with Monica, and Becca was so excited to have a woman that passionate and skilled and invested on board.

Of course, Becca was more than a little curious about the way Alex had paled when the woman had thanked him for his service. It reminded her a little bit of his expression when she'd told him "welcome home" at the airport.

The man thought he was Mr. In Charge and In Control, but Becca was beginning to see a thread of something underneath that. She hoped Monica's presence would help all three of the guys. They might not think they needed some therapy, but Becca was quite certain they did.

She nudged Pal to turn and head back to the ranch. Pal needed little encouragement to take off. She was a calm, steady horse, but she loved to gallop as much as Becca loved the freedom to enjoy it.

As a teenager, she'd been afraid. Afraid of testing her limits and the way any testing might hurt her mother. But Burt had encouraged her to take a few risks. To find her own way. Now, she couldn't gallop across the ranch and not miss him.

The pain of missing him was starting to get to be an almost-good type of hurt. It still made her sad he wasn't here, but it felt good to know he'd be proud of what she was doing. He'd be proud of her.

She wondered if Alex knew how proud Burt had been of his son the soldier, the SEAL.

Out of sheer habit, Becca pulled on her reins and slowed Pal down before she reached the view of the house. Mom wasn't there to scold, but it wasn't easy to break ten years of habit.

She nudged Pal to walk toward the stable, but she heard voices on the opposite side of the stable and rerouted Pal to go around instead of inside. They turned the corner of the building and found Alex, Jack, Gabe, and Hick standing around Magnolia, the horse Burt had bought for Mom.

A good horse, stable and calm. Used to nervous or finicky riders, which made Becca think this was some kind of lesson.

Hick was shaking his head and Alex looked stern and disapproving. Gabe was laughing. Considering Jack was leaning against the stable wall and scowling, Becca had a feeling he was being uncooperative.

"I'm not getting on the fucking horse. You never said getting on a horse was part of this."

"You've stared down men with assault rifles, Jack. How the hell are you scared of a horse?" Gabe asked, clearly needling him.

"I'm not scared of the horse. I grew up on a damn farm," Jack retorted. "I got a chunk blasted out of my leg. I'm not looking to break it trying to get on that thing."

Becca urged Pal closer to the group, finally garnering the attention of the men. Gabe and Hick smiled and nodded their greeting, Jack cursed, and Alex looked at her with a focused intensity she didn't understand. She didn't think she'd ever understand him.

"Look, Becca's not afraid of a horse, Jack."

"Shut the fuck up, Gabe."

"Why don't you hop on, Gabe?" Becca offered, smiling sweetly.

Gabe grinned. "Touché. I like her."

She rolled her eyes and dismounted, walking Pal over to the guys. So far, she'd heard them all swear at Jack and accuse him of being afraid, but she hadn't heard anyone offer any kindness, especially considering he was worried about his injuries.

Maybe that would be her role here, with these three very different men—a little kindness.

"You know, when I moved here, I was intimidated by the size of the horses."

"Okay, if she's going to try and psychoanalyze me, I'm getting on the damn thing." Jack finally moved off the wall and over to the horse. Though irritation and maybe anger radiated off him in waves, he approached the horse exactly as he should have.

He used all the right holds, had all the right footing. Though his overall mount was a little bit clumsy, it was technically perfect.

"There. Happy?"

Becca grinned. Maybe it had been accidental—she hadn't thought kindness would spur him on quite *that* way—but *she* had been the one to get him to do it. Still counted.

"Do you want me to teach you how to—"

"Fuck off," he muttered. He very cautiously but correctly nudged the horse forward. He had the appropriate grip on the reins, best posture in the saddle.

"You're doing an excellent job for a beginner," she called.

He flipped her off and she laughed. It very nearly felt like having a brother, or what she'd imagined having a brother would be like. When she turned to face Gabe and Alex, they were staring at her somewhat openmouthed.

She ignored the errant thought she didn't feel particularly *sisterly* to Alex, and she was step-related to *him*. "What?" she asked.

"We've been trying to convince Jack to get on that horse all damn day. It took you about three words." Alex was frowning at her.

Becca flashed him a smile. "I bet you never tried to be nice."

"He hates when people are nice to him," Gabe returned.

"Well, apparently the thing he hates is the thing that got him up there." She shrugged. "You're welcome."

"She's smart," Gabe said, somewhat in awe, as though he were surprised.

"And *she's* right here," Becca said. "You can stop talking about her as if she weren't."

Gabe laughed, good natured as ever. "Yes, ma'am."

"So, when are *you* going to get on a horse?"

Gabe cleared his throat. "Today was Jack's lesson."

"Uh-huh. And what about you, Alex? Did *you* get on a horse, or did you just give Jack shit all day?"

Alex's eyes narrowed a fraction. "I grew up here. I know how to ride a horse. I don't need any lessons."

"Really? Want to race?"

He took a step forward and opened his mouth to say something, but his leg seemed to give out a little bit on the hard step forward. He corrected quickly, but up until that point, she'd thought Alex completely healed of his injuries. He didn't noticeably limp the way Jack and Gabe did. Clearly he was mostly healed, but that near stumble pointed to some residual effects.

"It's almost dinnertime. It's your turn, isn't it?" Alex said, his voice flat and his expression inscrutable.

"It is indeed," Becca returned, forcing a pleasant smile. "Come on, Pal," she murmured to the horse, giving his reins a tug as she walked toward the barn. "Hope you like salad," she yelled over her shoulder, hoping to get a laugh or a smile at least.

She got both from Gabe, neither from Alex. Not exactly a surprise.

Though she felt good about herself for helping get Jack on the horse, she was a little bit concerned about how she might have made Alex feel in regards to his injuries. She needed to be more careful. She couldn't let the fact that the guys gave each other shit make her think she could do the same.

She didn't know them as well as they knew each other. She didn't know their vulnerabilities, though it was hard to imagine Alex having any. Still, she had to be more careful.

She took Pal into the stable and led him into his stall. She talked to the horse as she brushed and groomed him. Since she'd never had friends, had never actually gone to school, she had always talked to the horses. She'd participated in a few homeschool outings once she'd gotten older and Mom had finally relinquished some of her tight-fisted control, but the ranch animals had been her friends. It was a one-sided relationship, sure, but when it was all she had, she had to go with it. Had to get what satisfaction out of it she could.

"It's not so one-sided, is it, baby?" she murmured, brushing Pal down. "But I do need to get better with actual people since actual people are going to be here." Actual people. Mostly men. Soldiers. Hurting. Healing.

"I just have to remember no matter how obnoxious they are, I can't provoke them. It isn't fair."

"Neither is treating us with kid gloves."

Becca screeched and dropped the brush. She pressed a hand to her heart as she turned to find Alex walking toward her.

"Why are you eavesdropping on me?"

"Why are you talking out loud if you don't want to be overheard?"

She turned back to face the horse, grabbing the brush and focusing on finishing the job. Brush, comb, wash. All while trying to fight the embarrassment swamping her. "I wasn't talking about treating you with kid gloves," she muttered.

"It's exactly what you were doing." He'd gotten closer, had to be standing at the entrance to Pal's stall for his low voice to be that clear. "Unless you can explain some other reason why you think provoking us would be unfair."

Becca frowned at Pal's flank, trying to find the words that would refute that, but he had a point. Maybe she was talking about treating them differently, but there was a reason. A good one.

"Your leg buckled," she said, her voice so quiet and squeaky it was a wonder he could hear her at all, but she could tell from the way the air went tense and still he had heard.

"I can race you. Race right now," he finally responded, his voice cool and sure.

She shook her head, irritated enough with him to get over her embarrassment and meet his challenging gaze. "You're going to let your pride hurt your injuries?"

"I'm healed." He was standing at the entrance of the stall, far too…broad and foreboding and clearly angry.

"Look, I'm sorry if something I did or said hurt your pride or whatever, but—"

"You didn't."

"Then why are you looming there?" she said, gesturing at him with the sponge she'd grabbed to wash Pal down with.

He opened his mouth but eventually only closed it without saying anything.

"Exactly. Your knee gave out. It's nothing to ignore. Certainly nothing to be ashamed of."

"I damn well know my injuries are nothing to be ashamed of." But he said it with a fervor she almost didn't believe.

She didn't like him still standing there, so she did the same thing she'd done to Jack. Employed some kindness. "Would you consider telling me what happened?"

He stiffened and backed away, the fierceness in his nearly golden-brown gaze dimming into that shuttered thing he did. Though his reaction had been what she'd expected, his words surprised her.

"It was a crash. A grenade was thrown into the back of the vehicle I was driving."

Becca couldn't have hidden her horror if she'd tried. He said it so flatly. She couldn't imagine it—not that she'd been able to imagine any scenario that wasn't horrifying.

"Most of my injuries were sustained when I ran into an embankment due to the explosion. Gabe was next to me and in the seat that took the most damage from the crash. Jack was in the back. His injuries mostly stem from the grenade blast."

She'd lost track of washing down Pal, was blindingly aware of how *hard* she'd thought her life was being sick and having an overprotective mother. But Alex, and Gabe and Jack, had gone to war. *War*. As a choice.

"You didn't get any injuries from the grenade?"

His eyebrows drew together, the only not smooth, not calm thing on his face. He squinted out the barn doors. "There was another man in the car who stepped on the grenade and positioned his body so he'd get most of the force of the blow, which lessened its impact on the rest of us."

Becca blinked. She couldn't bring herself to ask, but she had a bad feeling she knew what had happened to the fourth man.

"My lingering injuries stem from the vehicle folding

in on my knee, requiring what amounted to a knee replacement. My knee is fine now. I just sometimes don't have all the strength it needs, but it's only a matter of time until I'm completely recovered."

"Is that what the doctors say, or is that what you say?" When he didn't respond, she knew what the answer was. "I see. Well, I have no intention of treating you or Gabe or Jack like some sort of delicate invalids. I just want to strike the right balance. You three know each other. You've been through hell together. You have the right to jab at each other, and I don't…I don't know you well enough to get into that."

"If they're jabbing at you, you can jab right back. You don't have to feel bad about that. Jack can be a surly ass, and Gabe's an obnoxious moth—" He stopped and cleared his throat pointedly.

She smiled, happy for the bit of levity. "What about you?"

"*I'm* a perfect gentleman."

She laughed, and though he frowned, she saw a little glimpse of humor behind it. It was a nice moment to have some humor. It'd been a long few days of…well, not really understanding each other. It would take time to find that understanding, but she liked the progress they were making.

What she didn't quite like—or maybe more accurately didn't know how to feel about—was that little tickle in the bottom of her gut whenever their gazes met. Like nerves, but not like the nerves she knew so well. It wasn't about not knowing what to say. It wasn't even not knowing what to do. It was something else. Something she'd never felt before.

She got the strangest notion he felt it too because he wasn't saying anything and he was staring at her. Just as she was staring at him. The moment held too long, and a prickly awareness spread across her skin as though he'd touched her. He hadn't, wasn't even close enough to.

"My mother's coming to dinner tomorrow night," she blurted. She had no idea why all of a sudden she was nervous with him again.

"Well, we can give you your space."

*If only.* "You misunderstand me. She's coming to dinner to meet you. I mean, all of you. This is fully a check-on-Becca dinner and all three of your presences will be required."

"Not necessary. We'll make ourselves scarce and you can have a nice meal with your mother."

"You obviously haven't spent enough time with my mother to understand that *no* is not an option."

"I'm a grown man and a soldier."

"But you are no Sandra Denton."

He gave her an odd look, almost like he didn't believe her. But he'd see. Oh, he'd see, and Becca could only hope she wouldn't be too embarrassed to enjoy it.

# Chapter 6

ALEX WASN'T SURE HE'D EVER BEEN SO WRONG ABOUT someone in his entire life. Usually his initial impressions of people stayed pretty much the same throughout his knowing them. Jack had certainly changed since the beginning, but Alex had always known there was the potential for Jack to turn into the angry, bitter person he'd become since the explosion.

Gabe was Gabe, and though Alex didn't think too many people saw underneath the facade, Alex always had.

Everyone he'd ever met fell into the rigid assessments he'd made of them from the beginning.

Except Becca Denton. Who was currently treating them to an inspection that would have rivaled any general's. She'd insisted Gabe change clothes, and when Gabe had laughed at the idea, Becca had not. She had gotten right up into Gabe's face, finger wagging, and Gabe had promptly hurried upstairs to change.

Even though it wasn't her turn, she had made dinner because she had some clear-cut plan about what to serve to get her mother's stamp of approval.

Alex didn't understand it. He'd met Sandra Denton a few times. He'd attended his father's small, intimate wedding celebration and then had to return to base immediately after. He'd spent two Christmases on the ranch before he'd been either deployed or made sure he'd be otherwise unable to get home.

He'd barely been conscious through his father's funeral due to the pain he'd been in and had gone back to the recovery center in Texas immediately after. After that, there'd been no reason to come home.

Still, in those short meetings and the conversations with his father over the years, Alex had gathered an impression of Sandra. Nice enough. Eager to please, but also willing to give him his space. He'd liked that about her.

Though it had been a little too weird for him to fully embrace her as the woman of the house, he'd never disliked her for taking that place. His issues had nothing to do with her or how she'd handled anything.

But if he were to judge Sandra by Becca's behavior, he might've guessed she was Attila the Hun. If he went by how Becca was acting, his analysis of the situation would be this dinner was life-or-death.

"Now, I just need you three to understand that for a lot of different reasons, my mother is very protective of me and she can sometimes be a little overzealous in her concern. Hopefully I can convince her that this is fine, and I'm fine, and all of this is…fine."

"You don't seem fine," Gabe replied.

Alex gave him a little nudge in the stomach. Clearly the girl didn't need any poking right now. "We're prepared to have a nice supper. We'll eat. We'll converse."

"It's hardly worth having a stroke," Jack muttered.

"Glad you think so," Becca returned.

"Knock, knock," someone called from the entryway.

Sandra appeared in the living room and looked exactly as Alex remembered—a healthy, middle-aged woman who clearly cared about her appearance. She was dressed well and neatly, makeup subtle but there.

It was interesting he could see a resemblance to Becca if he looked hard enough, since they were clearly very different women.

Sandra was smiles and charm and control. She moved through the world sure of her place in it. Becca... Lord, she did none of that. Though that was part of her charm.

Not that he found her charming. Just that she was... not terrible to be around. That was all.

"Well, aren't you three veterans quite the picture?" She smiled at all of them, and for the first time, Alex wondered if Becca might actually have a better read on the situation than he'd thought. Because that smile was... He didn't have a word for it, but it made him uncomfortable. Nervous almost.

"Alex, it's so good to see you again." She didn't reach out to hug him, and for that he was more than grateful. "You're looking well," she said, clearly assessing every inch of him. Much like his dad used to assess a horse or cow.

"Thank you," he offered, trying to get a handle on the weird atmosphere.

"I'm so excited to hear more about your venture. I know Becca had her heart set on this, and I'm so glad it's happening." She moved over to her daughter and enveloped her in a hug.

Alex could have been wrong, but he thought she whispered something about losing weight in Becca's ear. Which made no sense whatsoever as Becca was a tiny thing.

"Come into the kitchen. Dinner is almost ready," Becca said. Her posture was rigid, but she looped her arm around her mother's waist affectionately.

"Now, Becca, no rushing. We should sit in the living room and chat and catch up. You still haven't introduced me to these two other men."

"Right. Right." Becca's smile was a dismal failure. "What can I get you to drink?"

"Lemonade."

Alex knew Becca hadn't made lemonade, but she smiled and agreed, so he requested lemonade as well, giving Jack and Gabe looks to make sure they did too.

"I'll be right back out with that."

"Excellent." There was something predatory in Sandra's expression that continued to poke at Alex's unease. "Let's sit, gentlemen."

He exchanged a look with Gabe, who didn't look quite so amused as he had five minutes ago. Yeah, this was weird.

Sandra settled herself on a chair, and he and Gabe sat on the couch, with Jack in the chair across from Sandra. "The three of you are living in a house with my daughter. I think that gives us much to discuss." Though she spoke to the three of them, her gaze honed in on Alex.

"Only until we get the bunkhouse settled," he returned coolly and evenly.

"And when will that be?"

"As soon as we're able. But regardless of the time it takes, there's certainly nothing for you to be concerned about."

"Nothing to be concerned about?" Sandra made a sound, something like a laugh or a scoff that rubbed Alex the wrong way. "My daughter is an innocent, sheltered young woman. Alex, I know you're a good man. I wouldn't have agreed to give Becca her living space if I didn't believe that. So I need you to understand I'm entrusting you to make sure nothing hurts my daughter."

"I have no intention of hurting your daughter."

"Burt had no intention of leaving us, but things happen. I don't care about intentions. I care about results. But above all else, I care about my daughter. Her safety and well-being and health. I want make sure all three of you understand I hold you personally responsible for anything that happens to Becca while you are living under the same roof."

Alex had a few retorts for that, but he tried to keep them to himself. This was Becca's mother and his father's widow, and it would be best and fairest if he bit back his irritation. Still, Becca was a grown woman, in charge of her own well-being and happiness. Didn't he have enough to worry about with Gabe and Jack and this business? Becca was *not* his responsibility.

He'd been telling himself that for days now, and he wouldn't let Sandra derail his determination not to take another person under his care.

So as kindly as he could manage, Alex smiled. "Noted."

Becca returned and everything about Sandra's posture and expression softened. Alex didn't understand this dynamic at all. He didn't care for that feeling of being out of the loop.

He looked at Becca, who was timidly serving them all lemonade, and it bothered him—no matter how much he didn't want it to—that her shy discomfort was back.

She wasn't his responsibility—she *wasn't*—but that didn't mean he wasn't going to figure this whole thing out.

Dinner was exhausting. Becca had known it would be, but it was even worse than she'd anticipated. Trying to lead her mother away from comments about her health or her ability to take care of herself required second-to-second diligence.

Then there was dealing with three men she didn't know all that well interacting with her mother, on top of getting used to interacting with them herself. Becca didn't know how to navigate those waters. This was all so much.

By the time she ushered her mom to her car and watched her drive away, it was nearly ten o'clock and Becca was completely and utterly beat.

But as she walked back up to the porch, she didn't immediately head inside. She sank into the little rocking chair her mother had always used in the evenings. Burt and her mom would sit out here every night that was warm enough and watch the sunset, talking comfortably, happily—always after her mom had told her to go inside and stay warm.

Becca missed those days acutely. She'd always wondered if she'd ever have anything like that. She still did.

She rocked back and forth, watching the big, starry sky above. She could have drifted off right here, even though it was freezing. Instead, she eyed the moon, counted the stars, breathed in the icy spring night.

When the door opened and Alex stepped out, she didn't have the energy to be surprised or uncomfortable.

"That was quite an evening," he offered into the quiet night.

"I told you it would be."

"That you did." He sank into his father's chair. Not a cushioned rocking chair like hers, but a hard, straight-backed wooden piece. It had been a surprise to her over the course of living here that a man like Burt, hard and tough in everything he did down to the chair he sat on, had so much softness inside of him. She wondered if Alex might have the same thing. Which shouldn't—didn't—matter one way or another.

"Your mother is a little different than I remembered."

"You were never around much."

"True, but as I was sitting at that table with the both of you, I realized neither were you. Whenever I was home, you were scarce."

Becca wasn't sure how much to tell him. She didn't particularly like broadcasting her weaknesses, but at the same time, they were basically living together. Keeping everything a secret didn't make any sense.

"Mom was never sure about us spending much time together."

Alex straightened, his gaze sharpening on her in the yellow porch light. "Why the hell not?"

"It's not personal. She actually didn't want me spending much time with Burt at first either. Or anyone, really. She's always been overprotective."

"Why?"

She bristled a little at the demand in his tone. "Does there have to be a reason?"

"There doesn't have to be, but I get the feeling there is."

She fidgeted in her seat, focusing on the stars and the reassurance she got from that sight. "When I was five, I got very sick. Meningitis. It was a serious case and it took me a long time to recover. I had a lot of auto-immune issues afterward. So even after I'd recovered from the meningitis, the threat of a common illness was much worse because my body had lost a lot of its ability to fight germs and the like. Flu—hell, even a cold. It was dangerous to my well-being."

"So she kept you away from anyone who might have germs?" He sounded so judgmental when it was actually completely reasonable, if a little…stifling.

"She was constantly worried I would get sick again. That I would *die*. I'm her only child. My father disappeared before I was even born, *after* her parents kicked her out for getting pregnant. I was all she had, and she did everything to protect me. Maybe it seems weird now, from the outside, but she did what she had to do."

"I had no idea."

"Mom didn't like to talk about it. I didn't really care to either. It's a very weird existence, knowing how precarious your health is and being a kid and… Well, anyway. She didn't even tell Burt at first. I think she felt guilty or to blame, but your dad did so much for both of us. My life was different for Mom marrying him, for moving here. Things were getting looser, but Burt dying so suddenly… She found him, and it kicked things into high gear again. So I know she can come off harsh, but don't be too hard on her."

"That's…a lot."

"Yes. It is. I worked really hard to get her to move into town where she'd be happier, but that doesn't mean trusting me to take care of myself is easy for her. If she said something about watching after me and making sure

I'm safe or whatever, ignore it. She thinks I'm fragile, and I haven't figured out how to convince her I'm not."

"You're not?"

It would have irritated her, but he asked the question with a hint of a smile, as though the idea of her being fragile *was* smile worthy.

"No. I'm not. I'm completely healthy. Admittedly people aren't my strong suit, but I'm getting there. I'm not a responsibility, Alex. Certainly not yours. I'm not anybody's responsibility but my own."

"So *that's* why she said something about your..." Alex cleared his throat and looked away.

"My what?"

"Ah, your weight."

Becca rolled her eyes. "She always thinks I've lost weight. Even when I've gained. She can't help her worrying and I just have to go with it. I dream someday she'll believe I'm fine, but sometimes I think that might just be a dream." Becca clasped her hands together. She needed to stop babbling and go inside and get some sleep.

But Alex had come out here and she had a feeling he had a mission. She had a feeling Alex didn't do *anything* without a distinct mission. "She did ask you to watch after me, didn't she?"

"I'd say it was more of a warning."

Becca had to smile at that. "And were you and your soldiers intimidated by a middle-aged woman's warning?"

Becca snuck a glance at Alex, and the way his lips curved made something flutter and tumble in her stomach. She could count the number of genuine smiles he'd flashed in her presence on one hand, and every time, it hit her like that—a flutter, a horse galloping underneath her dip of feeling. He seemed so different when he smiled.

"Intimidated isn't the word I'd choose, but she's certainly formidable. But then again, so are you."

"Me?" she scoffed. He was messing with her. She wasn't about to believe he viewed her as *formidable*. Maybe, *maybe* not a total basket case, but not formidable.

"What? You see yourself as some sort of retiring weakling?"

"No, but intimidating might be a step too far."

"You got Jack up on the horse. You made us dress and behave a certain way for this dinner. Intimidating, maybe not, but when you want to be, Becca Denton, you can be very, very forceful."

It was a compliment that shouldn't have warmed her so much. His opinion shouldn't have mattered. But it did. She was very nearly giddy at the thought—not just that she *was* a force to be reckoned with, but that Alex thought she was. A man who'd been through so much, seen more awful things than she could probably imagine. *He* thought *she* was something to be admired.

"Don't let that go to your head."

"No, it's too late. My head has swelled. I am a forceful presence. You can't take it back."

"Good. You have every right to lead your own life. We all do."

She stared at him a few minutes, trying to work through the surety with which he spoke, the odd note in his voice. Not gentleness exactly, but something close. "I can see why you were a good leader, Alex."

"Yeah? Because *I'm* so forceful?"

"No, because you know when to give someone

a hard time and you know when to give them a big head, and I think…this is going to *work*. Don't you think?" She grinned, couldn't help it. That surety that had driven her this far bubbled up. Strong and *forceful*. "This is a really good idea, and I think we'll make a really good team."

"Believing is the first step." Alex leaned forward, resting his elbows on his knees, clasping his hands together. He looked out over the night sky and she watched him. The grooves around his mouth, the lines fanning out from his eyes, the way the yellow light glinted off his tawny hair.

He watched the stars as if they spelled out the answers to all the world's problems…in a language he didn't understand.

"I didn't realize how much I missed this place, I don't think. Not until…this."

"How come you so rarely came home?"

He flicked her a glance, one of those shuttered gazes where he cut off any and all emotional response. She wished she could dig under that and read him better. Understand him.

"Being a Navy SEAL takes a lot of time. I was deployed a lot. Hard to come home."

"You…" It probably wasn't any of her business what kept him away—because it had to be something. He'd had a good relationship with Burt, and Burt had always wished he'd come home more.

Not that Burt would have ever admitted it aloud, to Alex or Becca, maybe not even to Mom. Becca wondered if it would be a comfort or another wound to tell them how much Burt had missed his presence on the ranch.

Maybe there was a way to get that across without coming out and saying it. "I know how happy he'd be that you came back."

Alex's expression didn't change, but he immediately got to his feet. "Good night, Becca. Early morning." He strode inside without a look back.

Well. She'd hit a nerve, and she was a little tempted to hit it again and figure out what was at the bottom of it.

But for tonight, Alex was right. Tomorrow was an early morning with lots of work to do.

# Chapter 7

ALEX SLEPT LIKE SHIT, THOUGH HE DIDN'T HAVE A CLUE AS
to why. He'd gotten into bed later than he'd wanted to
for his five o'clock in the morning alarm, but it hadn't
been late enough to feel this beat up.

He scrubbed his hands over his face, not wanting to
dwell on the whys of it. Time to get up and get to work.
Hick was going to run them all through the cattle paces
today. Alex had no doubt it would come back to him
once his body got to doing the work.

Regardless, getting up, getting on a horse, *working*
would all feel good. It would settle some of that restless
discomfort from last night.

Becca's words about Dad...

No, he wasn't thinking about that this morning. He
was thinking about the future and not the damn, unfixable past.

He needed a hot shower and some hot coffee and
his head would be clear. Luckily, Becca took care of
coffee in the morning, so he could head straight for
the shower.

On a yawn, Alex crossed the hall to the bathroom and
ran through the shower.

He stepped out and toweled off, dreaming about that
first cup of coffee and a morning spent working with his
hands. It was a good way to start the day, no matter how
tired he felt.

He pulled on his boxers and his jeans and frowned at the now-gone pile. He must have dropped his shirt and socks somewhere along the way.

He scratched a hand through his wet hair and then shrugged. At least he hadn't dropped the boxers.

He stepped into the hallway and reached out to open his bedroom door when Becca crested the stairs, clearly returning to her room from starting the coffee.

"Oh." She stumbled to a stop, wide-eyed and deer-in-headlights-esque.

"Morning."

"You're naked."

He frowned and looked down at his *clearly* clothed bottom half. "I have pants on."

Her pale cheeks turned bright red and she squeezed her eyes shut. "Right. Right. I just meant…"

Alex didn't understand why she was acting so weird, but he pushed his door open and went inside to grab the shirt he'd dropped. Surely she'd seen a shirtless man before.

*Or maybe she hasn't.*

He shook that thought away and looked around his room, but there was no dropped shirt, no misplaced socks. No clothes anywhere. He'd never grabbed them. He frowned, looking around the room one more time to be sure.

He'd just…forgotten half his clothes. Which was completely out of the ordinary for him. He was always prepared. Always had everything he needed.

He took a deep breath, settling that flutter of panic in his chest that didn't belong. Sleep deprivation was messing with his head was all. Of course, he'd been a

SEAL and dealt with a lot less sleep while leading harsh, important missions.

"You have a tattoo. Of a star."

He didn't jump or flinch, though it bothered him she was standing there behind him and he hadn't noticed. "Are you just going to follow me around and point out the obvious?" He knew his tone was snippy, but he didn't need her talking to him while he was trying to get his brain to function without caffeine. Lack of caffeine was his only problem for sure.

When he turned, she was standing there in his doorway, staring still with that wide-eyed expression.

"What?" he demanded.

"I'm trying to figure out why you would get a tattoo of a star." She chewed on her lip, staring at him as though she could see things in his expression he didn't want anyone to see. Ever. She smiled. "That doesn't seem very...manly."

Teasing him. On purpose. It pissed him off even as that band of something close to panic eased. "It's the North Star. It's supposed to lead you home. Now, if you're going to insult me, at least wait until I've had my coffee."

"Should be ready," she murmured, and then she stepped away from the doorway, and he heard the slow footfall of her walking away.

Alex jerked a shirt out of his dresser and then his socks. His brain was fine. He just needed time to adjust.

And his tattoo was not unmanly.

He headed downstairs toward the smell of fresh coffee. That was all he needed. A hit of caffeine and a few quiet moments, and the rest of the day would be fine. He could get over the weirdness of this morning. It was just forgetting a few clothes on the way to the shower. Why was he so worked up about it?

"Your brain is fine," he muttered into the kitchen.

"You know my fourth-grade teacher told me people who talk to themselves are insane, so maybe your brain isn't so fine."

Alex glared at Gabe.

Gabe grinned and found himself a mug. "Worried about the state of your mental health?"

"Hell no. Forgot something this morning. I'm sure it's fine. Hard to sleep here."

"I think I finally got a decent amount last night," Gabe said, pouring his coffee.

"Good because I'm getting your ass up on a horse this afternoon."

Gabe grimaced. "I don't know why the damn things are so much bigger than I imagined."

"I never took you and Jack for such a bunch of wusses."

"Watch how you throw around that word. I may have to let it slip to Jack you're sitting here worried about your brain."

"I'm fine."

"Of course you're fine. We're all fine."

Something about the way Gabe said it made Alex uncomfortable. Almost as if he wasn't convinced.

"Where's Becca?" Gabe asked. Subject effectively changed.

Alex shrugged. "Ran into her in the hall as she was headed back up to her room." After spending a little too much time studying his tattoo.

"You ever figure out what her mom's deal is?"

Alex wasn't much for keeping secrets. At least not from Gabe and Jack. But at the same time, he wasn't sure Becca's past was really any of their business. It was probably one of those things she would tell them if she felt comfortable doing so.

"Not really." Alex yawned and stretched as he waited for his coffee to cool.

Becca appeared after a few minutes, expressly not meeting his gaze, though she smiled at Gabe. "Morning, guys." She crossed to a cabinet, but instead of pulling out a mug, she pulled out her thermos.

"Isn't Jack supposed to make breakfast?" Gabe asked.

"I'll go wake him up," Alex offered, setting his mug aside and pushing off the counter.

"Don't do it on my account. I'm just going to grab a protein bar. See you guys at lunch." She put some coffee in the thermos, offered a nod and awkward wave, then headed immediately out of the kitchen.

Alex frowned after her. She was different now. Back to jumpy and a little shifty, like she'd been that first day he'd arrived. She wasn't stuttering over her words or anything, but she certainly wasn't comfortable.

Which was weird after last night, when she'd been very open and…a lot of other words that meant things he didn't particularly care to dwell on.

*Enticing.*

Nope.

Without thinking about it, he followed her. She'd had her boots and coat on when she'd gotten her coffee, so she was already out the door while he had to pause to shove his feet into boots.

He grabbed his coat, shrugging it on as he jogged after her. "Hey, what's your deal?"

She didn't stop striding toward the stable. "Nothing," she returned, not looking back. "I mean, I don't have a deal."

"You're being weird." He quickened his pace so he could catch up with her. Luckily, his long legs and her shorter ones gave him the advantage. He stepped in front of her so she had to stop.

She frowned up at him. "Am not." She let out a piercing whistle and the dogs appeared from under the porch while the damn goat hopped over the gate of its pen. While he was staring at the goat, Becca stepped around him and resumed her quick strides toward the stable.

Alex watched her go, completely and utterly confused all over again. What on earth had he done to get her flustered again? Was it because he'd left abruptly last night? Was she mad about that?

He frowned after her, trying to ignore the little sliver of guilt. He hadn't wanted to talk about his father or what Dad might have felt about his return. All he'd done was say good night, quite cordially if he did say so himself. She had no reason to be mad at him, or weird around him.

Damn it. He was going to have to apologize. Even if he didn't think he'd done anything all that wrong, clearly he'd hurt her feelings.

———

Becca checked the non-work-animals' water, refilled feed buckets, and chattered idly to the animals. Usually, she dumped her problems on them, but knowing Alex, Gabe, and Jack were wandering around meant not airing what was currently on her mind.

Which was mainly shirtless Alex.

With a tattoo.

She blinked, trying to get the image out of her head, except every time she did that, she only seemed to bring up the image more clearly.

Abs and hair and…stuff. Maybe it was her imagination and her memory combining to create an image, but his shoulders seemed broad enough to fill the whole hallway, and she didn't understand what it was about a guy with broad shoulders and narrow hips that made her skin all hot and her imagination go places it normally didn't.

Because normally, shirtless guys weren't walking down her hallway, and even more normally, she didn't blurt out they were naked. In front of them. Out loud.

She groaned loud enough that Ron Swanson bleated at her, which caused Ranger to give him a doleful look.

*These* were the things that roamed her halls. Animals on four legs with fur. Incapable of speaking or embarrassing her because, hey, they ate each other's shit. They were not paragons of acceptable behavior.

Now she had three former Navy SEALs walking around her house, completely *fine* with being shirtless. All skin and scars and muscles and tattoo.

A star. Apparently the North Star. *It's supposed to lead you home*.

Why did he have to be so fascinating? And hot? Couldn't he just be one or the other? She could probably ignore one or the other. Mostly. It was just…not only did she not know how to be around people all that well, but she'd also never had to pretend like she wasn't staring at a guy shirtless before.

Lord, what if they *all* started walking around shirtless? Becca's mind drifted to that possibility. It *would* be summer and—

"Get a grip."

She'd worked outside all morning with the animals, but she had more things to do today. Horsemanship things. Foundation things. They hadn't even come up with a name yet, and they'd need to, so they could start filing the correct paperwork.

There were things that definitely needed to be done if they were going to start by winter, and *that* was far more important than spending her morning all worked up over a shirtless guy.

Probably.

"You ever planning on coming in for lunch?"

She jerked, spilling feed and making a little screeching noise in the process. Did he sneak around everywhere so darn quietly? She turned to glare at him, working on the reality of Alex fully clothed in front of her—and not the memory of him *not* clothed. "You scared me!" She glared at the dogs, who'd given her no warning at all. They lay lazily, panting in Alex's direction as if he was just part of the landscape now.

Nothing to bark at or move for. Just part of the place.

"You are easily scared," he returned with literally no remorse.

"I'm not used to people wandering in," she muttered, turning away from him and the dogs. Everything felt off today. She didn't like it, and she didn't have to face it or him if she didn't want to.

"I was hardly wandering. It's past noon and you didn't come in for lunch."

Okay, maybe she did have to face him. "I guess I lost track of time." Which was mostly true. She'd been so busy in her own head she *had* lost track of time. Of course, her stomach had reminded her a few times, but she'd ignored that reminder.

"Is that all it was?"

He was staring at her with that intense focus she didn't particularly care for. She just *knew* he was trying to figure her out—not because she was interesting or worthy of figuring out, but because he thought if he could figure her out, he would know how to maneuver her.

"What else would there be?" she returned, feeling cool and dismissive and full of not wanting him here.

He frowned at her, so she frowned right back. Did he honestly think she was going to admit to being all worked up over him? Not a chance in hell.

"Look," he said so gently she bristled. "If you're upset that I walked off last night when you were talking about Dad, I'm sorry. I wasn't really looking to have a heart-to-heart."

"And you think I was?" *That's* why he was being all tenacious about figuring her out? He thought she was upset about their conversation and his abrupt ending of it? She very nearly wanted to laugh.

"You brought Dad up."

"Yes, because I thought it might comfort you to know he'd like having you here. But I also understand if you didn't want to hear that. I knew it might be more of a painful thing than a happy thing, and I was ready to back off. Don't apologize for walking away if you felt uncomfortable or sad." Especially since that was not the reason she was currently having trouble looking him in the eye.

Was this why guys got tattoos? So girls couldn't stop thinking about them even when they absolutely had to?

"If you're not mad about that, then why are you acting so weird today?"

"I'm not acting weird. I'm acting like me. I'm jumpy and—"

"This is the first time you skipped out on a meal with us. And you're trying to skip out on a second one."

"Are you always going to keep tabs on me like this? I traded in one mom for another?" God, that was the last thing she wanted. Especially from *him*.

"What is this really about?"

"Nothing! Why are you so certain it's about something? Can't I just be *myself* without you questioning everything?"

"Well, the only other thing that's happened between then and now is… Surely this morning was not the first time you've seen a guy walk around without a shirt on. You can't honestly be offended by that."

Offended would not have been the word she'd have used. "Of course I've seen shirtless guys." In movies and on the internet. Not in her house. Within…touching distance.

"This whole thing we're doing only works if you're straight with me, Becca. I don't want to make you uncomfortable. So if something I did upset you or bothered you, you need to tell me. Connor thinks we need a new roof, and it's going to be weeks before we get that bunkhouse ready for Jack and Gabe and I to live in. So you're going to have to stick up for yourself and tell us when something bothers you."

He just wasn't going to give it up, was he? He'd keep poking and poking, just like her mother.

"Okay, fine. I'm acting weird because you were walking around shirtless. I am not accustomed to someone all up in my space." She waved an arm up and down. "Especially someone who looks like you."

"What does that mean?"

She stared at him for a second before she looked away. What was she supposed to say now? That he was hot? That she was attracted to the man who was or at least had been her stepbrother?

Becca's face heated and she had to have been a bright shade of red at this point. But it was his damn fault for pushing it. Why couldn't he let things go?

"You're not exactly out of shape," she grumbled, embarrassment so acute she almost felt sick to her stomach.

He didn't say anything to that for the longest time. Finally she glanced up at him quickly, just in an effort to read his expression. His eyebrows were drawn together and he still looked confused. She rolled her eyes. "Could you just go away and let me do my work?"

"Right. Right."

Still he didn't move and she didn't know what to do with that. She certainly wasn't about to say anything else. She'd embarrassed herself enough.

Why did people have to be so complicated? She wasn't complicated. All she wanted was to live on this ranch and do something that mattered.

And maybe touch a hot guy. *This specific hot guy.*

Okay, so maybe she was a little complicated.

She closed her eyes, frustrated with herself and embarrassed and one million other things.

"What do you want from me, Alex? You want to understand me? Maneuver me? Good luck to you if you think you're going to make sense out of me when I can't even make sense out of myself. It's going to be a lot of long, frustrating years though, I can guarantee you that."

"Years," he repeated.

"Unless you're planning on quitting, we're in this for the long haul. Together."

"Together."

"Don't tell me the man with the six-month, detailed, day-to-day plan hasn't thought about years in advance?"

She could tell by the confused and blank look on his face that he actually *hadn't* thought that far ahead. Which was interesting. She tended to take it one day at a time because she knew how much could change in a moment, but she had a long-range goal and she knew she wanted to do this for years and years and years.

But she didn't think Alex knew what he wanted to do in *years*.

"I'll be inside for lunch in a few minutes, okay?" she said, working some gentleness into her tone since he seemed shell-shocked by *something*.

"Yeah. There are, um, sandwiches waiting."

"Great. Thanks."

He stood there for a few more seconds, and if she wasn't totally mistaken, he was confused. A little lost. Her irritation with him faded, because she had been lost a few times herself.

"You don't have to have it all figured out, Alex. I

hope you know that." His brown gaze met hers, and much like he had last night, he turned on a heel and walked away.

# Chapter 8

THERE WAS SCREAMING. SMOKE. ALEX TRIED TO SEE through it, but everything was pitch-black. He couldn't breathe. He couldn't make out the noises that sounded like screams.

He had to calm himself down and focus. If he panicked, he'd never get out of here.

But that was the question. Where the hell was he?

His eyes flew open, though he hadn't known they were closed until that moment. He managed to suck in a deep breath as he looked around the dark room. He still didn't know where he was, and the fear and confusion completely paralyzed him.

It was too dark to see. The screams had stopped. Where the hell was he?

He realized then that he was lying on the floor. Quickly, he got to his feet in a defensive position. Nothing in his brain was working together. Everything was all a jumbled confusion.

Afghanistan.

The crash.

Becca Denton.

He forced himself to breathe in and out. He counted to ten, inhaling the familiar smells of the ranch. He was in Montana. He was in Blue Valley. He was in the house.

*Christ.*

It was fine though. He straightened, trying to breathe

evenly instead of the panicked gasps that were working through him.

He must've dozed off. Had a bit of a nightmare. That was fine. To be expected.

But…in the dark, he didn't know what room he was in. He'd been on the floor, and he couldn't quite make his body move to find a wall or piece of furniture.

He tried to work out the last thing he remembered. He'd eaten a dinner that Jack had made, and Alex had done his dish duty for the day. Jack and Gabe had wanted to watch some baseball and he had…

He heard footsteps and crouched, those old instincts humming along with the adrenaline of the dream he had woken up from. He forced himself to stand back up, but his body was shaking. He was shaken.

"Who's there?" It was Becca's voice. Surprisingly… not timid, but not confident either.

Scared.

"It's me." Except the first time he said it, no sound came out. He had to clear his throat and repeat it to get her to hear.

The light flicked on with no warning, and Alex flinched. Not just at the sudden light—the sudden movement in general bolted through him like panic.

"Alex?" It was only her voice that kept him centered in the present. He glanced at her. In her pajamas. Carrying a gun?

"What the hell do you have a rifle for?"

"What the hell are you doing in Burt's office?"

He looked around then and realized that's exactly where he was. In his dad's office. In the dark.

He didn't…he didn't remember coming into his

father's office, and that prompted a new bolt of fear. He didn't remember coming in here.

"I guess I had too much to drink tonight." It was the only possible explanation. He'd...he'd wanted one, hadn't he?

"You didn't have anything to drink tonight. You went up before I did."

"I must've come back down after you went to bed."

She stared at him and he could see a myriad of emotions on her face. Confusion, fear, and worst of all, worry.

There was no reason for her to be worried about him. He'd gotten a little drunk and forgotten some things. It wasn't like him, but that didn't make it impossible.

He *had* come back downstairs for a drink after everyone had gone to bed. He remembered that now. He'd come back downstairs, but there hadn't been any alcohol in the kitchen, so he'd gone to Dad's office because Dad had always kept a bottle of whiskey in the bottom drawer of his desk.

Alex glanced toward the desk. There was a bottle on top of the desk, one he specifically remembered pulling out of the drawer. He definitely remembered doing all of these things.

"See?" he said, nodding toward the bottle. "One too many, I guess. Nothing to—"

"Alex, that bottle's not open." She visibly swallowed. "I bought it for Burt for his birthday and I... He died, and I put it in the drawer because... But he wasn't here to open it."

Alex blinked at the completely sealed bottle of whiskey. Then he looked down at his hands, because that's where Becca was looking now.

Huh. His hands were shaking. Uncontrollably.

"I'm fine," he said, though his voice sounded strained and far away to his own ears.

"No, you're really not."

"Okay…" There had to be a reasonable explanation. There *was* a reasonable explanation. He'd come down here and fallen asleep and had a dream. He'd rather admit he had a dream than any other part of this…

It was a nightmare. That was all.

"I have…" God, it killed him to have to say this to her. To anyone. But she was going to think everything was worse than it was if he didn't explain himself. So… "I have…" He cleared his throat. "Occasionally, rarely, I will still have a nightmare. I came down here to have a drink, and I fell asleep, and I had a nightmare."

"You fell asleep where?" She gestured around the office. There was a desk, a chair, and not a whole heck of a lot of floor space.

He had no idea. No idea how he'd ended up on the floor, why the bottle was on the desk and still sealed. He had *no* idea, but he couldn't let…he couldn't let anyone know that.

"I was overcome with grief." Which as much as it pained him to admit, was far better than admitting he had no idea what happened. Grief was acceptable and true. He would always miss his father. Always.

It wasn't a lie, no matter how hard it was to breathe or how it seemed ghosts and memories slithered in the corner.

Becca took a few steps into the small, cramped room, setting the gun down against the wall. The dogs were with her, flanking her, but at some motion she made with her hands, they stayed put in the doorway as she moved closer. Closer and closer and he wanted to back away, but he wasn't afraid. And he certainly wasn't ashamed.

He didn't know why she was standing so close to him, in front of him, looking sleep rumpled and gorgeous. She held her hands at her stomach in some sort of awkward move as she curled her fingers together and then loosened them.

He didn't understand what she was doing at all until she finally reached out and placed her hands on his at his sides.

"You're still shaking," she said quietly, looking up at him with pained, green eyes.

Her hands were warm and rough. They were sturdy and strong.

"Why don't you sit?"

"Why don't you go back upstairs to bed and leave me be?" he returned, afraid of what any more of her kindness might do.

"I'm not going to leave you like this."

"Even if that's what I want you to do?"

"Yes. You shouldn't be alone right now."

"I'm fine," he said through gritted teeth.

"So you keep telling me."

"It was a nightmare. I'll live."

She gave his hands a squeeze, but then she released them. He would never admit he wished she would put her hands back on him. Her warm and capable and strong hands.

But he was strong too, and he was fine. He could be alone. He didn't need *comfort*.

Becca walked over to Dad's desk. She pulled the wax tab and opened the bottle of whiskey. Then she grabbed the shot glass Dad had always kept in the same drawer as the whiskey.

She poured a shot and shocked the hell out of him by taking it herself. She coughed a little on it, but it was clearly not the first time she'd shot whiskey. Which was most definitely a surprise.

She poured herself another one, but before he could warn her off hitting it that hard, she handed it to him.

"Your turn."

He thought about refusing. He thought about a lot of things, but in the end, he just took the damn shot.

"Let me guess. You're going to want to keep this a secret from Gabe and Jack."

"I do believe you're a genius, Becca."

She gave him a doleful look.

"It was just a nightmare. That's not to say they're pleasant, but they're rare and normal and not magically going to go away with time or therapy or whatever. So telling anyone, worrying about it—it's pointless. Gabe and Jack have their own nightmares to deal with."

"You don't think talking to each other about them would help?"

"Yes, reliving the hell that was Afghanistan helps. Remembering it all in great detail. Hearing screams, smelling blood. Feeling the pain again is fantastic bonding time."

"I'm sorry." She sounded so genuine it made him sick.

He didn't want her to be sorry, and he certainly didn't want to be standing in his dead father's office talking about nightmares and war. "Thanks for the drink, but I'm going to bed now."

"Alex?"

He didn't say anything in return, but he did stop his hasty retreat.

"I know you don't want to talk about it. And maybe the other guys don't want to talk about it. You're all fine. I know you want to believe that."

"But?"

"There's no but. Just me saying I get it. I mean, I don't, but I understand why you'd want to work it out yourself. Why you wouldn't want anyone else worrying over you. That…that I get."

Then she walked past him and grabbed her rifle. She murmured something to the dogs, and left the office, Ranger following her while Star stayed put.

Somehow it was worse that she didn't push. Worse she hadn't given him a reason to be angry, because he wanted to be fucking angry at everything and anything. Anger he knew how to channel.

But she just…understood.

He stared at the dog waiting for him and thought maybe understanding was the worst thing she could have done to him.

—⁓—

Becca rocked in Mom's chair—no, it wasn't Mom's anymore. It was hers. Her house. Her chair. She smiled at that, tried to focus on the thought, but…

It had been a week since she'd found Alex shaking and out of sorts in Burt's office, and though she hadn't said anything to anyone, including Alex himself, she couldn't get it out of her head. No matter how often she saw Alex being all rancher-y every day, in charge with the guys every night, she thought about that moment of weakness.

No, not even weakness. Just… Well, it made sense he'd have nightmares. If he'd been in his own room, she wouldn't have thought twice about it.

Why had he been sleeping in Burt's office? Why had he claimed he'd been drunk when he hadn't even had a drink? Why…

She blew out a frustrated breath, wishing the stars had those answers, but all they had was light a million miles away.

"I hope you're out there," she whispered, thinking about Burt on this porch. Burt, who'd loved his son. Burt, who'd surely know what to do.

But Burt wasn't here.

"Maybe you could show me what to do," she murmured into the dark spring night.

"Talking to yourself, Bec?"

She was getting better at not talking aloud to herself, but she wasn't cured. "Hi, Gabe." She glanced at Gabe's progress around the porch and up the stairs. "Where're the other two?"

"They're arguing over bunk beds of all damn things. Don't even have a new roof yet and they're bitching about furnishing. I told them I was going to get a drink." He leaned down and patted the dog at her feet. Star was off with Jack and Alex, something Becca'd started to find comforting instead of traitorous.

"Can I ask you something first?" she asked before Gabe went for the door.

"If it's asking me on a date, I'm going to have to respectfully decline. Wouldn't want to ruin a business partnership with any funny business."

"Ha-ha."

"You think I'm joking?" He grinned, but there was something in his expression that... Well, she wasn't interested in Gabe that way, but... She wrapped the blanket a little tighter. She was losing her marbles.

"What is it you want to ask me then?"

"It's about Alex."

"You want to ask him out on a date?"

"Good Lord, is that all you think about?"

"You'll notice the lack of female companionship around here," Gabe returned, gesturing around the ranch.

"Go into town. Pioneer Spirit. Pick up a girl, though I'll have to warn you off the bartender."

He frowned over at her. "You want me to pick up a girl?"

"Well, I don't know. I'm just saying, though young women aren't exactly crawling over Blue Valley, there are women. Of a reasonable age. A few are even single."

Gabe grinned, clearly pleased. He leaned against the porch railing and crossed his arms. "Gonna set me up, Bec?"

"If you want me to." She imagined Gabe and she had different ideas of what that meant, but she couldn't help but think Gabe and Jack needed some...softness. A nice woman who cared about their well-being would be a start.

"Hmm."

"But first, I want to talk to you about Alex."

"What about Alex?"

"A few days ago, I found him in his father's office. It was late. He was disoriented. Said he had a nightmare."

When she moved her gaze from the stars to Gabe, she saw an expression she'd never seen on his face before. Cold fury.

"And?"

"And," she continued, trying to find some balance between concern and...she didn't know. She didn't know what to do. She only knew it felt wrong to hold it in. It felt really wrong to ignore it. "He says he's fine. He *believes* he's fine, but he isn't."

She looked imploringly at Gabe, trying to find his usual softness. But there was nothing. Clearly, this wasn't what Gabe wanted to hear, and he wasn't about to be her ally.

"I'm sure you mean well, Becca. I'm sure this is some misguided sense of...something."

"I know Alex and I were never really family, and there's no relationship to speak of, but I did have one with his father. I loved Burt, and I can't sit by and let his son—"

"What? Have a bad night? Have a nightmare? If you're looking for soldiers who are perfectly healed, who never have a bad night, you're barking up the wrong damn tree." He looked away, shaking his head. "Don't step into this. It isn't your place."

It hurt. She might have expected this kind of harsh reaction from Jack, but not from Gabe. It also hurt because a friendship *had* been developing between all of them. She finally had friends, and she was screwing it up.

She tried to blink back the tears. Tried to be strong and honest at the same time. "I'm sorry," she managed, her voice little more than a whisper. "I was worried because I care."

"If we wanted any of that, we would have gone home. Do us a favor and keep it to yourself."

A tear slipped out, and she could only hope the dark obscured his view. He could think she was wrong, but she didn't want him to think she was *weak*.

"Good night, Becca," he muttered, pushing off the railing and striding inside. When the door closed with a slam, she jumped.

She wiped hurriedly at her cheeks, knowing it was only a matter of time before Alex and Jack came back too.

She'd grown to like all of them. Even surly Jack. She wanted to help. But she didn't know how. Apparently caring wasn't it, and Gabe had something of a point. Neither he nor Jack had gone home in the aftermath. They were here. Away from people who presumably loved them.

But Gabe was wrong about Alex, because Alex *had* come home, and maybe his father was dead, but he had people here who cared very much.

She heard Alex and Jack's approach, arguing as they stomped toward the house. She tried to sniffle and mop up best she could, keeping her face averted as they crested the stairs.

"Bit cold out for stargazing, isn't it?" Alex asked.

Which was possibly the worst thing he could have said to her in the moment. Oh, he could be her mom, worrying over it being too *cold*, but she couldn't express legitimate concern over his behavior the other night?

Bullshit. Bull. Shit. She pushed herself out of the chair and stood to face him and Jack. "I'll survive."

"Hey, what's wrong?" he asked, his eyes taking in what had to be the signs of tears on her face.

"Nothing," she replied. Because he was always telling her that. Nothing was wrong. He was fine. They were all fucking *fine*.

"You're crying," he said, glaring at the house, then back at her.

Like this was Gabe's fault. Hardly. It had started with the man standing right in front of her.

She looked him straight in the eye, knowing he would see every last trace of tears. *Let him. Let them all see it. Maybe then they'll get it.*

"I'm fine," she said, making sure to say it in the exact tone of voice he always did. "Just fine."

Alex wasn't going to swoop in and demand she tell him when she was feeling weird or awkward. He didn't get to lecture her about standing up for herself to the guys. She certainly wasn't going to let this turn into the three of them deciding what was best for her while she got shut down if she even expressed some concern. Rightful, thoughtful concern.

They wanted to shut her down and out? Well, they'd get the same treatment right back. And if Alex tried to push her on that, boy but he would be sorry.

# Chapter 9

ALEX STOOD ON THE PORCH AND WATCHED BECCA STRIDE inside, Ranger trailing after her.

"What the hell was that?"

Jack shrugged.

"It had to have been Gabe." Alex moved for the door to follow her, but Jack stepped in the way.

"Why do you say that?" he asked in a way that had Alex bristling.

"Because he's the only one here. Becca doesn't sit around crying for no reason."

"Because you know her so well?"

"It's been a few weeks. I think I've got a pretty good read on her. What the hell are you interrogating me for?"

"Why the hell are you accusing Gabe? You don't know the full story, but you're going to blame Gabe?"

"I'm going to *get* the full story from Gabe."

"Look, if you wanna fuck her, do it, but stop bringing us into it."

Alex took a step forward before he could stop himself, and when Jack smirked, it took everything Alex had not to curl his hand into a fist and land a blow right in his face.

"What are you going to do, punch me?"

"Maybe you need someone to punch you, Jack. Your shit attitude is getting old. We *all* got messed up in that accident—not just you. We *all* lost a friend—not just you. And I'm real sorry your personal life was sucking so hard, but it's been a lot more than a year since that shit with your fiancée went down, so maybe you could stop taking it out on everyone around you."

Jack stood there, no longer smirking. He looked grim and blank, and Alex hated he'd spewed all that at him. They didn't need this. Fighting and accusing. They needed to focus on the future.

But, *damn*, if Jack didn't need someone to shut him the hell up.

The door swung open, and Gabe stepped out. "Oh, are we having a Jack intervention? Why didn't you invite me?"

"I was defending you, asshole. So Alex decided to pick on me."

"I'm not picking on anyone. I wanted to know why Becca was crying. Everything I said to you was spot-on and you know it."

"Shit," Gabe muttered, but his jaw firmed and he looked out over the dark night around them.

"You did something to her then," Alex demanded.

Gabe's gaze, surprisingly cold, landed on Alex. "You two seem to be real concerned about each other. Do us all a favor—talk to *each other* instead of me."

"What the hell does that mean?"

"It means Becca was real worried that she caught you having a nightmare. I told her to mind her own business, because this is *our* deal."

Alex tensed. He hadn't expected Becca to tell anyone. He'd been certain she would respect his wishes to keep that to herself. But she'd confided in Gabe? He was already pissed, but that…well, that fucking grated.

"Yeah, not so quick to jump to her defense anymore."

"She's an innocent bystander in all this," Alex forced himself to say, though he didn't quite *feel* it. Innocent bystanders didn't go poking their noses where they didn't belong. "I'm sure she thought she was doing the right thing."

"Of course she did, but she had no business going behind your back. That isn't loyalty."

Which was when Alex finally got where this was coming from. He didn't know a lot about Gabe's family, but he knew Gabe was estranged from them, and he felt betrayed by it. So much so that *loyalty* had always been Gabe's rallying cry. You didn't tell a guy's secrets.

So whatever Gabe had said to hurt Becca's feelings, it had been in defense of Alex himself. Christ, this was getting complicated.

"We're all in this together," he said, using his best officer's tone, no matter how tired he felt. "I don't have a problem with you setting Becca straight, but she... Come on, man. She's sheltered and naive. You don't have to go at her like a soldier."

"Not your call."

It took every ounce of control Alex had honed as a Navy SEAL to keep from shouting at Gabe. To keep from saying it damn well *was* his call if *his* men were making an innocent woman *cry*.

He might not agree with Becca nosing around, telling Gabe things, but he'd learned a lesson—keep his shit together and in his room, and things would be fine. They would be fine.

"It doesn't serve any purpose for all of us to be at odds," Alex said as calmly as he could manage. Both

Gabe and Jack snorted and grumbled in a way they never would have if they were still deployed.

But they weren't deployed anymore. They weren't active SEALs anymore. They were…here for a reason and a purpose, damn it, and Gabe's surprisingly hard-ass line with Becca and Jack's consistent bad attitude was not going to get in the way of that. Alex wouldn't allow it.

"She may have crossed a line, but we have a purpose here. Maybe it takes a little while for Becca to understand we've got our own shit under control. Losing it on her doesn't help your case."

"My case? *My* case?" Gabe laughed, but it was bitter, one of those rare flashes of the temper Gabe kept buried very deep. "I wasn't helping anyone's case, least of all my own. You stand there and insist to everyone, including yourself, that you're fine. Everything is great and we're not scarred and fucking damaged. I told her to mind her business. I didn't tell her we were *fine*, because I'm not a liar."

"I *am* fi—"

Gabe stepped forward, jaw clenched, dark eyes glittering with something Alex didn't want to identify. "We're not fine, Alex. You want to pretend. And you… you want to be pissed about it," he said, flinging his arm toward Jack. "But I *know* I am not okay, and I *know* I never will be, so I don't see much point in denying it. It just is. We're not going to fix shit here. Geiger is dead. We don't fix that. All this does is give us something to do so we don't turn into nothing."

Alex had arguments for that, but he couldn't seem to get them out of his mouth. He kept opening it, trying to force them out, but his throat was tight and completely uncooperative.

"I like the girl, I do, but I'm not going to pretend like it's okay when she steps over the line. She might be our partner, but she isn't a brother. Her blabbing your business to me proves that, and I will not stand by and accept it."

"You will treat her with some respect. She didn't do anything not to deserve that."

Gabe shook his head. "You're not in charge anymore, Alex. This is civilian life, and you don't get to throw orders at me. And you're sure as hell not responsible for any of us—including her. So stop. Just stop."

Alex swallowed. Stop? What might happen if he did that? Who might get hurt? What lives might be screwed up if he *stopped* trying to make things right?

"He's right," Jack said, his voice quiet and lacking its usual edge. "You're not the officer anymore. Not the leader. You've got to give it up."

"No, I'm not the leader, but we're in this together. And there's nothing to give up. We know exactly what we're going to do."

"No, Alex. *You* know exactly what you're going to do. I don't have the first fucking clue what I'm doing here." Gabe shoved his hands through his hair. "Look, I believe in it. I get it. And I want this. I want to do something that helps guys who've been through shit, but I'm not the same as you. This doesn't always make sense, and I don't always know exactly where I'm going."

"And we don't all need to," Jack added.

"You have to step back from this idea that you can fix us," Gabe continued. "That it's your *job* to fix us. Us. Quite frankly, maybe you ought to worry about fixing your damn self first."

Panic was clawing at Alex's chest and his throat was still tight and everything about this was wrong. Gabe was purposefully poking where it would hurt, and Alex needed to neutralize the situation. He just didn't know how.

"We're all here for a reason," Jack said, grave and hard. "Gabe's right. You gotta let us do our own shit. But Alex is right too. Becca's got nothing to do with this. She's an easy target, and we shouldn't be hitting it. I'll be the first to admit I've been wrong in that department. I think we need to start over there. Make a pact. Whatever shit we've got going on, we don't get her mixed up in it. Agreed?"

It was a sharp pang to realize that if Jack had been afforded a few more years as a SEAL, he would've made an excellent officer and leader himself. He could've led missions and saved lives, but here they all were.

In the middle of Montana, learning about riding horses and driving cattle. Trying to put together a nonprofit.

*And fucking up right and left.*

"All right. I'll ease off." As much as was reasonable. "And we'll all agree that Becca is…" There were quite a few words he could think of, but none of them were appropriate for this conversation.

"We'll think of her like a partner and like a sister. Someone to protect. Right?"

Alex knew he had to agree with Jack's suggestion. Hell, Becca had been his stepsister for ten years even though he hadn't really had anything to do with the family for most of that time. But still, he should agree. Why was that just so damn hard?

Gabe laughed, and it wasn't that bitter angry thing from before. This was the usual cheerful, easygoing Gabe.

"Give him a break, Jack. It's hard to treat someone like a sister when you want to get her into bed."

Everything inside of Alex tensed. "I do not."

Gabe just grinned. "Your nickname in the SEALs may have been 'Dad,' but here in Montana it should be 'Denial.'"

"Can we get some fucking sleep before we have to get up and shovel cow crap tomorrow?" Jack muttered.

"I don't want to sleep with her," Alex said with as much unemotional conviction as possible.

Gabe and Jack exchanged a look that clearly said they did not believe him.

"I don't," he repeated. Because he did not. If he had ever noticed her…attractiveness, that was not the same as wanting to sleep with her.

"Guess you'll have to prove it," Gabe offered as he and Jack opened the door and walked inside.

Alex looked down at Star, who panted happily up at him, the tension of the argument having not affected him at all.

"Oh, I'll damn well prove it."

———

The trouble with crying herself to sleep was waking up feeling like her eyes were sandpaper and her head was stuffed with cotton.

But Becca had gotten the crying out of her system, and today was a brand-new day. She tried to find some strength in that as she walked downstairs to make the coffee.

But Gabe had beat her to it and was standing there stirring something into her mug. She thought briefly about not going into the kitchen, about scurrying back to her room so she didn't have to face this.

But that would be cowardly, and she hadn't been wrong. So she steeled her courage and stepped forward. "Morning, Gabe."

"Hey." He nudged a full mug of coffee down the counter. "Doctored up just the way you like."

Becca stared at the mug suspiciously.

"I didn't poison it, if that's what you're worried about."

"I was more worried that you put salt instead of sugar, but sure, poison too."

Gabe chuckled, but any amusement quickly died. In fact, everything about him kind of changed. His posture straightened and his expression was grim. She figured this was what soldier Gabe looked like. None of the easy smiles or big laughs. Serious, ramrod-straight stillness.

It made her more than a little nervous, but his dark gaze met hers head-on. "I'm sorry for how I spoke to you last night," he said, his voice clipped.

"Oh." Becca didn't know what to say to that. She didn't…have a lot of people apologizing to her. What was the gracious way to accept one?

"It was out of line, and I promise that while I may disagree with you in the future, I will not speak to you as harshly as I did. It was unacceptable, and it won't happen again."

"Aren't you supposed to call me 'sir' when you talk in that military monotone?" Which wasn't what she should have said. It just tumbled out because she didn't know how to respond to this in any of them. The way they adopted these blank, rote ways of talking.

Gabe smiled. A *real* smile. "You're a trip, Bec," he said, shaking his head. "And for what it's worth, I think you're good for this thing we're trying to build. We need someone like you, even when we push against it."

"Thank you. I appreciate that."

The front door creaked open and Jack poked his head in. "Um, Becca," he called. "There is a goat on the porch roof."

"Damn it, Ron Swanson." She looked longingly at her mug of coffee and then resigned herself to reheating it later. She headed for the front door. Ron hadn't gotten up on the roof in a while, but whenever he did, getting him down was quite the production.

She tried to hide a smile, imagining the guys' reactions, but it was nearly impossible as she shoved her feet into her boots and pulled on her coat.

"What are you grinning at?" Jack asked.

"You'll see." She followed him out the front door and down the porch steps. Alex was standing in the middle of the front yard scowling up at the roof, and Jack joined him with his arms crossed over his chest.

Becca turned around and glanced up at the goat on the porch roof. "Ron Swanson, get down here right this instant," she said, clapping her hands together.

The goat merely bleated at her.

"One of you, go grab Rasputin."

"Ras...who the fuck is Rasputin?" Jack returned.

"The rooster. He's the only one Ron will listen to."

"Listen to? He's a goat. It's a chicken. Is this a waking dream?" Alex said, his puzzled and slightly horrified gaze never leaving Ron.

"Try waking nightmare," Jack returned.

"Fine, I'll get Rasputin. You two stay put and make sure he doesn't start eating the gutters."

"How do we do that?" she heard Jack ask as she walked quickly to the chicken coop. But she didn't have time to explain. She took her gloves out of her pocket and pulled them on, as Rasputin probably wouldn't be too keen on being grabbed.

He was the only one left after Becca had finally given up the fight against the coyotes. Becca had no idea how Rasputin managed to stay alive, but she liked that inexplicable part of his story. It made impossible things seem possible.

She cooed softly to Rasputin as she entered the coop. He flapped around, trying to avoid her, but she eventually cornered him and managed to grab him, holding her arm around the rooster to avoid as much of his pecking and clawing as she could.

She marched back toward the house. Gabe had joined Alex and Jack and all three men were staring helplessly at the goat on the roof.

"I've seen a lot of crazy shit, Becca," Gabe said as she walked up holding the rooster. "But you officially win."

Becca smiled but turned her attention the goat. "Ron Swanson. Look who I've got." She held up Rasputin, who flapped his wings until she let him go. He squawked and crowed and Ron bleated in return.

"What the fuck is happening?" Jack said, shaking his head.

"Just wait," Becca said as Ron started to pace the edge of the porch roof. Rasputin crowed again, starting to strut back toward the coop. Which was when Ron clattered down the slope of the roof and jumped the distance to the ground.

"That did not just happen," Gabe said, something like awe in his voice.

"Afraid it did," Becca returned cheerfully, walking toward the animals, who were now circling each other. She had to separate them before Rasputin took a chunk out of Ron.

"Need...help?" Alex offered, clearly hoping the answer was no.

Becca lunged and came up with Rasputin. "Nope. I'm good. Just have to put him back in his coop. Ron can wander a bit. He's never gotten up on the roof twice in the same day before."

She heard all the guys muttering, but she ignored them and walked toward the coop.

It wasn't such a bad way to start the day, all in all. A little animal shenanigans to get the blood pumping, and it never failed to make her laugh when three Navy SEALs looked dumbfounded.

She placed Rasputin in the coop, then exited, locking up behind her. She should probably get Ron in his pen, but she knew he was restless after a winter of not being able to roam very much. Becca turned.

Alex was there, standing outside the coop as though he was waiting for her. He looked so serious her stomach fluttered with nerves.

"Why...why is the rooster named Rasputin?" he asked eventually, knocking any nervousness right out of her.

She grinned. "Well, I was just calling him Rooster at first, because Burt told me to stop naming the chickens since they just kept getting eaten by coyotes. But one day Rasputin got himself in a tizzy and flew into the pond and just kind of sank. So, you know, we figured he was dead. But, weirdest thing, next day he was back crowing up a storm. So, Rasputin."

Alex started laughing. A real, booming laugh she'd never heard out of him, and it didn't stop. He kept laughing until she was laughing right along with him.

He scrubbed his hands over his face as his laughter dissipated. "Well, that isn't how I expected to spend my morning."

"I hate when that goat gets in the way of drinking my coffee."

He chuckled again, and for the first time in all the time she'd known him, that smile stayed in place. It didn't melt into that military stoicism, and that warmed something inside of her she was afraid to analyze too closely.

"Well, let's go get that coffee, huh?" And he did the strangest thing. He slung his arm over her shoulders. Like they were friends or something.

Maybe if she felt nothing but *friendly*, it would have been easy to accept, but his body was warm and close and very clearly masculine. Just big and hard and...

She was a little afraid the squeaking noise she tried to swallow came out anyway since Alex tensed and started to draw his arm away.

"I came up with a name," she blurted, hoping somehow that would keep his arm on her shoulders. "For the foundation."

He paused, but his arm still left her shoulders. He stood next to her, slowly turning that dark gaze to hers. "Yeah?"

"I mean, obviously if you guys don't like it, we don't have to go with it, but since you didn't want to use any words like *center* or *rehabilitation* or whatever, I thought we'd stick with *ranch*. Revival Ranch."

He stared at her silently for the longest time. So long she couldn't keep holding her breath like she wanted to. "We can... We don't have to—"

"I like it," he said, all traces of that smile and levity gone.

This was Alex Maguire, Navy SEAL, and while she respected this man a lot, she missed that little glimmer of what was underneath.

She tried to force a smile, but she knew she failed. What would it take to unlock this armor he'd wrapped around himself? Something probably far more than a silly girl with goats on roofs and roosters named Rasputin.

"I'll ask the guys what they think," he said, walking back toward the house.

"Sure," Becca said softly, trudging after him.

# Chapter 10

IT HAD BEEN A HELL OF A WEEK. SNOW MONDAY, THEN RAIN ever since. Spring really was upon them, as the ranch became little more than a vehicle for mud.

Alex was thrust back into every calving season he'd endured as a kid, and it was a weird kind of nostalgia. He was living this thing he'd done as a kid, and there were things he remembered, things he didn't, and things he'd clearly glorified or vilified at turns.

Then, in between all that, he and Gabe were trying to get the bunkhouse in some kind of order and finding problem after problem they couldn't fix. It poked at Alex in a way he didn't want to examine, so he always went in search of something he *could* fix.

"Lunch," Jack barked from the doorway of the bunkhouse, the sun shining through it making him nothing but a dark shadow.

"In a sec."

"You said that ten minutes ago. Get your ass out here."

Alex sighed and looked at the floorboard he'd been carefully pulling up so he could replace it with a non-warped plank.

It could wait. This wasn't the navy, where you didn't take a break until the task was done. This was just life.

He rubbed at the tight band around his chest and got to his feet. It didn't matter what he felt, as long as he kept moving. It didn't matter how everything felt off-kilter on the inside, as long as on the outside he appeared perfectly normal.

He walked through the narrow bunkhouse and into the bright, spring day. Becca had insisted on making up sandwiches this morning, so they could enjoy the first sunny day in weeks with a picnic lunch.

Gabe, Jack, and Hick were sitting next to the bunkhouse, where a picnic table that Alex thought might predate his existence was situated on a little concrete pad. Star was happily waiting for scraps, while Ranger was likely following Becca around.

The other guys had already passed out the sandwiches and drinks and had started eating. Alex didn't feel hungry, but skipping lunch would either earn him looks or questions, so he decided to choke down a sandwich one way or another.

"Where's Becca?"

Hick nodded toward the stables. "Something about a rooster and a goat, and that's about the point I stopped listening," he said in the same smoker's gravel he'd had since Alex could remember.

"Why don't you go get her, Alex?" Gabe suggested innocently. Way too innocently.

Alex narrowed his eyes. "She's a grown woman. She can eat lunch when she wants."

"I'm done," Hick said, tossing his baggie into the trash can next to the bunkhouse. "I'll get her. Girl gets lost in her own head sometimes, grown woman or not." Then he strode off to the stables.

Alex slowly unwrapped his sandwich, glancing at where Hick had gone. Becca had stepped into the doorway of the stables and was talking to Hick. The sun teased red highlights out of her dark braid, and her smile was wide and pretty even this far away.

He couldn't hear her or Hick, but somehow he could think of exactly how it would sound if she were standing next to him laughing, instead of yards away with Hick.

"I don't know. Maybe we should cut her out," Gabe said in an overloud voice that had Alex jerking his head back to the conversation.

"What?" he demanded. "What are you talking about?"

"Yeah, I know what you mean. I'm not sure she's made of stern enough stuff for this," Jack said before polishing off his sandwich.

"Stern enough stuff for what?"

"I don't know," Gabe said with a shrug. "Ranch work. A bunch of guys hanging around. She's a skittish little thing—maybe we should keep her separate. Cut her out of the ranch stuff. Let her handle the easier stuff. You know."

"I do not know. She's tough as nails and knows more about ranch work than you ever will," Alex retorted. "Where the hell is this coming from?"

Gabe and Jack suddenly exchanged grins that didn't make any sense to Alex whatsoever.

"How long until he breaks, ya think?" Gabe asked.

"I've got ten bucks on a month."

"Oh, she's going to get to him before the month is out. I take that bet," Gabe said, holding his hand out to Jack, who shook it wholeheartedly.

Alex scowled at them. "What the hell are you two assholes talking about?" he growled.

But they got to their feet, walking around the picnic table on either side, then slapping each shoulder as they passed.

"Just proved a point for us, that's all," Gabe said jovially, heading for the house.

"What point?" Alex demanded after them, but they walked away laughing to themselves and Becca was approaching and...

*What damn point?*

"Uh-oh. The guys been messing with you again?" Becca slid next to him and dug through the cooler to get her sandwich.

"I don't know what the hell they're doing," Alex grumbled, staring down at his untouched sandwich.

"Well, pissing you off, if your look is anything to go by. Which I assume was their intention based on the way they're laughing themselves hoarse. Is this a guy thing or a Navy SEAL thing or what?"

"What?"

"The whole purposefully pissing each other off thing?"

"I think it's a Gabe and Jack thing."

Becca laughed, and though they'd been at this thing for weeks, cohabitating and working together, he wasn't quite over the sound of her laugh. It was always so effortless and joyful. It always spiraled inside of him like a firework ready to go off.

But he never let it go off, because he was a little afraid of the man who'd be left.

"Here, have a Coke," she said, sliding the red can his way. She gave him a sidelong glance. "You okay? You look..."

"I look what?"

"I don't know. You look peaked—and don't ask me what that means. I only know that's what my mom said whenever she thought I was coming down with something."

"I'm fine," Alex muttered.

"You should try tea."

"Tea?"

"Yeah, there's this sleepy-time stuff—"

"I'm not drinking something called 'sleepy time,' Becca. I'm a grown man."

She smiled at that, but then she reached across and touched his hand. A brief brush of her fingertips across the top, nothing that should jolt through him like electricity. "Grown man or not, you still need to take care of yourself. We need you around here." She gave his hand a little squeeze, then moved to leave, but before her hand could leave his, he grasped it, holding her in place.

He didn't know why, but he couldn't seem to force himself to let her go. This was some link to something that didn't feel bleak and dark. Her small, strong hand in his—a lifeline.

To what, he didn't have a clue.

"I told the guys about the name," he said, his voice too rusty, his grip too tight. "They liked it."

She held his gaze, though her pulse clearly fluttered in her neck. "I'm glad," she returned, her voice sounding a little…whispery.

His skin prickled, as though he were neck deep in water on a freezing cold night. As though something important was waiting for him if he only held on to Becca long enough.

But he didn't have his uniform, and he didn't have his gun, and what could be waiting for him without those tools?

*You're not a Navy SEAL anymore.*

He blinked down at this beautiful piece of civilian

life. A cheerful woman with a heart the size of Montana and a smile that did unbidden things to some place in his chest he couldn't name.

*It might be your heart.*

"I, um, better get back to work," he said hoarsely, forcing himself to let go of his grasp on her hand. He got up and started walking toward the bunkhouse.

*Walking or running?*

"Alex?"

He paused in his retreat, though he didn't say anything.

"You didn't eat."

He blinked over at the untouched sandwich on the picnic table and swallowed. "Right." He grabbed it, not looking at her. "I'll eat while I work."

Which was a lie. He was going to give it to the dogs looking at him longingly and work away all the swirling, confusing thoughts in his head.

---

Becca woke up three days later to the sound of her alarm and the fleeting memory of a dream she couldn't quite piece together. Alex had been there, which wasn't all that uncommon, she had to admit to herself.

But there'd been an...urgency. His hand grasping hers, as though he had to hold on to be saved.

She shook her head and slid out of bed. Dreams were just that, and there wasn't much point wasting time wondering over it.

She pulled her clothes on to head down to start the coffee. Once they had a break in the calf watch, she needed to head into Bozeman and get one of those programmable coffeemakers. Burt had been wholeheart-edly against most technology, and that was one thing she would happily change about the ranch. Introduce some modern practices. Starting with a coffeemaker.

Becca got downstairs to find the coffee was already made and three mugs were set out on the counter. She found her mug and deduced based on the three that were left who had made the coffee—Alex. Whether he knew it or not, he always took a mug her mom had bought Burt for his birthday a few years ago.

But the question remained: Where was Alex? He didn't generally take food into the living room or bed-rooms. He was a little too anal for that.

"Where would I drink my coffee if I were a control-ling, neat freak of an ex-soldier?" she pondered aloud into the kitchen.

She had no idea where a former Navy SEAL would take his coffee if not the kitchen, but she did know how to find him. She whistled for the dogs. They usually slept in the mudroom, trained too well by her mother, so they followed around whoever was up first until every-one woke up.

When the dogs didn't immediately come, she figured he must be outside. So that's where she headed with her mug of coffee.

She stepped onto the porch and there Alex was, staring off into the early-morning dawn. Both dogs were curled at his feet, and he sipped his coffee as he looked out over the ranch. He looked...focused, but not at peace—which was what *she* always felt sitting there as the golden ball of sun climbed its way up over the mountains.

Alex's expression was hard, those grooves around his mouth prominent. He had dark circles under his eyes and Becca frowned. He was working too hard and not getting enough sleep. She was pretty sure he had not eaten that sandwich the other day.

And none of that was her business.

Still, he made quite the picture, even before he turned that golden-brown gaze on her. "Mornin'."

"Good morning. Do you mind if I join you?"

"It's a free porch in a free country."

"Partially thanks to you, I believe."

He rolled his eyes, but she took a seat in the rocking chair. She sipped her coffee and watched the sun rise in the east.

"You guys have been scarce this week. Must be putting in long hours."

"Trying to get the bunkhouse ready, plus trying to learn as much about calving as we can before they get here. Funny—when I was a kid, this was my favorite time of year."

"And now?"

He flashed a grin that hinted at someone who wasn't completely devoid of fun or humor. "Still is. I never was one for downtime."

"Funny, Burt always complained about spring."

"My mud has mud has mud."

"Yeah, exactly that."

"He had a few sayings that never changed."

"That he did."

But she didn't want to dwell on Burt. Not just because Alex usually left when she did that, but also because she wanted there to be more between them than just memories of Burt. "Going to have to start thinking about the garden soon enough."

"You have a garden?"

"Well, Mom and I..." From one sticky subject to another. With Alex, it seemed like there wasn't much else.

Nothing was simple or clear. She wondered if that was why she liked him. Because she was finally at a point in her life when she wanted a challenge. She was ready to deal with the hard things, done with being sheltered from them. Alex was a million hard things.

"We tried to revive your mother's garden."

It didn't surprise her that he stiffened. Didn't surprise her that he looked down at his coffee with that tensed jaw.

"She did love that garden," he finally said. And that *was* a surprise. For him to say anything at all about his mother.

"Do you think it gets easier?" she asked, since he was giving pieces, and she'd gather all of them she could.

His gaze met hers, and she knew he understood that question and exactly what she was asking.

"You're asking the man who left for sixteen years? I'm not sure it ever gets easier if you run away."

"You're here now. Is that why you stayed away so much? You missed your mom?"

"No, actually. I always wanted to be a soldier." He took a careful sip of coffee. "I was four or five maybe, and I snuck downstairs and Dad was watching this movie. Some war movie. I never figured out what it was, but things were exploding and people were being shot, but one man stays calm, saves his men. I always wanted to be that man, but..." He trailed off.

There was more to that story, she would have bet money on it, but whatever it was, he pushed it away.

"I'll admit Mom being gone probably made it easier to do it. But that was always the dream. Serve my country. Save people."

"It's a very admirable dream."

"I don't know that it's admirable."

"Many people wouldn't do it. Most people are too scared." She couldn't imagine facing what he must have faced.

"Some men are born soldiers. It's in the blood or the brains or something. It's who we're supposed to be, but some people are born to other things."

Becca chewed her lip as she worried her thumb over the handle of the coffee mug. She caught the faintest sliver of gold peeking over the mountaintop in the distance. "What if…you have no idea what that thing is?"

"You figure it out. Knowing you, belonging here is a start."

It left a little hitch in her chest that he would say that, think it. "I'm not sure I know that. I think I hope it, but *knowing* it is something else, isn't it?" She wanted to be certain, and some days she could muster it, but… ever since the guys had come back, there were moments when she questioned her place.

"It's a leap of faith," Alex said as though it were a simple fact. "Belonging where you're supposed to be."

"A leap of faith." She smiled at that. A leap of faith— yeah, she liked that. Because this had all been, from square one, a leap of faith. To trust Burt. To find her freedom. To make this deal with these men.

Belief and faith and hope. It was what propelled her, and if practical and sturdy Alex believed in leaps of faith, there had to be something to that.

"Is this the place you're supposed to be?" she asked, not wanting this easy, open conversation to end. There were so few easy, open conversations in her life. She wanted to stretch it out and soak it up.

His eyebrows drew together, but not in confusion or frustration. It was as if he was giving her questions serious thought. "Yeah. I always planned on coming back. Maybe not this soon, but eventually. This is all...different than I planned, but in some ways, it isn't."

"We're going to build something that matters." The more she said it, the stronger her foundation from which to take that leap of faith grew.

His mouth curved—not quite a smile, but something soft. "Yes, ma'am, we are."

They sipped their coffee in the icy, rain-soaked air. But the clouds had mostly cleared, and the promise of a sunny day offered the possibility of warmth and drying out a bit.

"The guys and I were talking about going to town tonight. Dinner at Georgia's. A few drinks at Pioneer Spirit. Relax a little. Get our minds off the mud for a few hours. Show them what Blue Valley has to offer."

"I think that's very overdue. You guys deserve a night of fun. Hick and I will be able to stay on calf watch."

"You should come with us."

She blinked, and though she gaped at him, he kept staring straight ahead. "Me?" she squeaked.

"You deserve a little fun too, don't you think? Hick said he can handle it, and he'll call us if we're needed. You should come with us. Think of it as one of those corporate team-building exercises."

"I've never..." Georgia's was one thing, but Pioneer Spirit? She'd never been in a bar before, especially *that* bar, which was not exactly known for its upstanding clientele. Mom would have locked her in her room for even *thinking* about going to Pioneer Spirit.

"I'm not going to be offended if you say no."

"No. I want to go. I just… A bar." And three men who intimidated her on a social level. *Well, that's what you need to work on, right?*

"Tell me you've been to a bar before," he said, clearly amused.

"Sheltered, remember?"

"You shot that whiskey the other night like you had some practice."

He'd obviously said that without thinking, because tension crept into him. Likely at the reminder of when she'd given him a shot of whiskey—after his nightmare. She was so tempted to poke him, to press him about it, but after her…whatever it was with Gabe last week, she had no desire to relive that.

So she answered the question without any mention of that night in Burt's office. "A couple months after I turned twenty-one, there was this church trip Mom wanted to go on, but she didn't want to leave me. Somehow, someway, Burt convinced her to go. Which was a big deal—she'd never been away from me for more than twenty-four hours. Somehow he convinced her to go though. Three days, two nights. The first night she was gone, Burt took me up to the barn and gave me my first drink. Developed a taste for whiskey, gotta admit." She grinned at him, but there was an odd look on his face.

"On the west side of the barn? Next to the fence?"

It was her turn to give him a quizzical look. "Why do you know that?"

"I came home for a couple days before I was deployed the first time. This was before our parents got married. I'd just turned twenty-one. Granted, I'd had my night out with my buddies at a bar, but the night before I left for Afghanistan, Dad took me out there and gave me a shot of whiskey. Wished me luck and told me to make sure I got my ass home and mostly in one piece."

Even though it wasn't her story, Becca felt a little emotional over it. It made her miss Burt and what Alex and Burt might have had.

"Guess I should have told him to keep his ass alive."

Becca's throat tightened, but she couldn't keep herself from talking, from offering, from trying to soothe. "I know you don't like it or it hurts or whatever when I say things like this, but I can't keep my mouth shut. He was so proud of you, and he missed you so much."

"I know you mean well when you say that, but I don't really want to hear it right now. I'm..."

"Still grieving. That's okay. I just... I'll try to stop myself."

"What's it matter to you if I know he was proud of me anyway?" Alex muttered, his grip on his coffee mug so tight his knuckles were white.

"Because I loved him. And he loved you. I'll go inside. Stay. Enjoy your coffee and the sunrise, and I will..." She mimed zipping her lips together.

He shook his head. "You're a funny girl, Becca Denton."

"Not a girl," she muttered, pushing out of the rocking chair.

"I've got almost ten years on you."

"And Burt had almost ten years on my mom." Which

was so not what she should have said. Because that was insinuating…things.

He was quiet for a while and whatever he had going on in his head was all in his head. An unreadable secret. If she had an ounce of sense, she'd stop trying to figure it out.

"FYI, I don't want to sleep with you."

She jerked hard enough some coffee sloshed over her mug and spilled onto her fingers. "Excuse me?"

"The guys seem to think I want to sleep with you, and I just want make sure it's clear that that is not the case."

She could only stare at him, mouth gaping open, eyes practically bugging out of her head. She'd never even been kissed by a guy, let alone slept with one, and he was sitting there saying…

Well, what she would've known always and forever. Of course he wouldn't want to sleep with her! He was older and mature and had seen and experienced a million things. She was a girl who talked to animals and had never been kissed. Yeah, him not wanting to sleep with her was no surprise. Him announcing it though… What the hell?

He got to his feet. "I just wanted to make that clear."

"Believe me, I never thought otherwise," she muttered, even as a blush suffused her face. How were they talking about this?

"The correct answer is, you don't want to sleep with me either," he returned.

Before she processed that, he walked inside, Star tagging along after him as Ranger stayed put next to her.

She blinked after Alex, emotions grappling for purchase—embarrassment or shame or the undeniable truth that sleeping with him was quite the interesting prospect.

She tried not to think about that. She'd rather be irritated that he'd declare what the "*correct*" answer was. Rather be offended he'd be so up front about something like sleeping together. She'd rather be all those things, instead of embarrassed.

And she'd especially rather be all those things than *interested*.

# Chapter 11

It had been a long, hard day of work, and being such, Alex didn't feel much like getting cleaned up and heading into town. He'd have preferred a nice cold beer on the front porch and then a long, solid night of sleep.

But Becca had been right this morning about this being overdue. The guys needed some fun, some flash of life off the ranch to remind them there *was* life off the ranch. There was life, period. Not just work and missions.

There had to be balance for all of them. He'd agreed to back off on the leadership stuff, but he was still the resident expert, so to speak. He was the one who knew how to do all the ranch stuff and knew what ranch life entailed. He was the one who had lived it. So there was still a certain element of knowing things the guys didn't know.

It wasn't being an overbearing leader to make sure they dealt with ranch life in a healthy, sensible way.

He looked at himself in the bathroom mirror after having taken a shower. The little spot of hair in the back that stuck up when it got too long was being obnoxiously stubborn. He pushed it down again only to have it pop back up.

He scowled at the reflection—one he wasn't sure he recognized. Who was the man looking back at him? What was he trying to do?

He certainly didn't want to dwell on the fact that the man in the mirror was some kind of stranger. That this wasn't the plan. So, he focused on pushing the stubborn lock of hair down till it stuck.

He turned away from the mirror when it wouldn't. Who cared? He was going to go out to dinner, have a few drinks, and relax. His friends were going to enjoy themselves and he...

He didn't know. He wasn't sure he could enjoy himself, but he would put on a good front for them.

He left the bathroom and headed downstairs. Gabe and Jack were standing in the living room looking at their phones. Becca was nowhere to be seen.

"This restaurant better have steak," Jack muttered.

"If Georgia's is anything like I remember it, you won't be disappointed."

"I'd take a pretty view over steak," Gabe offered. "What's this Georgia look like?"

Before Alex could answer, Becca jogged down the stairs.

"That'll work," Gabe said with a grin that had Alex bristling.

But Alex couldn't deny she was quite the pretty view. She wasn't particularly dressed to kill. Nice jeans that actually hugged her hips instead of hiding them. She had a flannel shirt on over a tank top that scooped low enough for Alex to purposefully keep his gaze from following the curve of fabric.

Besides, he was a little too distracted by her hair. He'd never seen it down. She always wore it in a braid, but today it waved and tumbled over her shoulders, thick and shiny and distracting.

"What? Am I not dressed right?" she asked, straightening her shirt.

"You look fine," Alex replied gruffly.

"Then why are you all staring at me?"

Alex glanced at Jack and Gabe, who were still kind of slack jawed. Clearly, they all needed some…maybe not female companionship per se, but just getting back into the land of the living. They couldn't all be standing here drooling over a perfectly conservatively dressed woman.

"Is someone going to answer me?"

"We've just…never seen you with your hair down."

"Not exactly what I was looking at," Gabe muttered low enough Becca wouldn't be able to hear.

Alex narrowly resisted elbowing him in the stomach. So she had breasts and an ass. Plenty of women had those assets just as nice if not nicer. Plenty.

If only he could bring one of them to mind. "Let's go, huh? Gotta beat the rush."

Becca rolled her eyes. "Georgia's doesn't get busy, Mr. Sarcasm."

Alex grabbed his keys from the end table. He'd come to hate what keys symbolized, what he'd have to do with them, but that didn't mean he was going to chicken out of driving.

He could drive just fine.

"Let's take my truck. I gassed it up yesterday," Becca said.

They walked out toward the door and stepped out into the cool spring evening. The sun had already set behind the mountains, but the sky was a swirl of pink and purple. They walked over to where her truck was parked on a little gravel square in the front.

Alex held his hand out for her keys, ignoring the hitch in his gut and the hard knot in his throat.

Becca wrinkled her nose at him. "Why are you holding out your hand?"

"I'll drive."

Gabe cleared his throat, but when Alex glared at him, he didn't say anything or make any more noises.

Becca's attention was on Gabe, as if she stared at him with that soft, probing look in her eye, he'd explain. But after a few seconds, she turned that gaze to Alex. "No one drives my truck but me," she finally said. Firmly.

He could argue. He probably should. He didn't like being protected or whatever this was. He could drive. He'd driven in Texas when he'd been out of the hospital and waiting for Gabe and Jack to be released.

Sure, maybe he'd avoided it as much as he could, but that didn't mean he couldn't do it. It certainly didn't mean he would step down from doing it. He'd gotten over the resulting…trauma of being the driver of the accident. For the second time in his life, he'd had to get over a fear of getting into a car. And he wasn't a kid anymore. Not afraid.

"You know as well as I do your father never let anyone drive his truck," she said.

"What does that have to do with anything?"

"It means I thought that was a particularly good personal rule to follow. So I'm not letting you drive my truck, and there's no point taking your dad's truck, considering that it's not gassed up. So you can get in the passenger seat and let me drive, or you can stay home."

The funny thing was, as much as he wanted to be irritated, and as much as he was actually relieved he didn't have to drive, mostly he was just…sort of in awe of her.

Because he could see a change in her. It was actually

a lot like watching a new soldier get used to the rigors of military life. Some people withered away or shriveled into something else. Some people got used to it and managed to survive. And some people turned into something amazing—strong and certain where they weren't before. That was Becca. Growing into this person she wanted to be. By her own sheer force of will.

He admired that about her. Too much for his own comfort. But there it was.

"If you don't get in the passenger seat, I call shotgun," Gabe offered in the ensuing silence.

Alex grumbled halfheartedly, but he climbed into the passenger seat as the other guys got in back.

With an all-too-pleased smile on her face, Becca hopped into the driver's seat and started the truck. She drove them into town, chattering about the history of Georgia's diner. Mostly stories he'd heard growing up. Histories he'd always known. Nearly folklore and like pieces of him.

They drove down Main Street of Blue Valley, and the stories and the same storefronts he'd always known—they worked though him. He loved it. He still loved it.

Becca parked the truck in the gravel lot of Georgia's. The last time Alex had parked in this lot, he'd been with his father.

He hadn't realized that everyone else had started getting out of the truck until he was the last one in it. He slid out, but he knew Becca was staring at him in that way she had. As though she could read every piece of grief he couldn't seem to quash.

But he ignored her discerning eyes and focused on the small building ahead of them. It was squat, lined with a row of big windows with pretty, red-checked curtains behind them. When he stepped inside, he was greeted by the smell of burgers frying and the sound of people chattering. Two sheriff's deputies sat at the counter and a variety of old men and families littered the booths and tables in the small restaurant.

Memories assaulted him. Places he'd sat, conversations he'd had, old friends. His mother. High school. Dreaming of making a difference. He'd accomplished all that. And lost it.

It was only when Becca put her hand on his arm that he realized he'd stopped. While the other two guys had moved to an empty booth.

He cleared his throat and followed suit, continuing to ignore Becca's concerned gaze. She could be concerned all she wanted, but that didn't mean he had to acknowledge it.

Coming home was weird—that was all there was to it. The first few times he went into places where he'd grown up, it was natural he'd be assaulted by those memories. Natural it would feel a little out of body.

It wasn't…problematic. It was just one of those things you had to do. One of those things you had to experience. It'd wear off, like everything else.

Jack and Gabe had slid into one side of the booth, so Alex had to sit next to Becca on the other. He could smell her, something feminine and flowery. It was distracting but better than having to look at her.

The wavy hair, the all-too-shrewd green eyes, the compelling dusting of freckles across her nose.

Clearly he was just as desperate as the other guys. They needed to be around women more. But even as he tried to hold on to his usual denial, he couldn't get over the fact that Becca, well, she was a different problem than he wanted her to be.

She represented something he couldn't quite put his finger on. She was in none of those old memories, and yet she was connected to his father and his house and his ranch.

"Hey, Bec," Georgia greeted with a distracted smile. "And, Alex, it's been a while but I recognize you." She turned her attention to the other side. "And these must be your two soldier friends."

"Ah, small-town life is the same everywhere, I see," Jack muttered.

Meanwhile, Gabe flashed Georgia a grin meant to weaken the knees of any woman on the receiving end.

But Alex couldn't pay much attention to that. Georgia was nothing like he remembered her. She'd been a few years younger in school, named after her grandmother who had started this place fifty years ago.

She was older now. Of course he knew he was too. But instead of the bright, flashy teen who'd had dreams of getting the hell out of Blue Valley, there was a frazzled, harried woman waiting tables at a diner in the heart of Blue Valley.

What must have changed in her life? What must have changed in the lives of all of these people he had grown up with and known?

"Gabe Cortez," Gabe offered, inching the wattage of his grin up. "And you are?"

"Georgia. The proprietor." If she was charmed by Gabe, she didn't show it. "What can I get you fellas?"

They ordered drinks and Georgia disappeared.

"Please tell me she's single," Gabe said, watching where she disappeared behind the counter.

"Are you going to ask that about any young woman who crosses your path?" Becca asked.

"If they all look like that."

"Sad to say, I think she seemed wholly unaffected by your charm," Becca returned, clearly amused by Gabe. Or maybe Georgia's disinterest.

"Oh, don't be jealous, Bec. I'll ask it about ones who look like you too."

Becca rolled her eyes, but Alex noticed she didn't refute Gabe's claim. Would she be jealous if Gabe was interested in Georgia? Was she that into Gabe?

Which was none of his business. In fact, it'd probably be better for him if she were interested in Gabe. But not better for their business. Which did make it his business if they...

He was really losing it. What Becca did in her personal life was none of his business, no matter how his gut roiled at the idea.

But who wouldn't want her? Caring and sweet. There was a softness to her, but a strength too. She was beautiful.

*So, one hundred percent off-limits.*

He regretted inviting her. Especially if they were going to go to a bar. Especially if Gabe was going to flirt with her. Especially—

Georgia returned with their drinks and took their orders for food. She seemed completely immune to Gabe's flirtation, though Becca seemed amused by it. Jack was quiet and stoic.

Alex didn't know what was going on inside of him. He felt too jittery for his own skin. He felt like a ghost in a town that used to fit him like a glove. Every time a person walked by, he wondered if he'd known them, if he'd grown up with them. Had they known his father or his mother?

There were so many connections he'd lost without thinking about it, but now they were all around him.

When the food came—the same meal he could remember eating as a little boy—he had to excuse himself. He needed a minute alone to get his head together. And then everything would be fine.

Fine.

If the repeated *fine*s were getting a little hollow, that just meant he was *this* close to getting there.

---

Becca knew she wasn't the only one who thought Alex's abrupt departure was weird. But she was also a little leery of saying anything since Gabe had jumped down her throat the last time she had.

But she watched as Gabe and Jack exchanged glances.

Gabe nodded, then slid out of the booth and went in the direction Alex had disappeared.

Becca looked at Jack, who was sitting across from her with blank eyes and a blank expression.

"So do I just pretend like nothing's happening?"

"That's the way we work."

Ugh. Men. "Will you at least tell me what you think is wrong?"

"I'm not sure. And I'm saying that honestly, not because I don't want to tell you."

"I think he's homesick."

Jack's eyebrows furrowed. "But he is home."

"No, he's in this new, different Blue Valley. He grew up here, but everything is different now. The people are older. He's older. His parents are gone, and it's a different experience. I think it's a hard one, because you know..." Her heart pinched and her throat closed up a little bit. Because she'd had to go through a similar stage of her grief. When everything she had done reminded her of Burt.

"The thing is, you get to a point when you realize all of these things you knew for so long are never going to happen again. Since he hasn't been here to sort of see that change and evolve with it, he missed what it was." She noticed Jack's expression was hard. "Which you probably think is silly."

"No. I actually don't," he said on a sigh.

"You don't?" This was the most open Jack had been with her in all the weeks they'd worked together and lived under the same roof.

"There is a reason I didn't go home after I got released. I have a family and parents. Two little sisters, a brother. Grandparents and aunts and uncles and cousins. I have all of these people who would be very happy if I came home. But I came here. Which is not a short drive from Elk Grove, Indiana."

"So...you didn't go home because you were afraid it would be different?" she asked, wondering when he would cut off her questioning, wondering when he would clam up and turn into silent, stoic Jack again.

"Something like that."

She could tell he was debating telling her more, so she held her tongue. If she pressed now, she'd get that blank guy she was so used to. But if she let him do it in his own time, she might have a chance to find out a little bit more about him.

"I grew up in a small town. A lot like Blue Valley. Midwestern instead of mountains, and instead of ranches, we had farms. I had a high school sweetheart. She went to college. I joined the navy. We planned to get married. Before my first deployment, I proposed."

Becca had a bad feeling she knew what was coming, so she kept her mouth shut and tried to keep her expression from reflecting the pity she knew he would hate.

"I kept wanting to get married when I'd get some leave, and she kept pushing it off. Then on my last deployment, I found out she was sleeping with my brother."

It hurt. That people could be like that. Hurt someone who was already sacrificing so much. Even though she didn't know Jack all that well, she still hurt for him.

"So I knew going home wouldn't be the same. It would be nothing. It would be tainted by that. By change. By what they'd done. Now you know my life story. Happy?"

"I'll have you know, I didn't prod you to tell you me your life story."

"No, you just looked at me with those big, green eyes and didn't say a damn word because you knew I would spill my guts."

"I'm sorry that happened to you."

He gave one of those bitter laughs and shook his head. "You know the thing I don't get about you, Becca? You don't know me, and I haven't been particularly nice to you. But I know that you mean that, and that you care about people. I don't get it, but I see it."

"You have two little sisters. That's what you said, right?"

He nodded.

"I always wanted siblings. Someone to protect and vice versa. Someone to stand up against my mom with or someone who could help me help her. I always wanted a bigger family. And Burt was the first part of that. I hope you guys will be the next."

His eyes narrowed, not skeptically, but as if he was assessing her, much like Alex was always doing.

"You think of Alex as your big brother?"

Her face heated against her will. "I mean, Alex was my stepbrother there for a while, I guess."

"For a while, you guess. You know what's funny is neither one of you seem too keen on addressing that relationship full on. It's a lot of 'kind of' and 'I guess' and 'sort of.'"

Becca straightened because she wasn't going to let Jack intimidate her or make her feel uncomfortable. She gave him a cool, regal stare, or at least the best she could muster. "Is there a particular thing you're trying to get at, Jack?"

He stared at her for the longest time, and she did everything in her power not to fidget under Jack's icy-blue perusal.

"I think…you're a really good person, and you really care about people, and you want to see them happy. Alex is the same. He wants what's best for everyone… except himself."

"Why are you telling me this?" Becca asked, feeling like there was a point. Some point she was afraid of and so darn curious about.

But Jack looked behind her and Becca could only assume Gabe and Alex were on their way back.

She felt the cushioned bench depress before she glanced over. Alex sat stony faced and silent, immediately bringing the glass of water to his mouth.

Gabe slid back into his seat and if the look between Gabe and Jack communicated anything, Becca couldn't read it.

She was out of her depth here. All three of these men had dealt with things she had never even thought of happening to people. Not just in their Navy SEAL life, but apparently in their personal lives as well.

But Jack had it right about her. She cared about all three of them, damaged men trying desperately to find a way not to be. How could she not feel protective? How could she not care and want to see them heal? How could she not want to help them?

They wanted her to stay back and not get in their way. They didn't want her challenging their denial or whatever was going on in their heads.

But Becca was realizing that by following their orders to back off and give them space, she wasn't helping any. She wasn't being the strong, brave woman she wanted to become. Giving in to what they wanted, rather than what they needed wasn't going to help anything.

She thought what they needed was more than just work. More than just the foundation. They needed life. They needed this—going out to eat and flirting with Georgia and being human. Being civilians.

She was in no way equipped to be their therapist or psychiatrist or whatever. But she was equipped to help them find lives outside of their goals with the foundation.

She could give them Blue Valley and people, though people weren't *her* strong suit. Still, she knew…things, and she knew that belonging would give them almost as much as the foundation would.

"Do you guys want to hear the story about how the new Pioneer Spirit owner got the bar?"

"I take it he didn't just buy it," Alex offered, sounding so far away and lost.

She was going to help him find whatever it was he needed. She was going to help all of them. Her own personal foundation for these three *good* men. "No, *she* did not just buy it. Did you ever know Rose Rogers?"

"I am somewhat familiar with the Rogers girls. I don't remember which one Rose was."

"Well, as the story goes, Rose won Pioneer Spirit in a poker game. Many legends have sprouted from said poker game." Becca happily spent the next thirty minutes eating a hamburger and telling three men about Blue Valley.

Not the one Alex had grown up in, but the Blue Valley it had become in the past ten years. Not his old home, but his new one.

By the end of the meal, Alex was smiling. Becca would count that one as a win.

# Chapter 12

ALEX HAD NEVER SPENT MUCH TIME AT PIONEER SPIRIT. He'd left Blue Valley at eighteen. Most of his drinking days had happened in the navy. He'd been in one hundred bars in one hundred bad situations, flung all over the world, but he'd never spent much time here.

After dinner at Georgia's, even with Becca's stories of how Blue Valley had changed, he was glad to be somewhere that held no deep-seated memories for him.

There was a decent enough crowd for a small-town bar on a Thursday night. There was a jukebox blaring country music and two pretty bartenders sliding Budweisers down the slick surface of the bar.

Gabe was flirting with one of the women, who seemed maybe marginally more interested than Georgia, but only marginally. Jack was watching the crowd with assessing eyes. Becca also looked out over the crowd, but with wide eyes and a death grip on her bottle of beer. It was quite the evening.

"Why didn't you order whiskey?" he asked her over the bar din.

"Because I'm a lightweight and I have to drive us home."

"Drink. I'm only having one." Because he wasn't sure he trusted himself with a buzz—not to keep his shit together and not to keep from saying something stupid to Becca.

Like how he wanted to run his fingers through her hair or press his mouth to the graceful curve of her neck.

Yeah, shit like that was not even acceptable to *think*, let alone say.

"This is supposed to be your night of fun with Jack and Gabe. I think I can handle being the designated driver."

"I'm not drinking more whether I'm driving tonight or not. You deserve some fun too. Take it."

"Do people really think this is fun?" she asked, gesturing out at the crowd with her bottle. "I can't hear myself think over the noise. It smells like beer, grease, and…and I'm not sure I want to know what those other smells are."

"That's why you drink, so you don't notice it."

Her mouth curved and she shook her head, hair moving along her shoulders, and he found his eyes tracing one curl that ended right about where her shirt dipped low and—

He jerked his gaze back to the crowd. "Weren't you the one who said you want to be living life and breaking out of all that sheltered stuff?"

"Does that mean I have to get drunk?"

"Doesn't mean you have to. I'm just saying, drink if you want to. I'll drive us home."

She gave him a sideways glance, mischief dancing in her green eyes. "If you recall, I follow Burt's truck rules. My truck. Only I drive it."

He brought his beer to his lips and took a pull. "You know my dad let me drive his truck once."

"He did not."

"He did so." Alex smiled at her, couldn't help

himself. She was something like irresistible magic. He wanted her to smile, to laugh.

*You want her.*

"Anyway," he said, looking back down at his beer. "He might not have *known* he let me, but I drove the truck once."

She laughed, loud and pretty, and he wanted to lean forward into that laugh and then into her.

Which was why he was *not* drinking, though he could have used a fucking shot. Drinking and Becca could only lead to bad decisions.

He motioned to one of the bartenders, the one he was pretty sure was a Rogers girl. No, no longer girls. All grown up. He knew they'd lived in pretty crappy circumstances, and he couldn't help but wonder if they'd gotten out of them. It was one of the few changes he could get behind if they had.

"Two whiskey Cokes."

She nodded and turned to get the drinks.

"I thought you said you weren't going to drink," Becca said.

"I'm not. They're both for you." He flashed a smile and was a little too pleased by the blush that crept over her cheeks. He needed to get away from her. "I'm going to check out the jukebox. Be back."

He slid off the old stool and walked over to the machine. He pulled two quarters from his pocket and took his time figuring out what song he wanted to play.

Most of them were old, a lot of them rowdy bar songs. It seemed he couldn't go anywhere without being reminded of Dad, because half the available songs read like the man's record collection—Hank, Cash, Waylon.

In a fit of sentimentality that made him more than uncomfortable, he picked one of Dad's favorites.

He stayed there for a few minutes, letting the familiar strains of the Hank Williams song roll over him. Maybe he had to face the memories to get through them. Then he'd be able to move on. It was a theory anyway. A purpose.

Finally, he moved to head back to the bar and Becca. Gabe and Jack too, not just Becca. The guys were important, after all. He was here with them just as much as he was here with Becca. So he'd keep telling himself.

But as he walked back, he stopped short. There was a man talking to her. It wasn't Jack or Gabe. Jack had disappeared, and Gabe had finally caught the full attention of one of the bartenders, though not the one he'd originally been aiming for.

So there was some other *guy*, looming over Becca. Something uncomfortable reared in Alex's gut. It would be irresponsible for him not to step in and say something. Giving her space when she was clearly being bothered would be unconscionable, and if Jack had been around and Gabe hadn't been busy with his own agenda, Alex was certain they would have stepped in and done the same thing he was about to do.

"Excuse me."

The man reluctantly looked up from Becca. Like every damn person in this place and in Alex's life right now, he looked vaguely familiar.

"Alex Maguire! Heard you were back in town." The man smiled and offered a hand.

Alex knew the polite thing to do would be to respond and shake his hand. Instead, he just looked at the man who clearly thought he could…whatever he'd been doing talking to Becca.

"Mac. Mac Parker. You were friends with my big brother? Tyler?"

Tyler Parker. Yes, Alex had been good friends with Tyler growing up. He tried to think back through his recollections of Mac. A good deal younger, if Alex remembered right. Which put him much closer to Becca's age than Alex was.

He pushed that thought aside.

"He's over at that table in the corner," Mac said, gesturing toward a table Alex couldn't quite see. Okay, maybe he didn't try to. "I bet he'd love to see you."

Alex smiled grimly, though it flattened completely when he looked back just in time to catch Mac winking at Becca.

"It's been a while. Don't think I'd know him if I saw him," Alex said, making sure his tone was devoid of any emotion.

"Oh, well, you won't be able to miss him. He's in that table and I bet he'll recognize you. Your face was in the paper not all that long ago."

Fully aware Mac was trying to get rid of him, Alex stayed exactly where he was. Unfriendly and unyielding.

"You should go see your friend," Becca said, smiling encouragingly.

He only glared in response. Did she not have a clue what was happening here? Sure, she was sheltered, but she had to know a guy who *winked* did not have good intentions.

But apparently she didn't know that because she gave Alex a cocked-head, confused look for not scampering away as Mac suggested.

"So, Mac, what are you up to these days?" Alex asked, turning his glare to the young guy. He was wearing a button-up shirt and one of those rubber-band bracelets around his wrist. Alex didn't think it said *WWJD* based on Mac's glance down Becca's shirt.

"Not much. Work with Dad and Tyler on the ranch. Things are good for the Parkers these days." He smiled wide, and Alex wanted to punch him right in the target it made.

"I just bet they are." Alex stepped around Mac and took the barstool next to Becca, where he *had* been sitting not all that long ago. Mac looked at him, then at Becca, and then back out at the crowd. Alex took a sip from his near-empty beer bottle.

"Well, I guess I'll get back to my group. Come find me if you want that drink, Becca." He winked again and then sauntered back toward the corner table.

"You know only douchebags wink, right?"

"What do you think you're doing?" Becca demanded.

It was his turn to give her a cocked-head, confused glance. "Saving you from that turd."

"I didn't need saving from anything. I think he was flirting with me!"

"Exactly."

"Exactly?" She shook her head like he was being ridiculous. "The whole *not being sheltered* anymore thing includes flirting with guys. I was actually doing a decent job. I didn't get flustered and I didn't stutter. I blushed a little bit, but that's okay. Especially for my first time getting hit on in a bar."

"You're too naive, Becca."

"And you're not my father, Alex," she returned. "If

I am naive, it's my own damn business. I can take care of myself. I *know* the Parkers. Mac isn't exactly some strange guy."

"So has Mac ever hit on you before?"

"No, because Mac has been in Denver the past few years, getting his MBA, I might add. He just graduated."

Alex didn't know why that burned in his chest, but it did. So Mac Parker was a douchebag with an MBA. Was he was supposed to be impressed by that?

"I'm going to go over there and take him up on his drink offer and you are going to stay right here."

"Like hell I am."

She looked around and he thought she was maybe looking for Jack to back her up, but Jack was nowhere to be seen. And Alex knew Jack would back *him* up. Gabe and Jack would agree with his estimation of the situation. He was sure of it.

She raked a hand through her hair and then took one of the glasses of whiskey and Coke and drank it in one dramatic swallow.

He was not aroused by that.

He could tell she was working up to saying something, and based on the anger flashing in her eyes, it was going to be a scathing something. But that was fine. She could be a little bent out of shape about things right now, as long as she understood he was only trying to keep her safe. He wouldn't be sorry for that.

"You recall this morning when you told me you weren't going to sleep with me?"

Alex choked on the last sip of beer he'd taken.

"I'll take that as a yes, you remember. Well, here's the deal. I want to sleep with someone. Maybe it's not

Mac, and definitely not tonight or anything, but whoever and whenever, it does get to be *my* choice. I don't need some fake big brother trying to talk me out of it or getting in my way. I have a life to lead, and I damn well plan to have some *relationships*. So you can either get out of my way or…" She trailed off, that angry gaze dropping to the bar.

"Or what?"

She took a breath, then raised those flashing, green eyes back to his. She stared at him for the longest time, breathing angrily. Then she shook her head. "No. I have to… go to the bathroom." She got up off of the stool and fled.

---

Becca was livid. Absolutely furious. Unfortunately, she wasn't just furious at Alex. She was a little furious with herself.

She shouldn't have said that "or." She shouldn't have *thought* the "or" she'd been too chicken to finish.

Mac had come up and flirted with her. *Her*. She'd sat there like a scared animal and slowly realized as he smiled and chatted and offered to buy her a drink that it was time she had the types of experiences she'd always wanted.

She'd finally gotten out of her mother's overprotective shadow, but she'd hidden out there on the ranch. Hidden herself away from everything. But spending a month with the guys under the same roof, navigating a business with them, she'd learned something about standing up for herself and putting herself out there.

She didn't want a bar hookup or a one-night stand, but she did want to be open to the possibility that a cute guy might be interested in her. She wanted to be kissed or asked out on a date—all of those things normal adult women did. She wanted it. She was going to have it.

She didn't need Alex standing in her way when it was hard enough to not be in her own way.

She splashed cold water on her face and tried to get hold of her temper. Temper wasn't going to help her cause, and it wasn't going to...

She didn't know what. She didn't know what she wanted to be. She looked at herself in the mirror.

That was a lie. She knew exactly what she wanted. Alex's brown gaze on hers. It was *his* mouth she wanted to kiss her. That was probably all kinds of warped and whatever, but that's what she wanted. Even when Mac was standing there talking to her, smiling at her, she'd found herself glancing over at Alex...wishing it were him.

That wasn't his fault, unfortunately. That was her own dumb brain's fault.

Why didn't she have any girlfriends? She needed one. Someone who had done this before, who could tell her things she was supposed to know—mostly how to attract a guy and take things as slowly as she wanted to.

But she had no one. Except her mom, and that was a laugh.

She had to get back out there and... Unfortunately she didn't know what she had to do. What she should do.

Becca blew out a breath, giving herself a stern glare in the mirror. She was almost twenty-five years old. She had no guy experience and next to no friend experience. Which sucked, but it wasn't going to change if she didn't change. *Nothing* was going to change if she didn't do anything about it.

She walked back into the noisy bar and noted that Mac was sitting with his brother at the table in the corner. Alex hadn't joined them in an effort to reconnect with his old friend. In fact, Alex was nowhere to be seen. Jack had returned to the bar, but Gabe was now missing. She frowned and went over to Jack.

"Where'd everyone go?"

"Well, Gabe disappeared with the waitress. Alex went outside to get some air. Which I take it had something to do with you."

"No, it had something to do with Alex being an unrepentant ass."

For the first time in their almost month together, Jack grinned at her. "God, he *is* an ass. Means well." Jack gestured at her with his beer, and Becca looked at the line of empties behind him. He'd downed quite a few.

She decided to join him. She motioned for another drink, and the bartender complied. She sipped and glanced at Jack, who was just sitting there, drinking, watching the goings-on.

"Why aren't you trying to hook up with someone?"

"My heart is still deeply wounded, Becca," he replied, covering his heart with his hand in a mocking way, except she didn't think he was really quite as cavalier as the alcohol was allowing him to act.

"I wasn't talking about your heart." Clearly, if she was making comments like that, this needed to be her last drink. But Jack grinned again.

"Why don't you go hook up yourself?"

"Maybe I will. I have a hookup possibility." Not that she would take it, but there was something kind of confidence boosting about knowing a guy was willing to buy her a drink and flirt with her.

"Is he about six two and an ass?"

Becca choked on the sip of a drink she'd taken. "No!"

"Well, that guy is outside 'getting some air' and brooding over *you*. I don't know about this other guy."

Becca knew she turned a bright, bright red that would be visible even in the dim light of the bar. "The other guy was being very nice until Alex ruined it all."

"Of course he did. Jealous ass."

Becca snorted. "Jealous of what?"

"Um, a guy showing interest in you, the woman he can't seem to stop having interest in. I mean, don't get me wrong—he's gotta pretend he's not. He's Captain America, and you're off-limits, but that doesn't mean he's not interested."

She blinked at Jack, who was squinting into the crowd, closing one eye and then the other. She thought about this morning and Alex saying he didn't want to sleep with her, but...how did that come up if he wasn't *thinking* about sleeping with her?

Jack was drunk, obviously, but maybe she'd get better advice from drunk Jack than just about anyone else. "What am I supposed to do about that?"

"Well, you have two choices. You can go find the possible hookup to chat up and prove to Alex once and for all you don't care what he thinks. That he can't get in the way of your life, because he has no control over you. He's not in charge of you, can't order you around. It's a good feeling, all in all, telling him where to shove his orders."

"You are *drunk*."

"As a skunk. But drunk Jack is infinitely wise."

"Oh yeah, then what's my other choice?"

Jack screwed his mouth up. "Hmm. Other choice. Hmm. Oh! You go out there and you talk to Alex the Great. God knows you've got the skills to make his commitment to truth, justice, and the American way a little hard for him."

Again the blush washed over her face even though the first one hadn't receded. Skills? What the hell kind of skills did she have? "Isn't that Superman, not Captain America?" she managed.

Jack shrugged. "All the same, but you only get one life, Becca. So *you've* got to take the reins."

"So take the reins, Jack."

He closed one eye again and stared at her as if seeing her for the first time. His mouth curved and he gestured his bottle at her. "You first."

She turned around and leaned against the bar, looking out over the patrons. She glanced over at Mac. Mac would be the sensible choice. To go over there and let him buy her a drink, have a nice conversation. It could be...not easy exactly. She'd still be her nervous self, and she wouldn't have the first clue how to flirt back, but he wouldn't be complicated. Alex was nothing but complicated. *Everything* complicated.

And wasn't she tired of taking the simple, easy way out? Wasn't that the point of her whole life right now? That she wasn't a coward? That she could stand up for the things she wanted? Regardless of what anyone else wanted for her.

But she just wanted experience. She didn't need it to be difficult. Hard didn't mean good or worth it.

Did it?

She swallowed at the discomfort in her throat, took a breath against the jittery, tight feeling in her chest, and gave one last glance at Jack. "If I do this, you're up on the whole reins-taking thing."

"Aye, aye, Captain," he said with a salute, and there was something about the way he looked like he didn't believe her that spurred her on.

She made a beeline for Mac's table. Certain and sure and positive those were the reins she should take—until she got about two feet away, and then she paused.

Mac wasn't what she wanted. She wanted *experience*, yes, but Mac himself, as a person, wasn't the experience she wanted to have.

And this was about going after what she wanted. Or who.

# Chapter 13

ALEX STOOD IN A CLOUD OF CIGARETTE SMOKE OUTSIDE Pioneer Spirit. At least three people had offered him a cigarette, exhibiting the small-town kind of hospitality he'd grown up with.

Sadly, he wasn't looking for nicotine. He was after some clarity. He wanted something to make sense, and it wasn't making sense inside, with all that noise and darkness and Becca smiling at some tool.

He knew he had to get back inside. Make sure Jack hadn't drunk himself into passing out, make sure Gabe hadn't taken off with the waitress before her shift was over. He had to make sure Becca wasn't in there flirting with Mac Parker.

He had people to protect, whether they appreciated it or not. That had always been his job—to do things whether other people liked them or not.

It didn't change because he wasn't an officer anymore. It was a part of him, looking after people, wanting to help people. Ever since… He couldn't just shut that off because the person didn't want help.

He turned around to head back inside, but the door opened and Becca stepped out. With the battle light in her eyes that shouldn't do that thing it did to his gut. And lower.

He shouldn't have felt excited by the prospect of an argument with her. He should have been tired of it and irritated that she couldn't listen to him. Or understand him.

"So are you out here sulking or what?"

"Sometimes I think I prefer the Becca who picked us up from the airport and couldn't manage a word."

She gave him a curled-lip smirk. "That Becca is gone. As gone as I can make her be. But this isn't about me. It's about you. Your issues."

"I don't have issues. I have concerns."

"You know the Parkers just like I do. They're an upstanding family."

"An upstanding family doesn't mean someone isn't capable of doing something cruel. Doesn't mean they aren't capable of hurting you."

"Everyone is capable of hurting me, Alex. Believe it or not, Mr. Navy SEAL, there are people who are capable of hurting you as well."

He crossed his arms over his chest. "I don't see what that has to do with anything."

"No, you wouldn't." She shook her head, pressing her lips together more and more firmly until he wouldn't have been surprised if steam started coming out of her ears.

She grabbed his arm and began to pull. He considered fighting her—it wouldn't have been hard. She was strong, but not strong enough to forcibly move him. In the end, he let her drag him to the parking lot and her truck.

It was dark out here, though the moon and stars were bright. The air was cold and crisp and she didn't have a jacket on. He scowled. "Give me the keys."

"I'm not getting in yet."

"Just give me the damn keys."

On a frustrated grunt, she dug the keys out of her purse and threw them at him. Not lightly.

But he caught them and unlocked the truck, jerking the back door open and grabbing a coat. He didn't know whose it was, but it would at least keep her warm. "Put that on."

She shook her head and raked her fingers through her hair, ignoring the coat he held out. He curled his fingers into the fleece because if he thought about that, he wouldn't think about his own fingers following hers.

"I know when I need to wear a coat."

"I know you've got issues with your mom's overprotectiveness, but it's like thirty degrees out here. I'm not trying to smother you. I'm trying to..."

"What? Protect me?"

"*Yes.* That is what you do with friends. You protect them. I have protected Jack and Gabe for years. I made sure they had food before I did, made sure they had a place to sleep. It is what I do. It is who I am. You cannot change me because of your own baggage. And frankly, if you don't care for it, don't hang out with me."

"Did it occur to you we're not at war? That I know when to wear a coat, and I can figure out if a guy is talking to me because he's interested and what exactly he's interested in? Did it occur to you that I didn't ask to be lumped in with Gabe and Jack? If you want to talk about friendly concern, then let's talk about your nightmare the other—"

"No."

"You were shaking, and you didn't—"

"Enough!" He slammed his hand against the truck door and immediately regretted the outburst when she jumped in surprise. "I'm sorry." He cleared his throat and focused on being calm. "I am sorry."

"I know you are." She looked at him, concern radiating off of her in waves.

Her concern, her...whatever it all was, coiled inside of him, dark and ugly. He didn't want anyone's fucking concern. Most especially hers because it prompted some other thing inside of him he didn't know what to do with. Some kind of softening. A yearning, if he had to put a name to it.

He wouldn't.

"Let's go back inside," he muttered.

"No." She put her hand on the arm he had braced against the truck and her other hand on the wrist of the arm hanging at his side. Her fingers curled around his forearm as though she could keep him in place. It would've taken no effort at all to walk away, but...

She was touching him. He didn't want to walk away from that.

"Why are we really fighting?" She sounded soft, a little tired, and definitely a little drunk.

"Because you're obnoxious," he returned.

She gave a soft laugh, but her hands were still wrapped firmly around his arms and he was afraid to do anything. Because he didn't know how he would react if she slid her hands up his arms. If she touched his face. If she did any of the things he was imagining her doing.

He would have to be strong. He would have to put her in her place.

He was afraid he wouldn't be able to bring himself to do it.

"I need you to treat me like an equal. I think Jack and Gabe need the same thing from you. We're not asking you to change who you are. I know your instinct to take charge comes from a really good place. But we are all trying to figure out who we are and what we want and where we're going. I think you need to worry a little bit more about…"

She paused and he knew what she was going to say. He could've put her off. He could've told her to be quiet. He could've walked away. Instead, he stood there and let her talk. Instead of walking away from her hands curled around his arms, he let her say all the things he didn't want to hear.

"Try focusing on you instead of us. Please? For all of our sanities."

"I'm trying." Which was the sad part. He was trying to back off, but his brain didn't work that way. He didn't want to think about himself. He had his mission. That was all he wanted to focus on.

Becca leaned into him, and he was so lost in his own thoughts for a second, he didn't think to sidestep it or stop her. Her hands slid off his arms, but they came around him. A hug. She was hugging him.

And he couldn't…he couldn't move or speak. Partially because she felt soft and smooth and smelled so damn good, even after the bar. But partly because it had been so long since someone had hugged him. Since he'd been offered that kind of soft touch.

He had to swallow against the tightness in his throat and stiffen against the need to draw her closer.

For the first time, he wished the feeling in his gut was merely sexual rather than…whatever this was. Pain, comfort, longing.

"You try so hard for so many people. I know we keep snapping at each other lately, but we're trying hard too."

She didn't stop hugging him, but she pulled back far enough that she could tilt her head up and look at him.

If she had anything else to say, apparently meeting gazes put a stop to it. Her eyes seemed to take in everything, from his hairline, to the square cut of his jaw, to...

His mouth.

It would have been easy to kiss her. Lower his mouth to hers and sink into a sweetness he did not deserve. It would have been so damn easy, and it was so damn tempting. Especially when she moved on to her toes, that pretty, lush mouth closer than it had a right to be and...

"Don't," he managed to command.

She stopped on a dime, looking at him wide-eyed.

Her expression changed. The softness and surprise going hard. What was wrong with him that he liked all the different sides of her? Soft and stubborn and hard and good and sweet and honest and a little neurotic.

"Why did you send Mac away back there?" Becca demanded, her arms still around him.

"I told you. I was trying to protect you."

"That's the only reason in the whole wide world you didn't want him flirting with me?"

He was afraid she could see all of the reasons inside of him. She was still so close, and he needed to stop this. To walk away.

He could even tell her. All the truths inside of him he was trying to push away. He could tell her he didn't like some other guy flirting with her. And it had nothing to do with Mac Parker or this bar or whatever. He could tell her he didn't want *anyone* else touching her. That it physically hurt to think about someone doing that.

But how could he explain that he couldn't stand someone else even thinking about touching her, because then *he* thought about touching her? Having her.

So he had to lie. To both of them.

———

Becca had never been this close to a man before. Not in an embrace, not with her mouth close enough that it would take less than a second to kiss him.

Not that Alex was reciprocating anything. He remained frozen in place and she didn't know how to let go of him. How to step away. Even when he'd ordered her not to kiss him, she didn't know how to walk away.

Because he hadn't answered her question. Not fully. If he'd only tell her that…that all he cared about was her well-being and safety. That this had nothing to do with the attraction *she* felt, then she would give this up. She would go back inside and sit with Mac and know that nothing with Alex was ever going to happen.

But he had to tell her. She needed to hear it from his lips to really be able to give it up.

He lifted the hand that had been hanging at his side and curled his long, blunt fingers around her elbow. He removed her arm from around him, but as he pulled her arm off and released her elbow, his fingers trailed— probably accidentally—down her forearm.

It jittered through her, like nerves and electrical shocks. Something swirling low in her stomach, sparks rioting in her chest.

His breath hitched, but his gaze didn't meet hers as he pulled her other arm from around him.

"I don't know what you're trying to get at. I don't know what other reason there could be."

But he didn't *look* at her, which was so weird. Alex always looked her in the eye.

"You're lying." Which she hadn't meant to say out loud, but it was such a surprise to see it. To read him so well and so easily. "You're really bad at it."

His gaze finally met hers, and *that* she couldn't read, whatever war was going on in his dark depths.

"Maybe you think I'm lying because that's what *you* want."

Which was true, but there was too much lining up to her way of thinking. *He'd* brought up not sleeping together this morning. Jack's words—as drunken as they might have been—the whole not looking her in the eye and shuddering when they touched.

"Okay, that *is* what I want."

She could tell she'd surprised him. That he'd expected her denial or maybe her to stutter and scamper away, but she wasn't going to do that. "I'm attracted to you. Yup. Not going to deny it. You're hot. You're a good person—such a good guy, even when you're annoying the piss out of me. I feel comfortable around you in a way I don't with a whole heck of a lot of people. So, yeah, I'm not going to stand here and try to deny it, because I am not a coward—but you are."

The shock written all over his face sharpened. "Excuse me?" he said, dangerously calm.

Clearly the word *coward* got under his skin. But that's what he was being. Hiding behind lies and whatever else. It *was* cowardly. She should know. She was always a coward when it came to people.

Well, not anymore.

"I said you're a coward," she replied, giving a shrug she wished felt a little more nonchalant. "You won't admit you feel exactly the same way. Because you're afraid. Or is that for my protection too?"

He took a deep breath, clearly trying to find some calm, but his eyes were furious and his jaw was so tight it was a wonder it didn't crack in half. Everything about him vibrated with anger, and she felt powerful.

Her. Becca Denton. She felt *in charge* and *right*. Not a doubt or a second of uncertainty.

"A coward, huh?" he finally muttered through gritted teeth, one of his hands flexing into a fist and then open again.

"Yes. A big ole fraidy-cat over the fact that you've got some feelings for your much younger step—" But before she could get the remaining words out of her mouth, he used the front of her shirt to jerk her against the hard wall of his much larger body. She was too shocked to jump back or fend it off, and even though nerves slammed through her, well, she liked being this close. Not just hugging close, but *pressing* close.

Then his mouth crushed against hers, hard and unrelenting, and whatever powerful feeling she'd had evaporated on the spot. Incinerated completely. She didn't even have time to think about how she didn't know how to do this. His hands were in her hair, her *hair*, tangling and moving her head whichever darn way he pleased.

She grabbed for purchase, a little afraid her knees were wobbly, holding on for dear life. Letting his lips and tongue lead hers, *guide* hers.

It was fire and it was shock and it was *good*. It was good to be hollowed out and feel as though she was filled with liquid gold. Shimmering and lazy. To be pressed up against nothing but hard muscle and skilled mouth and know not a thing could touch her here.

Not a thing but him.

"Christ, we can't do this," he muttered, but it was against her mouth, his arms banded around her so that whether they *could* or not, they certainly *were*.

She wanted to keep doing it. Experiencing it. Participate instead of just letting it happen and soak it up—which was good, oh it was *good*, but she wanted more.

So she didn't stop. She pressed her mouth right back to his, wrapping her arms around his neck, and jumped head-long into that heat she would have never guessed existed.

# Chapter 14

ALEX DIDN'T KNOW WHAT WAS HAPPENING TO HIM. HE never lost control like this. He shouldn't. He couldn't.

Except all he *couldn't* do was stop. Stop touching those silky strands of hair, stop feeling the way her soft, lithe body molded to his, stop the impact of her tongue timidly running across his bottom lip.

So many things jolted through him—such deep physical connection, the taste of her, and something bright and happy and...foreign, really. He hadn't felt like this in years, and even then there was something different.

She felt small in his arms, and yet she was strong and certain. She was definitely the one leading this. Prompting this. She was somehow in charge and making him feel upside down and inside out and, strangest of all, like that was a good thing.

The arguments in his brain got quieter and quieter the louder the heartbeat in his ears grew. His skin burned like fire and his breath waged a war against his lungs. He was hard and desperate and tired of the tight rein on his control he always employed.

He nibbled at her mouth. She made a noise that was somewhere between a squeak and a moan. He held on to her for dear life, and it was only the thought that he wanted to press himself against her hard enough to back her against the truck, that he wanted to have his hands under her clothes and hear her make that sound over and over in a freezing-cold parking lot to a crappy townie bar in Blue Valley, Montana, that cut through the insanity buzzing though him.

He had to stop this madness. He had to stop. Period.

It took a few more seconds for his body to accept his brain's determination. He managed to pull her off of him, though she tried to arch against him instead. He was so hard and aching it nearly undid him. But he was a strong man. A soldier. He had to do what was right.

He untangled her from him and stepped a good few strides away. He didn't have a clue as to what to say, but even if he had, he wouldn't have been able to say it. His breath was still coming in short spurts. His heart was pounding so hard in his ears he wouldn't know what his voice sounded like even if he could get it to come out.

When he looked over at her, she was grinning, her teeth sunk into her bottom lip, palm pressed to her cheek. She was looking at him like he was some kind of…something.

He took a breath, everything sharp and painful centering itself in his chest. This had been a dereliction of duty, plain and simple.

She sighed. "You're going to be all weird now, aren't you?"

"I'm not…" He had to clear his throat to speak without that odd rasp to his words. "I'm not going to be weird."

"Okay. Then what are you going to be?"

He cleared his throat again and straightened his shirt, if only to give himself something to do while he tried to figure out what to say. "I'm going to be sensible and responsible and—"

"Boring?"

He glared at her. "You know as well as I do that was a mistake."

"I actually don't know that. I liked it. And I'd like to do more of that. With you."

Christ, she was just going to kill him. Stab him in the heart and jiggle around the blade, then maybe kick him a few times while he was down.

"We are starting a business together," he began, searching for the rules he'd laid out for himself.

"And?"

"And if we..." He had answers to that. He did. But maybe it was the wrong tack to take, because he needed this over. Or he was going to be a little too tempted by the moonlight reflecting off the moisture on her lips. "I mean, our parents were married. Which makes this weird." That was the other rule, wasn't it?

"Yeah, a little. But it's not as if we ever lived under the same roof or...you know, anything that normal stepsiblings do. Our parents were married and you were far away. If it were really that weird, I don't think the kiss would've been that good."

"I thought you were sheltered and nervous and scared?" he demanded.

Her grin widened, if that was at all possible. "I did too. I guess I'm not such a mess. At least, not as much of one as I thought. I've spent a lot of my life living for someone else. To make Mom happy and to hopefully make her see that I was safe and healthy and happy. She sacrificed a lot for me, and I did the same for her. I don't have to anymore. So I'm not going to. I guess that makes me... well, not as much of a scaredy-cat as I thought I'd be."

"This..."

"Was a really great kiss. Like, really great... Right?"

There was just enough of a hint of vulnerability that he couldn't lie to her, even though he should have. "Yes, it was a very great kiss, but that doesn't mean—"

"It means that we have chemistry, right? And when you have chemistry with someone, you explore it."

"Not when it's this complicated."

She did that thing where she cocked her head and stared at him as though he were some strange specimen she didn't understand. What was there to understand? Nothing about him would make sense when she was sweet and young and innocent as all get-out.

*And she kisses like a fucking miracle.*

He scratched his hands through his hair in frustration. He had to find his center. The thing that led him through every moment of his life, knowing what was next. Enduring. Surviving. Excelling. He had to channel it and use it. To nip this very dangerous, complicated, unwanted situation in the bud.

"You've been sheltered and you want experiences," he began, hoping he sounded like a teacher or an officer. Someone mature and in charge instead of a floundering asshole. "It's natural that you might fixate on me. But—"

"No. No, no, no. Don't ruin it."

"Ruin what?"

She patted him on the chest, then sauntered past him, back toward the bar. "My first kiss," she shot over her shoulder.

He stared after her, just another painful thing in a long line of painful things clutching at his chest. He'd known she was sheltered and innocent, of course. She'd made that abundantly clear. He wouldn't have been surprised if she'd said she was a virgin.

But first kiss? With him? In a cold-as-fuck parking lot? And she was smiling and sauntering away like that was a good thing. Something she wanted, something she didn't want him to ruin.

But this wasn't first-kiss material. It hadn't been sweet or someplace nice or after a charming dinner. It was in a crappy bar parking lot and...

He wanted to ignore the truth, wanted to deny it all, but it didn't matter where they'd been. It didn't even matter all the ways it was wrong and complicated and shouldn't have happened.

It was a damn fine kiss. Chemistry. Sparks. Like he'd never felt before. Something a little raw. Something bright and promising and so full of sweetness and hope, like a sunrise over the mountains.

Which was a fanciful enough thought to have him rolling his eyes at himself. Clearly they needed to go home. Needed to go back to the ranch and find some... sense. Rationality.

But first, he had to get rid of this erection.

---

Becca returned to the bar. Gabe was back, and he and Jack were laughing over something. She thought briefly about ordering a few more drinks and downing them in quick succession, but she didn't want to lose this feeling ricocheting through her.

She wanted to roll around in it. Revel in it. Attraction and want and lust. Even the frustration that went with it. It was so...amazing. All this feeling rushing around in her at once. To feel jittery and bubbly and hot and bothered and all of those other adjectives she'd never fully understood before. They jostled for space in her chest and in her stomach, and it was…absolutely perfect.

"You look awfully pleased with yourself. What have you been up to?"

Becca smiled brightly at Jack. "Just some fresh air."

He narrowed his eyes, clearly not believing her, but she wondered if he would even begin to guess what had transpired in the parking lot. That Captain America had lowered his morals so far as to kiss her.

Not just a little peck either. No, that was a *kiss*. A grade A obliterate-common-sense kiss. She wanted so much more than that from him. But for tonight, she was willing to dwell in that one first experience.

She wasn't going to let him ruin it, no matter what he said. She was going to cherish that moment forever. He couldn't take it away.

"So, you're all too happy and Alex just walked through the door like he's about to kill someone. What do you make of that, Jack?" Gabe asked leisurely.

Gabe and Jack exchanged glances, but all Becca could do was grin as Alex approached.

She actually didn't think he looked angry. He looked stormy. Confused. Okay, a little angry, but not solely that. There was a lot of *mixed up* in that look, and she was glad for it. Glad that she could mix him up. Because if she affected him, it meant…it meant this whole thing meant something. It meant it was not just okay that she was pushing, not just that she was standing up for herself, but that she was right in everything. She was right that this was exactly what she needed to be doing right now.

"All right, bus is leaving," Alex said, his voice low and gravelly and daring anyone to argue.

Apparently Gabe was willing to take the dare. "Still early, warden."

"You're welcome to stay and see if that waitress will give you a ride home, but I'm leaving. Anyone who wants to get back to the ranch tonight better get their ass in Becca's truck."

Feeling emboldened both by the kiss and probably at least a little by the alcohol in her brain, Becca slid right against Alex as she passed. She gave him a look that she hoped was flirtatious and not just giddy. "Yes, sir."

She could barely stop herself from giggling as she walked back out where she'd just come from. Whatever Gabe and Jack said to Alex as they walked out of the bar was lost on Becca. She was happily oblivious in her own world of, well, whatever this was. Having a guy interested in her. Having him be a little conflicted about it. Having something as exciting happen as a guy jerking her to him and kissing her senseless.

She sighed dreamily as they reached the truck.

The ride home was mostly silent. Occasionally Gabe or Jack would relate some story from their time at the bar, but Alex never showed any reaction, and Becca was mostly too busy reliving that kiss to pay them any mind.

Alex drove up the crest of the hill that led to the ranch. Darkness and starlight enveloped the entire vista in front of them. Alex pushed the truck into park, then gave them each a glare.

"You will go to bed. I'm going to go check on Hick."

Gabe and Jack got out of the back of the truck, but Becca stayed where she was, staring at Alex. He pressed his lips together in a scowl, then shoved out of the truck himself.

"Don't be difficult," he muttered before slamming the truck door behind him.

It was probably childish to want to be difficult, since he'd ordered her not to be, but she was a little too—well, not drunk exactly, but a bit tipsy—to care.

She thought maybe Alex needed a little bit of difficult. Someone to be a pain in his ass. So he could realize he wasn't in the military anymore. There were no rules and no codes or regulations on how any of them had to live.

It wasn't that she didn't empathize with him on how hard it must be to adjust to a brand-new way of living, but that didn't mean she was going to be easy on him. He had a whole amazing life ahead of him. He needed to realize it.

She'd help him realize it. That was *her* mission.

She slid out of the truck, but she didn't go to the house. She walked in the opposite direction, toward the fence that looked out over the mountains. Everything around her was dark, but with the moon and starlight, she could vaguely make out the looming peaks of those beautiful, majestic rocks that made up the landscape around them.

She wanted to breathe it in. Appreciate it. Feel in awe of it—and she wanted him to see and feel that too.

"Becca," Alex said in a warning voice she was sure he used on his soldiers.

"I'm not quite ready to go inside. Go check on Hick. I'll be fine." She stepped up onto the first rung of the fence, lifting her face to the moon.

"I'm not leaving you out here to drunkenly freeze yourself to death."

"Honestly, Alex, I am not that drunk, and you are not that overprotective. Or you need to stop trying to be. As we've discussed."

He didn't say anything for a while and she didn't move. She soaked in the clusters of stars and listened to the rustling of an early spring night. She listened to Alex's steady, even breathing, and she traced dark mountain peaks with her eyes.

She wanted to stand here and dream of summer and kisses and a million other beautiful things.

She should've known Alex wouldn't make it easy.

"Do not make me throw you over my shoulder and take you inside myself."

She glanced over her shoulder at him. "Is that an order, or like a sex thing? Because if it's a sex offer…"

He sputtered and she laughed—at the fact that she'd said something so outrageous. That she'd made Mr. In Charge Navy SEAL sputter. This really was the best night.

"What are you trying to do to me?" he demanded, pained and irritated.

"Believe it or not, Alex, I'm not trying to do anything *to* you. I am trying to live my life. I'm trying to enjoy a moment. I am trying to…" She stepped down from the fence and turned to face him. The moonlight gilded him silver or marble, some majestic, ancient Greek god standing there. He looked grim and angry, but underneath that was a sense of loss she understood so well.

He needed to come through the other side.

"The past year has been so hard and sad. I have fought my mother for independence. I've fought through my grief and knowing I'm never seeing Burt again. I have been barely holding on by a thread, and I am tired. I'm tired of being sad, and I'm tired of being frustrated. I am damn tired of not doing what I want. I don't want much. I want to work hard on this ranch and on our foundation. I want to help people. And I want to kiss you. Again and again and again."

"You keep saying you want…me, but you're drunk and…"

"Do you really think you're not worthy of that?"

"Are you trying to sound like a shrink?" he demanded, clearly at his wit's end with her. Which, by her estimation, was exactly where he needed to be.

"I'm trying to understand why this is so hard for you."

"It's not."

She stared at him for the longest time, realizing that in a weird way, Alex needed the same thing she had for the past few years—to break away from the cage he'd probably unwittingly put around himself. Open up and reach out and try. But it would be hard, and he wasn't quite at the moment yet.

But that was okay. Because she'd been there, and she could show him. "I'm going to break you, one way or another."

"Break me?"

She straightened, more and more certain it was exactly what he needed. "Yup." She took a few steps toward him, confident and sure. Emboldened. So damn happy and excited for the future it hurt. "I'm not backing down anymore. I'm not letting you pretend you're fine when you're not, or that you don't have the hots for me when you *do*."

"The *hots*?" he repeated as if he didn't believe what he was hearing.

"Yes. I know you think you're strong enough to deny this or resist it or endure it or whatever, but what you're about to learn, Alex Maguire, is that strength is not about what you can endure. It isn't about what you can accomplish when you have a mission to see through. It's about wanting something and not being afraid of going after it. It's about allowing yourself to admit you want something in the first place. That will be your biggest challenge. But don't worry, I'll be here to hold your hand."

Then she moved up on her tiptoes and brushed her mouth across his bottom lip. "Good night, Alex," she said before he could respond. And she walked back to the house, happier than she'd been in a long time.

# Chapter 15

EVERY TIME HE FELL ASLEEP, A NIGHTMARE CONSUMED HIM. Completely. At one point, he'd woken curled up on the floor, not knowing how he'd gotten there.

He gave up on sleep and not being a grumpy asshole sometime before dawn. Likely his crew had hangovers the size of Texas, and they'd be stumbling around all morning trying to get through them.

He would have zero sympathy as he worked his ass off. To keep his mind off of the thing he shouldn't have his mind on. He pushed himself off the ground and got dressed, having showered last night to get the smell of bar and Becca out of his clothes, and hair, and mouth.

When Alex walked into the kitchen, Jack was already there, yawning into a mug of coffee.

"What the hell are you doing up?" Alex demanded.

"Drinking always makes me get up way too early. Made coffee."

"Great. Thanks," Alex grumbled.

"You look like you've been through hell. Or should I say, Becca Denton?"

Alex didn't even bother to glare. He was too tired.

"I noticed she didn't come in when we did last night. Good twenty minutes after," Jack continued, clearly not taking a hint that Alex wanted nothing to do with this subject. Or maybe that was the point.

"Yes, because she wanted to needle me some more. Obnoxious woman that she is."

"She's sweet. Weirdest damn thing."

"Why is that weird?"

"I'd kind of forgotten sweet existed. If you'd asked me a month ago if I would've wanted anyone around me to be *sweet*, I would have said fuck no. But…I don't know. Not so bad coming from her."

"If you say so."

"She really bothers you, doesn't she?"

Alex didn't have to look at Jack to know he was grinning. "I don't know what you're talking about," he returned. Becca didn't bother him, she…she…jumbled up his damn soul.

"I think you do. She gets under your skin. And it bothers you that she does. Can't say I mind watching it happen."

"Can't say I mind watching you shut the hell up."

Jack laughed and, much like the woman in question, that created two very different responses in Alex. It annoyed the hell out of him, but it was good to see Jack laugh, even at Alex's expense.

"So, are you going to tell me what transpired between you two outside the bar last night?"

"No."

"And why's that?"

"Because it's none of your business," Alex replied, staring at the steaming, black liquid in his coffee mug.

"So, to be clear, what you're saying is that something happened outside the bar between you and Becca…but it's none of my business what that something was?"

"Yes, that's what I'm—" Alex looked over at Jack, who

was grinning broadly, and Alex realized he was playing a little too much into whatever Jack was trying to get at.

"So something *did* happen," Jack reiterated.

"Since when did you get to be such a gossip?"

Jack stretched his arms behind his head and leaned back into his linked hands. It reminded Alex, a little painfully, of a time before, well, war.

"I think it's something I'm going to take up in my military retirement," Jack was saying. "Gossiping about other people's sex lives."

Alex pointed a finger at Jack. "Becca and I are not having sex. Jesus H. What the hell is wrong with you?"

"You're not having sex *yet*. I think *yet* might be an important word."

"There is no important word."

"Why can't you just admit that you like her?" Jack asked, leaning forward, some of his easy smiles and amusement fading. "Why can't you admit that she is smart and funny and cute, and she doesn't take your crap too seriously, which I find the most endearing thing about her?"

"Why are you trying to matchmake? We have a foundation to start. With the woman in question. Who just happens to be—"

"No, you can't use the stepsister thing only when it suits you."

"Says who?" Alex demanded. It was a convenient excuse all in all, even if Becca had obliterated it last night.

Again Jack laughed. "I don't think I've ever seen you quite so…worked up. Or is it confused? Or is it"—Jack feigned a gasp of horror—"not knowing exactly what to do?"

"I don't think I've ever seen you quite so annoying, and that is saying something, Jack."

Jack was quiet for a while, and Alex could only hope that was the end of it. What he wouldn't give to shut everyone up—including his own brain.

"Can you just explain to me why you think it would be so monumentally awful if you let yourself enjoy something with her?" Jack asked, sounding far more sincere than Alex wanted him to.

"What kind of question is that?"

"It's an honest one. For as long as I've known you, Alex, you have taken on the responsibility of ten men. You've been a damn fine leader and even a good friend. You were one of the few people who didn't make awkward jokes or avoid me altogether when the shit with Madison went down. But you have never allowed yourself one ounce of freedom. Fun."

Alex tensed at the unfortunate truth in that. The past few years had not been fun. He'd been weighted. Drowning in responsibilities and the fate of others. Sometimes it had even felt like the fate of the country rested on his shoulders.

Which hadn't been right, but...well, he'd been in charge of keeping peace, ensuring freedom. He was making up for the thing he'd been too young to fix. He'd lost the ability to take that lightly.

"Maybe that's because I came into the regiment later and you'd already been deployed a couple times," Jack continued in that same maddeningly even and sincere tone. "Maybe I didn't know you at your fun-loving best. But she's a sweet girl and she likes you. The only reason you haven't started something with her is that we all work together—not that you're not interested in her right back. You wouldn't be conflicted if you didn't feel something."

Alex opened his mouth to stop this entire conversation. To bark out an order to cease and desist. Except he wasn't supposed to order anyone around anymore. He'd promised to back off on that, and the promise was the only thing that had him shutting his mouth.

"I get working together can be sticky. But I'd say we've dealt with a lot stickier situations in our lives. So you'll have to excuse me if that doesn't hold much water."

"What the hell is all of this to you?"

Jack drained the last of his coffee and gave a little shrug as he stood. "You know, believe it or not, Alex, you're my friend and I care about you. Which hopefully is the only time in my life I actually have to say that out loud, unless I'm present at your deathbed. Gabe and I want you to be happy because…maybe you were sacrificing things for us because it's how you're wired, but it doesn't mean it goes unnoticed. It certainly doesn't mean we don't appreciate it. We're here because of you. We made it through that accident and hospital stint in large part because of you. So why does it matter? Because I like you, and I care as much about your future and happiness as you do about mine."

With that, Jack walked swiftly out of the room.

Alex took Jack's vacated seat, a headache throbbing at his temples as though he'd been the one to kick back twentysomething beers last night.

He wanted to dismiss everything Jack had said. He wanted to ignore it. But that was the thing about Jack that always snuck up on Alex. Jack knew how to push a guy's buttons. He knew how to give reasoning so tight no one could get out of it.

He'd offered something Alex couldn't ignore. Because if part of Jack's happiness and healing was tied in with Alex being happy and healing himself…he was going to feel like a guilty ass until he did it.

But happiness was not intrinsically tied to *Becca*. Maybe she made him laugh, and occasionally talking about things he'd rather face an insurgent than deal with wasn't so bad with her, but that didn't mean he had to act on anything.

Maybe that kiss would haunt him for the rest of his life, but that didn't automatically mean he should repeat it. Even if she was more than willing. Even if it was a little bit more than perfect.

Maybe he wanted to be around her most all the time, kissing or not, but that didn't mean…

Hell. He might be an expert in denial, but even he could see how weak his "that didn't means" were.

Now, if only he knew what the hell to do about that.

---

Becca groaned at the high-pitched trilling way too close to her ear. Her stomach sloshed and her head pounded. Even with her eyes still closed and the noise stopping, she felt gross and vaguely ill.

When she managed to open her eyes, she whimpered as the sunlight streamed in through the sides of her curtains.

She'd slept in, and her phone was ringing again, and she felt like utter shit.

How was this fair? She knew some people could drink all the alcohol in the world, but if she ever went over one hard alcoholic beverage, she was toast the next morning.

Her phone stopped ringing and she relaxed with a sigh of relief. Only to groan again when it started squawking.

She pawed around for the offending phone and wrinkled her nose at the fact that her hair still smelled like the cigarette smoke from outside the bar, even though she'd showered after coming inside last night. Hannibal meowed irritably from his position at the end of the bed. A spot he almost never left.

When she finally grabbed her phone and looked at the screen, she groaned again. This time not in pain, but in frustration and possibly guilt.

She hit Accept and tried to work some cheer into her voice instead of gravel and hangover. "Morning, Mom. How are you?"

"Worried."

*How unusual*, Becca thought sarcastically. It was an unkind, snotty thought, and Becca winced at the way it almost escaped her mouth. "Worried about what?" she asked instead.

"Do you know how many people have told me they saw you at Pioneer Spirit last night?"

Becca scratched a hand through her still-stinky hair. "No. Why would people care if I was at Pioneer Spirit?" Becca tried to think of anyone last night who would have passed that on to Mom. Or why they would have.

"Because apparently they have more sense than you do."

"Mom, I'm so not in the mood for this." She didn't trust herself to be kind in the face of Mom's criticizing worry. Not this morning. Not when she was feeling crappy and late for her chores.

"Why, because you're hungover? Because you had some crazy night on the town?"

"Mom, I'm almost twenty-five. I get to go to a bar if I want to go to a bar. I hardly had some sort of drunken orgy." She probably shouldn't have put that idea into Mom's head. Now that's all she would be convinced of.

Mom's silence on the other end was damning. Flippancy had never calmed her mother's worry, and Becca knew better than to employ it. "Mom, I—"

"If this is the influence those men are having on you, then I absolutely want you staying in town with me."

"You know I can't stay with you and take care of the horses."

"Isn't that what we have Hick for?"

"No, Hick is for helping with the cattle and watching over things if we need to get out. He is integral, but I'm not having him do all my work for me while I sit in your house because you're afraid that I… What are you even afraid of? Mom, I haven't been really sick in years."

"Are you sleeping with them?"

"Sleeping with who?" Becca demanded, too sluggish to keep up with Mom's accusations.

"Any of them. Have they convinced you that—"

"Mom. Seriously. You can't do this. I am an adult."

"Yes. One I've protected your whole life. You don't know a thing about men or what they're capable of. I thought I could trust Alex, being Burt's son, but—"

"I am not completely unaware of the fact that men can be awful. That people can be cruel. That's life. I may not have experienced much of it, but I'm aware of it. You can't—"

"I never even had the talk with you."

Becca physically and emotionally recoiled. "And you don't need to. Please. Listen to me." Becca let out a breath and tried to think, but it was hard finding reason and sense with the pounding in her head and the frustration deep in her bones.

"I know I'm not very good with people—well, actually I'm finding I'm just not *used* to people, not that I'm bad with them. I certainly don't have a lot of experience with guys, but I know what goes on in the world. I know what sex is and… But I'm not…" She didn't know what exactly she should give Mom. The whole story? Just nip this in the bud? How did she cut these apron strings when they had been tied so tight and for too long?

"Can you just trust that if I have a problem or someone hurts me or I don't know what to do that I will come to you? I will tell you and I will ask you for help and advice. Can you let me figure some things out on my own if I promise to come to you the first time I don't want to or can't do that?"

"You are all I have left in this world," Mom said with a sniff audible over the phone. "I have tried so hard to give you some space like Burt wanted me to, but I hate it. I hate losing you like this."

Becca felt unwanted tears sting her eyes. That was the problem with this whole thing. She was all her mom had left. Mom had lost the few people in her life who had stood by her, and she had friends, sure, but Becca didn't know how much she let them in. Becca didn't know how much she needed to be her mother's crutch.

There wasn't an easy answer. Telling Mom to back off and hanging up wasn't fair, but giving in to everything she wanted wasn't fair either. It all just kind of sucked.

"I love you," Becca managed, because she didn't know what else to say.

"I love you too, baby. I just wish you'd come home with me. The house here in town is so sweet, and—"

"And far away from the business I'm trying to start. Mom, this is everything I ever wanted, and I really like being on my own. I don't say that to hurt you. I say that because I can't…I can't break myself to give you what you need. Can't there be a compromise?"

"What kind of compromise?" Mom asked coolly.

"I don't know. I don't know. I just wish you would… I need to do some things on my own. I want to make some mistakes on my own, and I want to do that without hurting you."

"You being hurt will always hurt me." Her mother's voice was still cool and pinched and Becca wished it could be different.

But it couldn't.

"I'm not sleeping with anyone, if that's what you're worried about. I'm not getting drunk, though every once in a while I might indulge in a few too many. I'm taking care of myself. And I'm old enough to make all those choices."

"Age doesn't have anything to do with it."

"It does. It *does*. At some point, you have to let me be an adult. You have to let me go." She didn't want to say it out loud, certainly not to her mother, but the truth of the matter was that losing Burt so suddenly had woken Becca up.

Mom wouldn't be around forever to hide behind. If Becca didn't learn now to stand on her own two feet.

If she didn't learn how to be someone who made her own choices and mistakes now, when would she?

"Mom."

"I didn't know the first thing about life when I got pregnant with you. Which is not a regret by any means, but your father…"

"I know the things that happened to you with him weren't great, but you taught me… You married Burt. How could that not be the best example of what to look for in a man?"

"I won't argue with you that his son is a good man, but you cannot replace Burt with Alex."

Becca inhaled sharply, anger mixing with her sadness and frustration. "That's not what I'm doing, Mother."

"Are you so sure about that?"

Becca was sure. She was totally sure. It wasn't… She wasn't looking for a replacement for Burt. She wasn't looking for Alex to be some father figure. Someone to tell her what to do and someone…

If she had been looking for a Burt replacement, she wouldn't have picked a man who made everything ten times more difficult than it had to be.

"I have to get to work." Her voice wasn't as strong as it should have been, but Becca had a hard time caring. Mom made her feel stupid and like she didn't know her own self, and Becca wasn't going to let that happen anymore. No matter how many good intentions her mother had.

"I want you to think about what I said, and I want you to think about moving—"

"Goodbye, Mother." She hit End more forcefully

than necessary. She scooted down to where her cat was glaring at her and let herself shed a few tears because she hated being put in a position where she hurt her mother or she hurt herself. She hated being in a position where Mom thought that somehow undermining everything Becca was doing would make her safe or happy.

Sometimes in life, a person had to do things that sucked. Sometimes she was going to have to experience things that felt uncomfortable and hard and shitty. She'd lost Burt, hadn't she?

She had to believe it was okay to feel sad and shitty and horrible about those things, as long as she didn't wallow in it. As long as she understood that she'd made her choice, and it was a good one, and she had to move on regardless of whose approval she had.

But mostly what she had to do right now was take a shower and get the smell out of her hair, and drink approximately a metric ton of coffee and then go check on her horses.

After all, her horses would understand her inner turmoil…but they couldn't talk back. They couldn't give advice and they couldn't reassure. They could do a lot, but they weren't exactly people.

She gave Hannibal a last stroke and then walked into her bathroom and grabbed a towel. She had thought she'd gotten over wishing for a real friend some time when she'd been a teenager, but the want was back. That wish for someone to talk to who might understand. Or in lieu of understanding, just support. Someone who would tell her she was right or her mom was wrong. No matter how childish it was, that was what she wanted right now.

She got in the hot spray of the shower and thought

of Alex and even Jack and Gabe. There were things she
knew about each of them that she didn't think very many
people did. Jack had given her quite a glimpse into his
life before the military, and Alex had told her about their
injuries, and maybe it wasn't so crazy to think of them
as friends who might support her.

Of course, they were also former Navy SEALs who
seemed as okay with discussing feelings as bulls were
about being castrated, but maybe this was another thing
she should push on. Ask for.

She smiled to herself for the first time this morning.
It wasn't castration season yet, so a discussion about
*feelings* it would have to be.

# Chapter 16

IT WAS A GOOD DAY OF WORK. ALEX AND GABE HAD MADE progress on the bunkhouse while Jack had spent most of the day on cow duty with Hick.

Alex felt...sore and sweaty and spent, but it was the good kind. The kind where you knew you'd accomplished something. Which was hard with the bunkhouse because most days, no matter how much work they did, it felt like they were getting nowhere.

But they'd finished installing new windows, just he and Gabe using the basic carpentry skills they'd picked up as kids. They'd taken a step forward, and there were few things in life that put Alex in a better mood.

Unfortunately, there was still that nagging thing at the back of his brain every time he looked in the direction of the horse stables.

Becca had come by and chatted once she'd finally emerged from bed. She'd looked a little worse for the wear and fidgeted a little more than normal, but she'd smiled prettily and joked with them as she'd gotten the update on the cows from Hick.

She hadn't eaten lunch with them, but she'd been meeting with the vet about one of the horses' weight loss, so he couldn't assume she'd been avoiding him. It didn't change the fact that he'd missed her presence.

Alex found his gaze drifting toward the stables, wondering what she was up to. It was Jack's turn to fix dinner, so he'd gone into the house, and Gabe was already walking toward the porch, cell phone to his ear, talking stiffly to his mother as Star trailed after him.

So Alex was left to walk to the house alone. With nothing pressing to do except shower.

He could always go talk to Becca. She had been acting a little off this morning. Which could've just been the hangover, but…maybe it was his duty to check it out.

*And maybe you're a pathetic dipshit.*

Probably that last one more than anything, but his conversation with Jack this morning had stuck with him, and he couldn't ignore the fact that it would until he did something about it.

What he *should* have done was ignore this. Avoid this. Get the foundation started and then see about personal happiness. Maybe. But as he slowly walked toward the stables instead of the house, he knew it wasn't going to work.

He was too practical of a man. He knew how bombs were made and what caused them to explode. Pressure. And applying pressure to himself to stop this inexplicable infatuation with her, or the insistent memory of that kiss, would only make the explosion that much bigger.

*That* was what had happened at the bar last night. It wasn't effective. He needed to be effective. To have a plan.

He peeked around the opening to the stables to find Becca in the stall with Pal. She was brushing him down and talking to him, clearly quite involved, as even when he stepped through the door, she didn't turn to look at him.

It amazed him, the way she had with the animals. Without any fanfare, she treated all the animals as though they were people themselves. With their own personalities and their own roles. His dad always had animals around, dogs and cats and cows and horses, and yet he'd never had that…whatever it was she had. Something so easy and natural he was certain that this was simply part of who Becca was.

"Well, I'll do it soon enough. Just need to gather some courage," Becca was saying to Pal.

"Do what?"

She screeched and whirled to face him.

He could've lied and said that he didn't do it on purpose, but he kind of liked the way she jumped and looked at him all wide-eyed whenever he caught her deeply involved in something. There was an unguardedness there that, surprisingly, he very rarely got out of her.

Even when she was half-drunk and telling him that she was going to break through his walls, there was a kind of armor around her, as though she was keeping something back. Or maybe she'd shielded herself with an armor she didn't even realize was there.

*Sound familiar?*

Whatever it was, in those moments when he caught her deep in conversations with her animals, he always got to see a flash of it. Unguarded, innocent, genuine Becca.

His heart caught a little and he thought of Jack's words. Letting himself be or feel happy. That seemed like such impossible bullshit before they got this venture off the ground—this thing was supposed to be what brought him happiness.

Yet when Becca looked at him like that, her wide-eyed surprise morphing into a little smile, he couldn't think of a single plan that didn't revolve around more of *her*.

"Why are you sneaking up on me today?"

"Just checking up on you."

"That is so the opposite of what I need right now. One compulsive checker-upper is enough, thank you."

"Your mom bothering you?"

Her eyes narrowed a fraction. Not in suspicion or in any emotion he thought he understood. It was a study, and it was… Well, whatever it was, it was Becca. And he didn't have a hope of making sense out of her.

The strangest part of all that was that he was a man who tried to understand everything. To make sense of the world. To figure everything out so he knew exactly what to do. There was something about the way Becca confused the hell out of him that was weirdly refreshing.

He was probably going a little crazy. It was the lack of sleep. He'd fix that soon enough.

"Apparently people were lining up to tell my mom they saw me at Pioneer Spirit last night."

"And your mother doesn't care for bars?"

"Mom doesn't care for her frail, little daughter to be in the public, where mean, awful people are lurking to ruin her life."

"Don't all parents worry like that?"

"Do all parents call up their adult children and lecture them about taking care of themselves? You know how long it's been since I've been sick? Five *years*. I've had a few colds, but nothing that kept me from work. But of course it's not just that, is it? How dare I be around other people and…" She shook her head and let out a little breath. "I don't have to dump this on you."

But she said it as though she would if he gave her the go ahead. Maybe even as though she needed to unload it on someone. If she needed to unload anything on anyone, he had to admit he'd be the first in line. He couldn't remember a time that the thought of a heart-to-heart hadn't made him want to run in the opposite direction.

Except with her. "But you can dump it on me."

She smiled at that. Something sweet and…pretty. So damn pretty even after a day of work with her hair falling out of its braid, even with dirt and dust smudges on her face. There was just something so appealing about her.

"She thinks I'm sheltered. And I am, which I think is what makes it frustrating. I know I don't know anything about a damn thing, but *she* made me that way. I have to experience to learn, don't I? She wants me to be a baby chick in an egg for the rest of my life."

"Did you tell her that?"

Becca switched from the brush to the sponge and washed Pal down with her eyebrows furrowed. When she spoke, it was into the horse's neck. "I did. I tried to be very reasonable and honest and…and she told me that I was hurting her, and it sucked. Because…"

"Because you feel like you're all she has." He grabbed a sponge from the rack and moved into the stall with her. Pal shifted, but he didn't shy away.

"I am all she has," Becca returned, watching him with an eagle eye, as if she didn't quite trust him to wash her horse. But she didn't tell him to stop, so he worked on Pal's opposite side.

"I feel like she wants me to be happy with her being all that I have, and I'm not. Does that make me a bad daughter?"

"You're asking a guy who joined the navy and barely

came home for ten years. I might not be a paragon of what makes a good kid."

"Burt never complained."

"He wouldn't have. The thing is, he didn't like me going. He would've preferred I stayed and ranched and, you know, not been in Afghanistan. But he never said it, and he never made me feel bad about the choices I made. I think that's because he knew—in a way that's hard for some people—that I needed to do that thing, whether he liked it or not. So he encouraged me to do it, not because he wanted it, but because I needed it. I don't think that makes your mom bad, or you a bad daughter, I just think that means my father was pretty exceptional."

"He was," Becca returned, having stopped sponging the horse. "I think she's lonely, and I think she's sad. But I don't know the right balance between giving her what she needs and doing what I need. She spent so much time when I was growing up giving me what I needed. I don't know how to…do it all right."

"There's something we were taught in the military. There will be times when you want to do everything, when you want to save everyone, and there will be moments when you can't. It's impossible to give everyone what they want, what they need, and especially what they deserve. I think that balance isn't about being fifty-fifty all the time. It's about giving and taking. It's about making the choice that's best for the moment, and that will change and be different from day to day. Some days you put yourself first, and some days you put your mom first, and worrying about which one is more right will only cause more problems than it ever solves."

She dropped her sponge in the bucket and stared at

him over the horse's head. He finished his side, then looked right back at her.

Her lips curved, and those green eyes sparkled with a mischief he shouldn't want to sink into.

"You know, for someone who's afraid to kiss me, you're pretty smart." She batted her eyelashes at him, and damn if he could even manage a frown.

"I'm not afraid of kissing you."

"Then why don't you do it again?"

"Are you thinking I won't?" It was flirting, plain and simple, and he couldn't help himself. He wanted this and her.

"I'm thinking you won't, but I'm hoping you will."

God, and he wanted to. To move around the horse and back her up against the rough stall wall. He wanted to taste her again until it was all that existed.

He needed to find some of his own *balance* though. Not give in to every damn impulse, but maybe not shove them all away either. Admit there were times when it was best for him to be in charge and take the lead, and there were times it was best to… He raked a hand through his hair.

No matter how he tried to get on even ground with her, she always seemed to find the upper hand. Maybe that wasn't such a terrible thing. Maybe that was *balance*.

But he still needed a plan. He needed to try to find *some* of that control. Which meant instead of kisses in parking lots and slightly drunk discussions, they needed something a little more…traditional.

"Instead of a kiss, I have an alternate suggestion," he managed to say, ordering the ideas into a plan.

"Intriguing. Go on." She stepped out of Pal's stall and so he followed.

"I could take you to dinner. Some night that would work around both of our schedules."

He watched the emotions chase across her face. Confusion, surprise, and then that beautiful bloom of a smile.

"Are you asking me out on a date?"

Alex reached out and touched her arm, though the bulky coat kept it from being much of a meaningful gesture. But this, this feeling she gave him, it was a thing he wanted—despite his best intentions. And much like the foundation, much like *she* was doing, he needed to have the balls to go after it. On his terms, anyway. "Yes, I am asking you out on a date. God help me."

She bit her lip, presumably to keep from grinning. "Okay. Um, well, I'm sure there's a day neither of us have meal duty, and Hick is always here for cow stuff, and, um, I mean, then we might have to tell them we… We don't have to, I guess, but, um—"

She killed him. Just…dead. He reached out and put a finger over her lips to keep them from continuing their trip down Stutter Lane. And if he put his hand there, he couldn't use his mouth. Which was what he *wanted* to do, but it wouldn't get their plans made.

"I'll handle the arrangements." He let his fingers drop from her lips, because he was a little too tempted to trace their shape.

Maybe with his tongue.

"Right," she said on something like a squeak. "That makes sense. You should do that."

"For now, I'm going to go shower today off of me and eat some dinner."

"Okay, yes. Yeah, I'm heading in. To eat. Dinner."

He nodded and turned, even though walking away from her was pretty much the last thing he wanted to do right now. She looked fresh and bright and like something he wanted to sink into until everything in his life made sense.

That was not an option. There was a plan. An order to things, and if he kept that order, things could work out in a way that would…well, work out.

He walked toward the stable doors and he wasn't sure he'd wanted to ignore a plan ever in his life so much as he did right now. He didn't want order. He didn't want *steps*. He wanted *her*.

And wasn't that what everyone was always on his case about? Planning too much? Controlling things. Jack and Gabe groaned over his schedules and Becca looked at him like he'd lost his mind.

So why not for once just do something without a plan? Everyone else seemed to. Everyone else wanted *him* to. So…

He glanced at her, walking next to him. Ranger had bounded ahead and around the house, probably to get in through the dog door out back. Becca had a small, self-satisfied smile on her face.

He wanted some self-satisfied too, so he stopped in front of her and took her by the arms, far too much like he had in that bar parking lot. Her body jerked against his, somehow soft and willing, no matter how strong and unbending she could be.

She looked up at him, those enigmatic, green eyes of hers wide, that all-too-sweet mouth hanging a little open. He shouldn't want this, want her, but he did, and she wanted him right back—and damn it, he was so tired of fighting everything.

"One of these days I'll kiss you nicely. But it's not going to be today." So he sank into her, just as he'd been telling himself not to do, devouring her mouth until she was breathless and shivering in his arms. He wanted her with an intensity that scared the crap out of him. She broke things inside of him, plans and order, and yet all he wanted was more.

When he finally managed to take his mouth off hers, she looked up at him wide-eyed and breathing heavily.

"For the record," she said, her voice a shuddery whisper, "you're welcome to kiss me like that whenever you want."

He let out a shaky breath of his own. "One of these days, it'll be a nice kiss." Because he'd find his control. "One of these days."

# Chapter 17

BECCA BLINKED AT THE ODD GLOW CREEPING FROM BEHIND her curtain. It wasn't the warm shaft of light that existed when the sun rose in the morning, and when she glanced at her clock, it was only one in the morning, so there shouldn't be sun at all.

She pushed out of bed and pulled the curtain back, something in her heart catching at what she saw. The light outside the bunkhouse door was on, as were a few lights inside. All lights that hadn't been on when she'd gone to bed a few hours ago giddily dreaming about her date with Alex.

Alex, who was probably the culprit. She sighed, worry lodging like an uncomfortable weight in her stomach. He worked too much and too hard.

She knew he'd want her to pretend she hadn't seen this. He'd want her to forget it and go back to bed, but…

Well, they had kissed, and they were going on a date, so didn't she have some…well, not say necessarily, but input? She could voice her opinion, and that didn't mean he had to take it, but she had something of a right to speak up.

Someone had to say something. Gabe hadn't liked her poking her nose into things, and she understood that. He'd objected to her telling Gabe about something that had been between her and Alex. What she should have done was take it up with Alex himself and not involve other people.

So now she would.

She dug through her closet for a hoodie and pulled it on before padding downstairs. In the dark, she felt around for her boots and coat, not wanting to wake anyone else up. She eased the door open and stepped out into the frigid spring night.

Moonlight lit her way to the bunkhouse, and she glanced up at the pattern of stars above her. "I sure hope you're looking down on me, Burt. I need all the help I can get with this son of yours," she muttered.

She steeled herself on a deep breath in and pushed the door open as she slowly let it out.

Alex glanced up from where he was working on something with the floors. He held a hammer in one hand, a variety of tools lined up next to the wall.

He got to his feet. "Becca. What…are you doing?"

"Wondering why a light is shining into my window." She hugged herself against the cold and bit her tongue against telling him he should be wearing a coat.

"Your window?"

"The light on the outside shines directly into my bedroom window."

"Oh, shit. I'm sorry." His forehead scrunched into lines of confusion. "How did a little light wake you up?"

"I'm always a light sleeper when I'm worked up about something."

"What are you worked up about?" he asked, clearly ready to swoop in and fix it for her. She wished she could decide if she liked that or hated it, but all she ever felt was some mixture of both.

So, instead of deciding, she went with a joke. "Oh, just this guy…" She sighed heavily, trying not to smile.

"He asked me out, and I have no idea what I'm going to wear."

She got the reaction she'd been hoping for—something very close to a laugh—and she grinned. But even with the levity, her heart pinched and her smile died.

"Why are you out here, Alex?"

"I...found mice."

"Gross." Becca wrinkled her nose. "But why are you finding mice at one in the morning?"

Alex glanced at his watch. "Oh. Huh. Must have lost track of time."

She forced herself to move forward, to be strong and determined. Not her area of expertise, but every new thing had to start somewhere. "I'm worried about you."

"Don't be."

"You do realize telling someone not to worry is like telling someone not to breathe. It's not a voluntary action."

"I'm fine."

"Do you ever get tired of saying that?"

His mouth firmed and she knew she was going about this all wrong. The problem was she didn't know how else to go about it. As long as he was so determined he was fine, what could she do?

"Go to bed," he said, and there was a touch of gentleness to that order that he didn't usually use. She'd hold on to that.

"I'll go to bed if you come with." When his eyebrows winged up, she realized how that sounded. "Oh, that's not what I meant," she stuttered, her cheeks flushing pink.

Alex chuckled, but then she kind of thought of it. Of

the kiss earlier today, and the kiss in the bar parking lot, and Alex. "But maybe it could be what I meant."

"No," he said firmly, though his mouth was curved in that almost-smile she liked so much.

"Don't jump to an automatic answer. We should consider it. You know, really think about—"

"No."

"Why not?"

"Because we haven't even been on a date yet," he said, as though people went around not sleeping together because they hadn't been out on some official date.

"So?"

"So that's how you do things," he replied, holding out his hand and ticking off steps. "You go on a date. You go on multiple dates and then you…"

"Then you what?" she asked as innocently as she could manage. "Rescue goats together?"

"Is that what the kids are calling it these days?"

"Oh, stop everything! We need to memorialize this day."

"What day?"

"The day Alex made an actual joke, and it was even about sex!" She grinned up at him, stepping closer, gathering the courage to touch him. This man so determined to do things the right way, who had this hidden sense of humor that was all the more special because she'd only seen it come out around her.

She slid her palm against his cheek and enjoyed the rough scrape of a day's worth of whiskers. She pressed her thumb to the corner of his upturned mouth because she wanted to commit to memory that expression. As though he was helpless against her charm. Or goat jokes.

He reached out, but sadly not to touch her. Instead, he pulled up the collar of her coat so it covered her neck better. "It's cold, Bec."

"Yes, it is, and you're not wearing a coat at all."

"I'm used to that."

"And I am used to Montana. You should have a coat on. Actually, you should be in bed. Again, I'd like to bring up, my bed is available, with me in it."

His hand left her coat collar, but instead of going back to his side, he gave her braid a little tug.

"You even wear your hair in a braid to bed?"

"Otherwise Hannibal plays with it."

He opened his mouth, she was sure to quiz her about Hannibal, but she found she didn't really want to talk about her cat or her goat or anything else. She wanted to press her mouth to his, so that's what she did. She kissed him.

When he didn't resist, when he instead wrapped his hand behind her neck and pulled her closer, she sighed into it and him. Into the feeling of a quiet, lazy exploration that had her insides humming with some mix of nerves and excitement she'd never experienced before.

She moved onto her tiptoes, pressing her body against his, wrapping her arms around his neck to give her better leverage against his much taller frame, and she kissed him with everything she had.

Clumsy or clueless, she didn't care. Because Alex would never make her feel those things. He would guide her somewhere sweet and perfect.

"What are you wearing underneath this coat?" he murmured into the cold.

"A hoodie."

"Well, that is disappointing."

"There's nothing underneath the hoodie if that helps," she offered hopefully.

"It does." His mouth lowered to hers again, this time the hand on her neck tightening its hold and his other hand sneaking under the hem of her coat and hoodie, cool, long fingers touching bare skin.

Alex's hand was touching her bare stomach, and he was kissing her mouth. Alex Maguire. And it felt like puzzle pieces coming together, like fate finally aligning in the right part of her universe. Like a perfect, electrified hope.

He groaned, pulling his hand from her clothes as he stopped kissing her. His eyes were a dark swirl of emotions she couldn't parse. "This has to stop," he said in a voice that sounded awfully strangled.

"Why?" she asked on a dreamy sigh.

"Because we are going to do this right."

"That sounds boring."

"Oh, does it?" he said, his voice a deliciously dangerous rasp before his mouth was on hers again, hard and hot and insistent.

Not boring at all.

⸻

He had to stop. Had to control this side of him. She was new to all of it, and she deserved it to go in the right order. She deserved it to happen the way these things were supposed to happen.

Not in the middle of the night in a crappy bunkhouse that still wasn't livable. Not before he'd even taken her out to dinner. There was a way you did things with women you cared about. There was a way his father would expect him to handle this.

Of course, that was laughable. He didn't have a clue what his father would think about him making out with Becca anywhere, let alone here, but it was the thought that helped him finally step away. Not just stop kissing her, not just stop touching her, but step away and put distance between them.

Her cheeks were flushed, her mouth curved in that beautiful smile he wanted to soak in like summer heat.

"You need to go inside." For her own damn good. And definitely his.

"I'm not going inside without you, Alex."

Oh hell. He didn't want to go back in there. Didn't want to be faced with all of the pieces of himself that didn't fit. The pieces all felt jagged and broken, and he didn't know how to fix it.

The bunkhouse he knew how to fix, and he was certain once it was finished, he would feel finished too. Once this goal was achieved, all those jagged hurts living in his chest would go away.

"What about this?" she said softly, still close and warm and all too pretty. "We talk."

"Sure? The calving is going well and—"

"Not about ranch stuff. Not about foundation stuff. Us stuff."

"I like football. Soccer is confusing as hell. I firmly believe Taylor Swift is not country and tequila was invented by the devil."

"Those are important things. More important, of course, is that baseball is superior to football, Taylor Swift is the best of country, and tequila...well, I've never had tequila so I'll have to reserve my judgment."

Damn it, why did he have to like her so much? He'd

never known someone who talked like this, who was unafraid to poke at the rigid way he held himself. At least not in female form. Not in a very, very appealing female form.

"As firm as my opinions about Taylor Swift are though, your feelings about her weren't really what I was getting at," she added.

He closed his eyes for a second. He'd known that and tried to sidestep it, and still, he'd known he'd side-stepped nothing. Not by kissing her. Not by changing the subject. Becca did not give up once she zeroed in on something.

It was the most annoying damn thing—and the most admirable.

"Then what were you getting at? What is it you want to know?" More about the accident? The things he'd done as a SEAL? Maybe she wanted to know about his mother's accident. Did she even know anything about it?

The problem was there were so many places he didn't want to go. So many compartments he kept locked down.

*Except in your dreams.*

"Why didn't you come home?"

He blinked. Of all the places he thought she might go, that wasn't it. "I don't know."

"You can ignore a question, Alex. You can say you don't want to answer, but I don't ever want you to lie to me. I think that's more than fair."

*Fair.* She had to throw that word out there. None of this was fair. He'd always thought of himself as a fair man, but a fair man would not drag her into his life when he wasn't one hundred percent on top of things.

But he'd get there. Once the bunkhouse was fixed, once the foundation was up and running, this thing lodged in his gut would disappear. It was just another reason the order of things was so important. If they dated, if they took things slow, he *would* be right and fine once... At some point. Maybe he didn't know the exact point yet, but it was out there.

"When, specifically, are you talking about me not coming home?"

"The entire time after our parents were married. You came home...what? Twice? And...the thing is I don't get it. I thought maybe you hated it or Burt, but you loved him and he loved you. You love this place. It's home. I know coming back and building this is complicated, but it's still so clear you belong here. So why would you have kept away so much?"

"How do you know all that?" he asked, surprised at how raspy his voice sounded, how affected.

"I have eyes, don't I?" she said with one of those sweet smiles he wished he could see as pitying, but from her it just felt like comfort. "I've seen you look at the sky, at your father's truck, at the mountains in the distance. I've seen you work with the cows with a smile on your face and laugh with Hick. You love this place. That's obvious to anyone who's watching, and I have... well, I've been watching. In a totally not-creepy way."

He laughed, and it was so easy with her to remember how again. To lose that weight on his chest and remember life had all this—humor and light. Love and people.

"So?" she prompted, a tenacious fighter to the end.

Alex sighed. He wanted to lie or to refuse to talk about it, but he was a fair man, and it was all too fair a question. "I didn't know I was doing it, I don't think. I just…" He raked a hand through his hair. It was easier to admit things to himself in the privacy of his own thoughts than it was aloud to another person. "I never wanted to see someone take my mother's spot. I thought Dad had every right to remarry, and I never took issue with your mother. I just…I didn't want to see it—this place that was my family's turned into someone else's."

She was so quiet he wasn't sure she was breathing, and he couldn't quite bring himself to look at her, because all of that still hurt. That he hadn't realized he was doing it to himself, and he'd lost all those chances to have another moment with Dad.

"I never knew my father," Becca said into the eerie quiet.

He did look at her then, not sure why she was offering that kind of confession.

She shrugged jerkily. "Mom was seventeen. He disappeared when she told him she was pregnant. Her family kicked her out. So it was always just…us, and then I was so sickly." She swallowed. "That's why Burt was such a miracle for us. For both of us. After all that bad. That something and someone so good could happen was a *miracle*."

"And you still believe that, even after he died so out of the blue?"

"Yes." She smiled, her eyes bright with tears, but she didn't shed them, and her smile was real. "Because… because once you know it can happen, that miracle, you have to believe it can happen again."

His chest was too tight, and so was his throat. Everything was squeezed, and for a few panicking seconds, he didn't think he'd be able to breathe. He might die right here—death by hope.

Except Becca reached out and touched his hand, a featherlight brush of her fingertips, and suddenly he could inhale and then exhale. Suddenly, she was close and she was all the air he needed.

"You are something like a miracle, Becca Denton." And he knew without a shadow of a doubt he didn't deserve that miracle, but somehow she was still here. "Let's go inside."

"Are you coming to my bed?"

"No."

She huffed. "You're such a stick-in-the-mud. No wonder your nickname was *Dad*."

"Who told you that?" he asked, stepping into the dark night with her and closing the door behind them.

"Jack told me."

"Jack needs to shut his mouth."

And she laughed as they walked, hand in hand, back to the house they'd both grown up in at different times of their lives, and somehow that felt just about right.

# Chapter 18

BECCA STUDIED HERSELF IN THE MIRROR FOR APPROXIMATELY the millionth time. How was she supposed to know what to wear on a date? Alex had said he was taking her to a restaurant in Bozeman.

As if that gave her any clue. Nicer than jeans and a T-shirt, but, well, not the dress she'd worn to Burt's funeral. But she didn't have a lot of in-between clothes. She didn't exist in an in-between world.

Eventually, she'd decided on a summery dress she'd bought on a whim three years ago, a sweater to go over, leggings to go under, and nice boots her mother had given her for Christmas. She'd curled her hair and put on makeup and she felt…

Well, like a fraud. And silly for putting so much effort into it. She didn't know what kind of effort *he* was putting into it. Dinner in Bozeman was vague, but it was a step above a booth at Georgia's. But *where* in Bozeman? What kind of date guy *was* Alex?

She didn't have a clue. She knew where he'd been stationed in the navy, and she knew different things about his childhood that Burt had told her. She knew about his accident and his neat-freak ways, but hell if she knew anything about the man as a romantic-date-type person.

Except kissing. She knew how he kissed. She grinned at that. Good. Excellent. Brain melting. Couldn't they just kiss all night?

Which was the answer to her current dilemma. Well, sort of. Because even with no kissing, when she looked at him, she rarely felt nervous. She never felt overwhelmed or scared. Sometimes he could make her heart pound like no one else, and she might stutter in the aftermath of all those little surprises he could evoke. But it wasn't this all-encompassing, shaky, nervy fear.

Maybe it stood to reason that if she didn't know how to act when he wasn't here, once she went downstairs and *saw* him, she'd be fine. She'd know what to say and how to feel. Maybe it wouldn't freak her out the way she was currently freaking out.

She looked at herself once more in the mirror. She felt a million different kinds of foolish, but she was also really, really, really excited. Her first date was with this *good* guy. Who knew she was not what anyone would call experienced, and not only didn't care, but who was also really sweet about it. He was the kind of guy who'd care that she was comfortable or nervous or whatever.

Alex was thoughtful, and this was going to go well. What was the worst that could happen? Something awkward? She could survive some awkward. She was intimately acquainted with awkward.

"Oh, for heaven's sake. Grow a pair," she muttered at her reflection. She had initiated almost everything that had happened between her and Alex, after all.

She forced herself out of her bathroom and into the hallway. She brushed her hands down the front of her dress and wondered for the millionth time if she looked too…something. Trying too hard, being too silly, whatever.

But it was too late now. Too late, so she had to bite

the bullet. She had to dive in, make some mistakes, maybe feel a little stupid, but *live*. Experience.

She walked down the stairs far slower than she normally did. It was hard to take a deep breath. It kept getting caught somewhere halfway in her lungs. Her heart was beating too fast and everything was too much. But that was good too. A new experience. Surviving the anxiety and the nerves and all of that.

When she reached the bottom of the stairs, all three guys were in the living room. Which obviously made her all the more nervous. It wasn't just Alex. She had to worry about Gabe and Jack's judgment too.

Except theirs didn't matter. All that mattered was that she was going on a date with a decent guy.

The decent guy in question's mouth was in that grim line while Gabe and Jack both looked inordinately pleased with themselves. So they were probably giving Alex crap for this whole thing. Which made her feel a little bad. That she was the cause of him being made fun of.

But they turned to face her, nearly in tandem, and they were all three just standing there staring at her in that open-mouthed-shock kind of way like she was...

The other night before the bar, it had made her feel like she'd done something wrong, but she was starting to realize that maybe that wasn't it at all. Maybe they actually thought she was...attractive. That they were surprised to see her dressed up or with curly hair or makeup or whatever. And that they liked what they saw.

Which would be different than what she usually saw—a mousy little girl who didn't know what the hell she was doing. Or getting herself into. But was doing it anyway.

"Hi," she forced herself to say when they were all just standing there staring at her.

"Hi," they chorused together.

"So am I going on a date with all three of you or...?" She smiled at herself, because that was the thing about them. They brought out this person who wasn't afraid. She still didn't know what she was doing, but the nerves didn't hammer quite so hard. She had full use of her voice and her humor.

"Is that on the table?" Gabe asked with a grin.

Alex elbowed him in the stomach. Hard, by the looks of it, as Gabe doubled over with an *oof*.

"Go find something to do," Alex said in that military-commander voice he had. One that brooked no argument.

"I want you two back by ten," Jack said in a mock deep voice. "I'm a very strict curfew parent."

"Fuck off and get the hell out of here, Jack."

Gabe and Jack laughed, and even though Alex scowled after them, she thought maybe...if she wasn't totally reading everything wrong, he kind of liked or appreciated that they were...

Happy, she realized. Even though they were giving him crap, he was glad they were because they were laughing and smiling and *happy*.

He watched them leave and didn't turn to face her until he was certain they were alone. Then his dark gaze met hers and he took a step toward her.

Her heartbeat kicked up, the breath she'd inhaled catching in her lungs. He seemed to take in all of her—her hair, her outfit, *her*. She swallowed.

"You're beautiful," he finally said, low and sincere.

The compliment fluttered in her chest and she could

only smile at him. He thought she was beautiful. What was she supposed to do with that?

"Are you ready to go?"

She nodded.

"Are you going to speak on this date?"

She nodded again, more out of humor than because she didn't have anything to say.

"Funny girl," he murmured. But he smiled and gestured toward the door and this was really happening. She was going on a date. With Alex Maguire.

She followed, relishing the little flutter of nerves as they pulled on their coats. It was different than the nerves from earlier. Because something about Alex set her at ease even as they walked out toward where the trucks were parked.

"Do you think we could take my truck?"

"Because you have to drive?" he asked drily.

"No. I just feel weird about going on a date in your dad's old truck."

His steps paused for a second, and when he continued, she noticed the little flinch of a limp before he smoothed it out. "Fair point. But I am driving. I don't care about your truck rule."

"If you insist." She didn't particularly care about it herself right now.

If he was nervous, it didn't show. He seemed completely comfortable as they got into her truck and started driving toward town. He didn't fidget. He didn't stammer. He asked a few questions about her day and everything felt normal.

Except for the fact that she knew she was on a date, which was not normal at all.

"The bunkhouse is going slower than we thought it would, but we're still making some progress," he offered into the silence.

"You know, I was thinking that I wish we had some place for women to stay on-site."

"Women? Plural?"

"Well, eventually we'll have to hire more staff. We could hire all former military for that, but it wouldn't have to be all male. It'd be nice for Monica and me to not be completely surrounded by gruff military men."

"We're not all gruff."

She slid him a look. "Sure. Gabe is very personable. Till you piss him off. Jack grows on you once you get past all the prickly stuff. You—you are gruff."

"Am I now?"

"Oh yes. And if three out of three have gruff tendencies, I'm going to need the rational, calming influence of women."

Alex snorted and she scowled at him.

"I like the idea of hiring as much former military as we can," Alex continued. "Men would be easier to start just because they could bunk in the house, but long-term, we can work on coed housing."

Becca chewed on her lip. "Should we be talking about this? Work?"

"What else is there to talk about?"

"Well, you could tell me about Navy SEAL life."

To her surprise, that's exactly what he did. They managed to have a nice conversation all the way to Bozeman. He took her to a more upscale restaurant than she was used to, and it was really…comfortable. Nothing exciting or nerve wracking, but it was nice and relaxing and sweet.

Either Alex was an expert at conversation or they clicked really well, because she never felt like she was breaking down the communication or making things weird. If she ever felt like she'd said something silly, he either didn't notice or pretended not to.

It was easy to see how he'd commanded a regiment. Easy to see how he was the kind of man who could walk into a dangerous situation and fix it. At least try to. He awed her.

He laughed at her goofy jokes, and he asked questions about whatever story she was relating to him. They talked a little about Burt, but mostly they had a conversation about themselves. As people.

She never would have imagined there was someone in this world who was this easy to be around. As much as she'd loved Burt like a father in the end, he'd still been someone she'd had to get used to in the beginning. Someone to learn to settle into. Someone she'd had to learn to trust.

But maybe because of that, she *had* learned. To trust. To open up. To give.

They walked back to the truck after their all-too-delicious dinner, and Alex took her hand. A very gentlemanly, sweet gesture, and there was so much about him that was...exactly that.

He had the truest, most intrinsic sense of goodness about him. She knew he wasn't perfect. No one could be, and she couldn't expect someone to be. But within all of his imperfections — including being uptight, a neat freak, and far too bossy — at the center of his being was true goodness.

He wanted to do right by people, and sometimes

that could be annoying and frustrating. But she could trust that he wanted what was best for her. He wouldn't do anything to hurt her, because that would hurt him, having hurt somebody.

She got into the truck, lost in her own thoughts, but it hit her then. What she wanted. What she *needed*.

"Stop," she blurted as he started to pull out of the parking lot.

Alex stopped the truck at the exit to the restaurant. "Why am I stopping?" he asked.

But wasn't that something? That he would, that he'd *do* it, and ask questions only after? "I need you to take me somewhere real quick."

"Somewhere?"

"Yes. I need you to stop at, like, a drugstore or the like."

"Okay." He pulled onto the street. "Why do you need to go to a drugstore or the like?"

"Oh, you know, to pick up something."

He gave her weird look, but he also drove toward the drugstore. Which made her even more sure of this spur-of-the-moment decision.

She was going to buy condoms. Even if that was awkward, and even if they didn't actually do anything tonight. She wanted to be prepared. She wanted to be ready. Because that was something she definitely wanted.

Maybe she should care more about what that meant for the future, but she found right now she couldn't. She didn't want to worry about what might happen in a month or two or six. She didn't want to worry about next year. She wanted to enjoy what she had, the possibility of what she had, right now.

She wanted him. To be with him and to experience all of these firsts with *him*. So she would do what she'd been doing all these weeks.

Go for it.

# Chapter 19

ALEX PULLED BECCA'S TRUCK INTO THE DRUGSTORE PARKING lot, trying to puzzle out this strange turn of events.

"You can just stay here," she suggested over brightly.

Such a damn puzzle. "You want me to stay in the truck while you go buy some mysterious thing at the drugstore?"

"Well, it's not mysterious."

"Then why can't I go in with you?"

"I'm…just…I'm going to buy something that's kind of embarrassing. So I just thought maybe you should stay in the car." Her eyes focused on the doors of the store. "I don't know when I'll have time to run to town again, and it's an item that, um, well, you know, I might need soon. Maybe."

"Is this some weird feminine thing?"

"No! No." She blinked at him, her cheeks turning pink. "Not that. Just…" She took in a breath and studied him. He knew she was assessing him in some way, but he never could figure out what she was looking for or what she wanted from him. She was so inherently difficult to figure out.

Who knew what the hell was wrong with him that he got something out of that? That he enjoyed it in some mixed-up way. "Okay, maybe I'll just stay in the truck," he said.

"Great. Be right back." She scurried out of the truck like a spooked animal.

Alex could only stare after her and wonder how he'd gotten himself into whatever this was. Wondered how he could muster up the sensible reaction, which would be anything that would stop this from continuing.

But the thought of stopping anything when it came to Becca was ludicrous. She was like summer and freedom. She was truly unique and smart and funny. It was a weird thing to admit, even just to himself in the privacy of his own thoughts, but he hadn't *dated* much. The navy hadn't left much time for relationship-type things, so most of his experiences with women were hookups. Maybe a week's worth of them. His one and only relationship had been his high school sweetheart, and they'd mostly fumbled through trying to figure the opposite sex out. It wasn't some great true-love thing.

It wasn't smart to get caught up in a relationship with Becca. They had a lot of things to accomplish that were very important before they started worrying about... futures. Futures with people.

But, damn, he'd enjoyed every second of this night. Every last ridiculous second. He liked watching her eat, and he loved listening to her talk. He liked the way she laughed at him and asked pertinent questions when he told her a story.

Maybe Gabe and Jack weren't totally off base that he should have some happiness of his own. Maybe that was an important piece of their life now. Maybe.

It took a few more minutes before Becca returned, and when she did, her entire face was beet red and she clutched the drugstore bag to her chest like it was a treasure. Actually, more like it was something she would be ashamed of anyone seeing.

"You okay?" he asked when she climbed into the passenger seat.

"Sure. Great. You know, new experiences."

"You know this is killing me, right?"

"What's killing you?" she asked.

"The curiosity."

The flush on her face did not disappear in the slightest bit. If anything, it got darker.

"I was just thinking about the future," she said in an odd, squeaky voice.

"The future?" he repeated. Seriously, something was wrong with him that he got such a kick out of the circuitous way she talked.

"Yes. The future. What I might want to do with it."

"And that necessitated an emergency drugstore run?"

"Yes," she returned with a firm nod.

"Are there any more emergency errands you need to run?"

She paused for a second as though seriously considering it. "No. I think anything else would take more time than I'd be willing to have you wait in the car for."

"Anyone ever told you that you're a strange girl?"

"No, but that's probably because I didn't have friends." She said it so matter-of-factly. As though that was just life. She never even seemed to expect him to feel sorry for her.

It...affected him. Bothered him maybe? Or was it that he wanted to fix it for her? Give things to her? He shook the thought away and backed out of the parking lot. "So is that why you talk to the animals the way you do? Because you had no one else to talk to?"

The blush that had receded returned, if a little different this time. Just two small slashes of pink across her cheeks.

"I guess. I mean, I could talk to Mom about a lot of stuff, but if I was mad at her or didn't agree with her or needed someone to vent to about her, the animals were good listeners. I was thinking about that the other day, actually, after the bar. I love animals and they've given me a lot, but they can't talk back. It's nice to have someone around who can talk back."

"Hopefully you don't kiss them too. I can share conversation, but…"

"Well, mostly not," she returned deadpan. "Ron Swanson requires a little extra love and attention."

Out of the corner of his eye, he saw her grin.

"I had you a little worried there for a second, didn't I?" she teased.

He chuckled. "I was mostly sure you haven't been making out with your goat, but I do have to say you're a constant surprise. One would never know for sure."

"A constant surprise and a constant delight, right?"

It was his turn to grin at her. "You are that too."

She settled back into her seat, her smile going a little soft. Pleased.

"You're very good at this whole conversation thing. I think you are my perfect first date."

He didn't know how to respond to that. *Perfect* made him nervous, and *first date* made him even more nervous. He hated to be nervous. Nerves created mistakes or made you miss important things.

But this wasn't war. It was just Becca.

"Well, I'm glad you think so because I certainly

don't have that much experience either." And apparently nerves also made him say stupid, stupid things.

She sat up straighter, though she still clutched the bag to her chest. "What do you mean you don't have that much experience?"

He didn't respond.

"Oh, you're a virgin, aren't you?" she asked with mock concern.

He snorted out a laugh. "Not a virgin, no. But not well versed in the ways of long-term relationships either. Not that…" Oh, so many stupid, stupid things.

"So you've never had a girlfriend, you've just had lots of one-night stands?"

"I think 'lots' is in the eye of the beholder. I did have one girlfriend. Once."

"I can't believe you've only had one girlfriend. We're practically on the same experience plane."

"I doubt that."

She just kept grinning at him. "Okay, tell me all about the one and only relationship you've ever had. Was she the love of your life and she broke your heart, so you had to find solace in a string of women's vaginas? I think that's the gist of James Bond, right?"

"No. And no." He shook his head, eyes on the road and mountains as he tried to stop himself from focusing solely on her. "She was a girl in high school. She was hot and she liked cows enough she'd come hang out on the ranch. We dated for two years, and then I joined the navy."

"Was she brokenhearted? Were you brokenhearted? Did she—"

"My but you are a curious one," he muttered.

"I don't have any experiences of my own. I have to live vicariously through other people's."

"I do not believe she was brokenhearted. In fact, I think she had someone lined up for once I shipped off."

"So *you* were brokenhearted?"

"Hardly. I was eighteen and joining the navy. I did plenty of experiencing in the years before I was deployed. But being a SEAL doesn't offer much stability to make a relationship work."

"And that would be very important to you, wouldn't it?"

"What? Stability?"

"The ability to give someone else that stability."

"I guess so. I wouldn't want to let anyone down. I wouldn't want my choices to be hard on anyone. Or at least harder."

She leaned over the bench between them and brushed her mouth across his cheek. Something sweet and light.

"What was that for?"

"I just think you're a really great guy."

Her gaze was a little too dreamy, and he fidgeted. "I am not without my faults."

"Oh, I know that. Trust me, I could list them for you if you'd like." She smiled at him when he slid her a look.

"I'll pass."

He drove them into and through Blue Valley, up to the ranch. Silence settled over them as darkness encroached. It was another beautiful spring night—cool and dark, with a clear, bright sky.

"I love spring," Becca said on a sigh. "There's so much to do and every time you get a chance to rest and relax it seems like there's so much promise in the air."

He glanced over at her as he brought the truck to a stop. Promise. Yes, there was definitely a lot of that in the air.

He didn't like putting too much stock in that or allowing her the idea that he had much to give. But he also knew he was a hard worker, and as Jack had said the other morning, they'd gotten themselves out of a lot of sticky situations. This couldn't be harder than dealing with crises in Afghanistan and surviving a car accident caused by a grenade explosion.

He could handle Becca Denton. He could handle seeing what they could do together. And if they couldn't do anything together…well, they could probably both deal with that too. How hard would it be to make some rational choices?

"You want to drive up to the north pasture and look at the stars?" he offered.

She smiled at him and then looked at the bag still clasped in her hands. She frowned a little, but soon enough the smile was back. "Yeah, let's do that."

---

Alex drove them up and around the barn to the north pasture. Because it was on a hill, most of the house, barn, and stables were hidden behind a swell of land.

All that existed were stars and mountains and moon. It never failed to make Becca feel small and awed and so darn hopeful.

Alex pushed the truck into park and Becca looked down at her bag.

"There are some blankets in the back. Stay put with the heater till I get it set up."

In another moment, she might have argued, but Alex
fussing with blankets gave her time to pull the box of condoms out of the drugstore bag. He slid out of the truck and
she scrambled to pull the box out of the bag and rip it open.
She tried to detach one of the condoms from its row, but
Alex knocked on her window and she jumped about a foot.

She shoved the whole box into her coat pocket. Luckily
it was as dark in the cab of the truck as it was outside, so
he likely couldn't have seen her guilty reaction.

She slid out of the truck and into the inky black of
night only punctuated by a steady beam of moonlight
and the faded glow of a million stars.

It was *cold*, and Alex handed her a heavy work coat
that must have been in the back of the truck. She pulled
it on over her own jacket as they walked to the bed of the
truck. She could barely make it out in the milky light of
a clear night, but a handful of blankets had been laid out
in the back of the truck, creating a nest of sorts.

Her heart fluttered in happy anticipation as she
crawled up into the lump of blankets. She rearranged a
little bit to roll one of the blankets into something like a
pillow for both of them. She made sure to sit where the
lumpy pocket full of condoms would be next to the truck
side, not Alex.

Her heart hammered at the thought of the condoms,
but…but life was short and who knew what would
happen tomorrow? Did she really want to put this off
and maybe put off the chance of it ever happening?

In an easy, fluid move, Alex maneuvered next to her,
laying his head close on her makeshift pillow. He pulled
a blanket over them, and it smelled like horses and hay,
but it was warm.

*He* was warm. Even through the layers of their clothes, she could feel it seep into her. She wriggled her way closer, until their sides were pressed together.

The dark enveloped them, cool but something of a comforting presence. The sky stretched out like their very own cinematic masterpiece. Stars winked, planets gleamed, the Milky Way swirled across a section of the great canvas above them.

She'd done this before—laid out under the stars, breathed in the vast beauty, wondered at the amazingness of it all, but she'd never had company. Not human company anyway.

"This is nice." Which, to Becca, was a million shades too muted for what this all was. The culmination of every fantasy, but real and something she'd hold close to her heart always.

He turned his head, brushing his lips across the hair at her temple. *Nice.* A sad, paltry little word in comparison to what that did to her insides—melted them, lit her up, made her feel like the world was too big and beautiful to bear.

So she tilted her head up, trying to see his face in the dark. Moonlight outlined his features, hard and sharp, sculpted with ruthless slashes.

Except for his mouth, which was a curve, warm and inviting. She knew it could go sharp, hard, but not now. It wasn't that now. It was irresistible and she pressed her own to it, stretched herself against him as much as she could.

He rolled onto his side, his arms coming around her, everything about that hard, strong body enveloping her into himself. The kiss was slow, poignant, his arm pulling her closer, his other hand brushing against her cheek and through her hair.

It was magic and hope, something indefinable in all her limited experience. Or maybe experience had nothing to do with it. Maybe kissing Alex would always be this warm, sparkling thing that itched along her nerve endings and soothed her heart all at the same time.

This wasn't like those first two kisses, all hard and demanding, fierce and desperate. This was as soft as the night sky. Shimmery as starlight. Magic like the moon. Everything about it was gentle and sweet, and she made a little protesting sound when he pulled his mouth away from hers.

But he pressed it to her cheek, and then her temple, featherlight brushes that made her shiver.

"There," he said, his voice a whisper against the quiet night. "Finally, a nice kiss."

"You should probably do another grabby one so I can immediately compare and contrast."

He chuckled into her hair, his fingers still tracing all the curves and angles of her exposed skin. "You don't need to compare and contrast."

"How will I decide which one I like better?"

"You could just like them both. Like them all."

She grinned, because that sounded about perfect. She nuzzled closer, experimenting with how her head fit against his chest, listening to the beat of his heart. Steady. Strong. So Alex.

Though she knew the air around them had to be cool, the little burrow they'd created was nothing but warm and comfortable. So she traced her finger up his coat zipper, grasping it and tugging it down far enough that she could get her hand in underneath.

"Are you cold?" he asked, rubbing his hand up and down her back, though with two coats and a sweater on she could barely feel it.

"Nope," she replied cheerfully. She nudged the zipper down farther and farther until she could get her hands under his shirt as well. His skin was hot and she could feel hard muscle and coarse hair.

She wanted to feel all of him. She wanted to see all of him. But mostly she just wanted…him. To experience it all and to give in to it. She didn't want to think or worry or feel nervous. She wanted to open herself up to all of the possibility. All of the feeling, regardless of what the ramifications might be.

"Though I do have a confession to make," she said, pressing the flat of her palm to the hard plane of his abdomen.

He cleared his throat. "What's that?"

Alex, of course, hadn't returned the favor of unzipping her coat, because he was probably too worried about her temperature. Too overly worried about a million things, and she wanted to be the opposite of that. For herself, but more for him. He deserved a little letting go and opening up too, and she'd probably have to pry that out of him. But she could. Maybe she could.

"When I went in the drugstore, I might have bought something that's pertinent to our current situation."

"What's our current situation?"

"Alone. With only the stars and possibly coyotes around us."

"You talk in the strangest riddles, Bec."

"Okay, no riddles. Condoms. When I went into the drugstore, I bought a box of condoms."

He was completely still and he didn't say a word and she had to bite her lip to keep from laughing. Because it was ridiculous. What she'd done. Telling him. It was just all so…silly.

Except it wasn't, because she was going after what she wanted. She wanted to have sex with Alex Maguire.

"And I was thinking we could use one. Now."

# Chapter 20

ALEX HAD KNOWN TONIGHT WOULD SURPRISE HIM NO matter what happened. There wasn't anything about Becca that wasn't surprising. He'd been ready to be surprised and was enjoying it so completely and utterly and deeply.

The way she felt perfect curled up with him in the bed of a truck with a beautiful Montana night stretched above them was one.

The condom thing? That was something more than a surprise. It was a shock, and if he was being completely honest with himself, he was damn scared of her suggestion.

"You want to have sex in the freezing cold? Here? Now? In the back of a truck?" God help him, she probably did.

"I can't think of a better setting, can you?"

"Yes. A bed. In a room with heat."

"You're plenty warm," she said, flirtation and innuendo dripping from her mouth all practiced and smooth, her warm, small, rough hand still pressed to his stomach. She was beginning to make him feel like the innocent.

Her hand slid up, over his chest. Suggestive touches and brushes and tracing. Yeah, he was plenty warm. And hard. But he also knew she'd never done this before and it seemed wrong and irresponsible to do it in the back of a *truck*. Even if the scenery was beautiful and the woman was willing. More than.

"I mean we could always go back to the house," she said, her fingers still tracing swirling patterns under his shirt. "But Jack and Gabe being there is a…thing. I'm not sure I like the idea of sharing the same house with multiple people the first time I do this."

"Then maybe we shouldn't do it." Even as all of the images and possibilities assaulted him. He already knew she was soft and something akin to heaven. The way she touched and kissed—fearlessly—it was like a drug. He had to resist this. It was a test. Of will.

"But I want to do it. Don't you?"

Oh, she was the queen of complicated questions that didn't have easy answers. Did he want to? Absolutely. Was it right? That's where things got dicey.

Her fingertips traveled down the center of his chest and stomach, but this time they didn't dance back up. No, this time, they ventured to his belt.

"Becca."

"Obviously, I haven't done this before, but based on what I've gleaned from movies and books and the internet, men seem to be very big fans of the sex thing."

"I'm not saying I don't want to have sex with you," he ground out, trying to recite all the reasons he was supposed to resist. Mostly his brain was static. "But…" But something. Something important, he was almost sure.

She let out a hefty sigh against his neck. "But you're overly responsible and worried about my well-being, I'm gathering. Which might be sweet except, you know, I'd like someone to trust me to make my own choices. I was hoping that would be you."

"I hate that…" He didn't know what to say. There

was so much to say and so much he didn't want to tell her. Including that he hadn't done this himself in a while. Sure, there was a certain "like riding a bike" nature to the whole thing, but this was different.

This was not hooking up with a woman. This was not meeting someone at a bar or knowing he was only in town for a week or a month.

This was Becca. She was *special*. This would be important. To both of them. And that was intimidating and…

"On the off chance this is more than just you wanting to protect me, you need to tell me that. Because if it's just you wanting to keep me safe or be responsible or whatever, I'm going to take hideous advantage of you."

He barked a laugh because it never failed—she made him laugh. She was funny and so insightful sometimes when he'd really rather her not be.

"I wasn't expecting this and I am a…planner."

"You're anal."

"I'm a *planner*," he returned firmly. "I like to work things out and know what's coming and be sure. If the question is am I attracted to you, then obviously the answer's yes, though it's more than that. I like you. I do."

"But?" she prompted, irritation simmering in her voice.

He couldn't see her in the dark, just the moon and starlight glinting off her face. A few of her features, the sharp, upended nose, the downward curve of her lips. Damn, how he wanted to lose himself in her.

Wasn't that all that mattered these days? He didn't have missions anymore. No codes or rules or regula-tions. Sure, he had a foundation to start and there were certain things he wanted to accomplish before he died, but that was pretty much it. A goal. Long term. There was no chance of being deployed. There was only his life, any way he chose to live it. There was only him, any way he chose to be.

So instead of finishing her "but," he lowered his mouth to hers. He kissed her slowly and softly, just lips at first before gently gliding his tongue across the seam of her mouth. She opened, not just her mouth, but her whole body. Pulling him in until they were a tangle of limbs and mouths and tongues. There was so much fabric between them and yet they seemed to spark enough body heat to warm the entire pasture.

He wanted to make it hotter.

She'd already unzipped his coat, had her hands under his shirt, and though her fingers hadn't ventured past his belt, he had a feeling that's where she wanted to go. He untangled himself from her and when she made a sound of protest, he stripped off his coat.

He placed it behind her, hoping if they had enough layers around them, they could remain warm even naked. Then he fumbled in the dark to unzip and remove her coat as well.

She sat up and stripped off the heavy work coat he'd put on her a little while ago. "Don't take this as I want you to stop," she said, shrugging off the second coat she was wearing. "I just wish I could see you."

And damn he wished he could see her. Because against his will, for more weeks than he cared to admit, he'd been driving himself crazy over that one, short moment that first morning when he'd seen her in her pajamas. All that skin, all that possibility.

Which was when lightbulb in his head went off. "Do you have a flashlight or something?"

She gestured toward the toolbox he'd shoved into the corner to make room for them. "I mean, I do, but I'm not sure how we can hold the flashlight and have sex at the same time. Unless there's some magic way of doing things I don't know about."

He chuckled. "Oh, Becca." He crawled over to the toolbox and pulled out what he would need to fashion a lamp of sorts out of the flashlight. It only took some fence wire, the gun rack already attached to the truck bed, and his knowledge of knots. He used the wire and tied one end around the end of the flashlight, then the other around the gun rack, so the flashlight hung down, creating a small circle of light on their pile of blankets.

"Wow, that's very handy. Did you learn emergency sex lighting as a Navy SEAL?"

"I don't know that I learned it as a SEAL, but I certainly learned how to make the best out of a complicated situation."

She sat cross-legged in the pile of blankets, smiling up at him. If she was cold, she didn't show it. So he reached out and undid the lone button keeping her sweater on over her dress. He let his fingers skim across her neck and collarbone and arms as he pushed the sweater off her shoulders.

It fell into the pile of blankets around them and he traced his fingers over the slopes of her shoulders. She shivered and he decided then and there that he wouldn't worry about cold unless her teeth were chattering. He wanted her shivering and shuddering under him.

He wanted her everything.

She moved to her knees and reached out for his shirt, quickly if not deftly undoing the row of buttons and then pushing the shirt off his shoulders. She moved her palms across his chest and then down, her fingers splaying out and taking in as much of his chest as they could, all the while trailing down until she got to his belt.

She unbuckled it with enthusiasm, but he took her hands in his and gave them a little squeeze. He had to be…something. In control or slow or all those things he normally admonished himself to be. Because he wanted her hands on him, but first…

"Hold on. Twist around." He motioned with his index finger for her to turn around so that he could undo the back of her dress. She turned and he found a tiny row of buttons that were nearly impossible to undo.

But he was a former Navy SEAL. He wouldn't be foiled by *buttons*. Concentrating hard, he undid them. Then he pressed his mouth to the back of her neck. Lingered there when she made a little sighing sound. He kissed his way up her neck to her hairline and then back down, all the way to the center of her back, where the buttons ended. He could feel the way goose bumps broke out across her skin, he reveled in the little shiver that chased down her spine, and he lost himself in the taste of her skin.

If he had ever lost himself in such a way, he couldn't remember it. Didn't want to. He slid his hand under the fabric and pushed it apart and then off her shoulders. The glow from the flashlight wasn't exactly romantic mood lighting, but it at least gave him a good view of the shape of her.

"Turn back around." She did so and the dress pooled

at her waist. The bra she was wearing was some no-nonsense thing, not an inch of frilly lace or bows or whatever. Which he supposed suited her to the bone. She was pretty in a completely unadorned kind of way. Simple—and in that was her beauty. And her poise. And the way she could make him laugh when it was the last thing he wanted to do.

So he pressed a kiss to her mouth and pulled her into the warmth of his body. She was warm herself, vibrating, and he feasted on her mouth and the bright, summer taste of her. She held on to him, all willing enthusiasm that nearly undid him completely.

But every time he was close to losing any thought of control or finesse, he simply moved forward the next step. He undid the clasp of her bra, still memorizing the shape and taste of her mouth as he did.

He didn't immediately pull the fabric off her body. Instead, his hands tangled in her hair and he deepened the kiss, further and further until he didn't know who was running the show anymore. Only that they were clinging to each other, desperate for each other, to see each other, to kiss each other deeper and deeper until his breath was just as shuddery as hers.

It was that realization, that he was as far gone as she was, that caused him to pull away. To pull the bra from her completely and give them enough space that they could see and that he could take in the beautiful view. Torture himself with looking and pausing.

Her breasts were small, but the rosy nipples were pulled tight into peaks from the cold or from excitement or from… It didn't really matter at this point. He wanted his mouth on them. So he lowered himself to do exactly that.

She squeaked in surprise and he smiled against her skin. She smelled like fruit and flowers and everything feminine and summery. She was such a fantasy come to life. The softness, the gentle curves, the utter femininity she exuded. All of it something he'd forgotten existed in the years spent in navy barracks and bases and camped in the Middle East. Forgotten anything could feel this good when he'd been stuck in sterile and unfeeling hospitals—just another patient, just another wounded warrior visiting friends.

To come home to this, to her. The softness and beauty. He wasn't going to let it go, and he wasn't going to screw it up.

He sucked her breast deep into his mouth and she clutched his shoulders, clearly surprised and aroused. His cock throbbed, desperate to be inside of her, but he had to hold himself back. Give her everything first.

"Lay down," he ordered, and if she had a problem with him ordering her around, she didn't show it, and she certainly didn't mount any argument. She did exactly what he'd told her to do. She lay down on their bed of makeshift blankets and coats. The harsh light of the flashlight gleamed over the perfect, beautiful woman she was.

He pulled her dress down over her hips and she lifted her butt to allow him to also pull her leggings off. She was lying in the cocoon they'd created in only her underwear.

"Why are you just staring at me?" she asked, a smile on her lips, so many questions in her eyes.

"Because you're the most beautiful thing I've ever seen."

She rolled her eyes. "I know I'm inexperienced, but that doesn't mean I don't know a line when I hear one."

"Not a line," he returned, shaking his head as he leveraged himself over her. "Absolutely…" He kissed between her breasts. "The most beautiful thing…" He kissed lower and lower. "I have ever seen." He stroked his fingers across the waistband of her underwear, watching her eyes flutter closed. He planted a kiss there too, underneath her belly button, felt her stomach jump.

She was heaven. She was everything he'd forgotten existed. He had to be careful, rein all this in and give her what *she* needed first.

He glanced up at her and she'd opened her eyes, was watching him intently. He could read both the nerves and the certainty on her face. Nerves she was determined to force back or overcome. And that was just Becca.

He couldn't take away her nerves, but he could give her something she'd never have cause to regret.

He inched her underwear down, using his fingertips to trail over as much soft, fragrant skin as he could. He followed each new exposed centimeter of skin with his mouth. Kissing, nibbling, tasting. Wanting to build the anticipation so tight, so hard that neither of them would be able to stand under the weight of it for very long.

He finally got the underwear completely off her, and then he spread her legs wide even though she tensed a little bit. But it was only for a second or two, and then she relaxed.

He kissed up one impossibly smooth leg, dancing his fingers across the other until mouth and fingers met at her center. He paused for a second because the noises she was making were about enough to send him over the edge.

His pants were far too tight, and his body was vibrating with the desperate need to sink inside her. Claim her, take her. It'd been so long, and she was everything he wanted. But he held himself back and touched her instead. The glide of his finger against her nearly made *him* moan, she was so hot and ready.

So he slid his finger inside of her, the tight heat. He tried not to think too hard about sliding there himself. The way she would feel against the impossible hardness of his erection.

It was too much, so he touched her with his mouth, his tongue.

She jerked at the friction of his tongue, so he moved his arms around her thighs and held her in place as he lost himself in the taste of her body.

She whimpered and moved against him, pressing harder and deeper, and it was such a powerful moment to know he was the only one to have done this for her. To bring her to this edge. She shattered on his mouth with a low, keening moan into the quiet night around them.

She went completely still as he unwound his arms from her legs and scooted up into a more comfortable position next to her. She was blinking up at the sky, the flashlight beaming straight on her breasts.

"So," she said on an exhale. "That was a thing."

He laughed, falling to his back, looking up at the stars himself. "You crack me up, Becca."

"Isn't that a bad thing? Sex shouldn't be funny."

"Sex should be everything. Funny and good and sweet and hot. It should be all of those things mixed together." Which he'd never thought about before, not really, but of course he'd never thought much about sex before. He'd just done it.

This was so much more than simple release, but he didn't want to dwell too much on that when he was trying to calm his breathing, the thick pulse of need in his cock.

She turned on her side and smiled at him, all wide-eyed and pretty and irresistible. "I like that. Sex can actually have *all* of those things?"

"Trust me."

Her smile widened and her eyes held that mischievous twinkle. "That sounds like a very important mission," she said with mock seriousness.

He reached out and ruffled a hand through her hair. He could tell she was flushed, but the cold air hadn't reached them yet. She was…something truly special.

Which he couldn't think about too much, or he might be tempted to think about feelings, and…well, things he wasn't quite ready to ponder.

Then she rolled onto him, eyes gleaming with mischief. "Well, we better get to it, soldier."

—◦◦◦—

Becca had never expected sex to be fun. She thought it would be a very serious affair, but she kept making Alex laugh, and he kept making her laugh in return. It was fun and it was nice, and she eagerly attacked his pants as though they had done her some personal affront. Which they kind of had, because they were hiding the rest of him, and she desperately wanted to see it. Feel it.

She carefully pulled down his zipper and gave a little tug at his jeans. He lifted himself up so she could pull them off. Even under the weird flashlight lamp, she could see the way he jutted forward. It was amazing how hard a man could be. Amazing *that* was supposed to fit inside of her.

Something she wasn't quite ready to contemplate yet. Even as it scared her though, she wanted it. She wanted everything about this experience. Even if it hurt. Even if it was imperfect. It would still be perfect. Alex was…

No one would be a better first. No man could possibly be a better start.

Or finish.

She shook the thought away and placed her palm against the thick line of his erection. He groaned, pleasure chasing over his face. He pushed up against her hand and then seemed to think better of it and relaxed.

She took a deep breath, steeling herself. "Tell me if I do something wrong, okay?"

"I don't think you can do anything wrong."

Which was something of a comfort even if she didn't quite believe it. She rubbed her hand over him again and again, testing the weight of him, the length.

It was all so much. So overwhelming and yet an irresistible kind of overwhelming. The kind she wanted to dive headlong into, even if it was crazy. And all this was crazy.

She tugged off his boxers and though she couldn't quite make out all of him in the light of the flashlight, she could make out enough to know that he was impressive and so very hard.

She found that she wanted to give what he had given her. But she wasn't quite sure how.

"Before you get any grand ideas, why don't you just get that box of condoms?" he said, seeming to read her thoughts.

"They were in the first coat pocket," she said, looking around the back of the truck for the coat she'd been wearing.

Alex found it first and rummaged around until he found the box. He pulled out a foil package and tore it from the row. He opened it easily as though he had plenty of practice—and he probably had.

She didn't want to think about that. She didn't want to think about another woman touching his beautiful body or feeling this way about him. Because all that mattered in this moment was him and her together. She was sure of it.

"On your back, sweetheart."

She gladly complied even as nerves fluttered from her toes to her temples. She liked how easy he made it for her to know what she was supposed to do. She wasn't a fan of being told what to do in any other arena, but when she didn't know what to do, it was pretty comforting.

She lay on her back and watched with complete and utter fascination as he rolled the condom on his erection. He was so beautiful, like one of those old statues. Perfectly carved. Art. Miraculous.

His gaze met hers in the dark, and it was perplexed maybe. Worried definitely.

"It's probably going to hurt a little bit," he murmured, positioning himself between her legs.

"I know," she said, brushing her hands down his shoulders and arms. She forced herself to smile against the battle of nerves. "It'll be all right."

"I'll make sure of it," he said, firmly and full of certainty.

How could she not believe him?

This was really truly, honestly going to happen, and even though she was shaking with all the unknowns, she was ready. She was *needy*. She was going to have sex with him, and she knew he would do everything in his power to make this experience something really important and special to her. That was a feeling beyond measure.

He kissed her slowly, sweetly, taking his time tasting her mouth. She wrapped her arms around his neck and let herself be drugged by this tender moment. When she felt the tip of him at her entrance, she did everything in her power to remain relaxed and calm. This was all very natural after all. People had done it and survived since the beginning of time.

Besides, people and time didn't matter. She wanted it and him. She was here because of that and that alone.

He moved inside of her. A slow, uncomfortable burn. It was definitely not magical in and of itself, but the act was so *intimate*—and though the pleasure wasn't immediate, it was amazing to be here with him in this way. It was amazing to feel him slowly enter her and become a part of her. It was amazing to feel herself slowly begin to accept him more easily.

He reached between them and found just the right place to give her a jolt of pleasure before he moved deeper and deeper again. It was a strange feeling, but it was a good one, a magical one. Once he entered her completely, he simply held her there. Wrapped up in his arms, completely joined. Skin against skin, hearts beating against each other.

Tears pricked Becca's eyes, though she fought them off. It was an overwhelming moment, but not in a bad way. She felt good, happy, *right*. She didn't want him to confuse her tears for something else. So she blinked them back and held on tight. She kissed his neck and his shoulder.

"All right?" he asked, his voice husky against her ear.

She nodded into the crook of his neck. "More than."

He brushed a kiss across her forehead and then across her mouth. He looked deep into her eyes and she gave him something of a tremulous smile. Not because she was nervous anymore. Not because it hurt a little bit. But because the things she felt were so overwhelming and so good, a new fear wiggled its way into her brain. The fear of losing it. The fear of wanting it more than she should. So many different fears.

He opened his mouth as if to say something, but in the end, he just pressed another kiss to her mouth. Soft and sweet, a direct contrast to the hard invasion inside of her.

But that was what they were here for. Sex and joining and finding release together like this.

So, she moved against him, an arch, a slow glide. Testing the different angles that might offer pleasure. She gasped a little when she found one, then smiled against his mouth when he groaned. Becca was thrilled that she could make a man groan, especially a man like Alex—so strong, so in control all the time—except with her. Except with *her*.

It was a marvel and a wonder. Alex's hands were everywhere. He glided and he explored. He touched and he ignited her from the inside out. He began to meet her movements, even as she set the rhythm, even as *she* determined the angle. He didn't try to take it over, but he didn't take a back seat either.

The desire built just as it had when his mouth had been on her. A slow meandering coil of pleasure that slowly felt better and better and better, a deep want that twisted tighter and bigger and stronger.

There had been a grace to Alex's movements up to this point, but it was lost now. Instead, it changed into something more frenetic and desperate. She reveled in being a part of that. She reveled in all of it. Chasing her climax with her own movements even as he chased his.

"Becca," he said roughly into her ear, and there was something of a warning note to his voice. But she didn't heed whatever warning he was trying to get across.

She went faster and harder against him. So close. So desperate. He pushed deep on a groan, shaking, and she realized he'd lost himself in release. It was that knowledge and something like power that sent her over her own edge. A blurring, sparkling tumble into warmth and sated satisfaction.

He crushed his mouth to hers, desperate and needy. Which matched the odd flutter beneath all that *yes*—those *desperate, needy* feelings she didn't know how to handle. A seedling off kilter even as she felt alive with light and desire and pleasure. She wanted to relive the moment a million times even though she didn't think she'd survive it.

She didn't *want* to survive it. She just wanted to experience it over and over again.

"So, that was a thing too," she managed to say once his mouth left hers. Her voice was rusty and barely audible.

He nuzzled into her neck, kissing her collarbone, her shoulder. She loved those little brushes of intimacy. Found she needed them in the aftermath. Not a surprise he would give them, that he would know to. Routinely when it came to what she needed, Alex gave.

"Yeah, well, you're quite a thing yourself," he muttered, curling around her, pulling her into him.

He held her there for she wasn't sure how long. She didn't want to count or think. She just wanted to enjoy.

So she did.

# Chapter 21

ALEX DIDN'T KNOW HOW LONG THEY LAY IN THE BACK OF THE truck in each other's arms. Time had ceased to mean much of anything there for a while.

Eventually the cold air of the night began to seep in and they hunted around for their clothes and pulled them on. It took some time, but they convinced each other they needed to head back. Though he got the feeling she wanted to do that about as much as he did. Which was not at all.

Because reality was going to be something they had to deal with, and in the warm afterglow, the last thing he wanted to do was think about reality.

For the first time in so many years, he didn't want to solve problems or achieve anything. He wanted to wallow in the perfect beauty of something.

But life didn't work that way. Silently, he bundled them both back up and got in the truck and drove back to the house.

When he pulled to a stop, Becca was twisting her fingers together, staring at the house with an unreadable expression on her face.

He wasn't quite ready to read any expressions. Or figure much of this out. Because he knew himself well enough to know what would happen when he started *thinking* and *figuring things out*—a plan, orders, a mission. Rules and codes, even if they were only his own, and that would most definitely irritate Becca into bolting.

Or maybe he wasn't afraid his brain would go in its normal, overly careful patterns. Maybe he was damn well terrified he'd keep living in the moment. Just keep enjoying. And where the hell would that lead him?

He wasn't sure. Everything about tonight had upended him. It was good, probably, but uncomfortable definitely.

"I have one last request for the evening," she finally said.

"Okay." Requests he could do. Whatever she wanted, he'd want to give it to her—if only to see her face light up in a smile.

*Chill the fuck out, dude.*

"It's kind of…silly," she continued, still twisting her fingers, looking nervous.

"I doubt that, Bec." She was funny, and she was quirky, but silly? No. He couldn't imagine it.

"Okay, well, you know, I was thinking or hoping… I mean, I thought maybe, it's probably dumb, but you could, uh…"

He frowned over at her, fidgety and stuttery, and completely the opposite of what she'd been all night. So he reached across the console between them. He took her hand and brought it to his mouth, kissing the top of it. "Just say it. Whatever it is. It'll be fine."

"Would you sleep with me?" she asked, blurting it out even as none of the nerves left her vibrating frame.

"I think that's what we just did."

"No, I mean like in my bed. Tonight. With me. I mean, we can have sex again. Or we don't have to. I don't know how that whole multiple-times, sore thing works. But you know, like, just a…"

Alex didn't think it was silly, but that didn't mean he

wasn't taken off guard. It was more than fair for her to want that. He should have no qualms about offering that, no qualms in giving her whatever she wanted, but...

This was the damnedest thing about the woman fidgeting next to him. She had no experience with people, none whatsoever, and yet *he* always ended up feeling like he didn't know what the hell he was doing.

He'd never spent the night with a woman before. Which he'd never thought about or considered. It had just been the way things had gone in his life.

"You don't have to," she said, trying to tug her hand from his. "It's not that big of a deal."

He held tight to her hand. "It's not that I don't want to," he managed to say carefully.

Her hand stilled in his and she peered at him with those big, assessing eyes. "Is it because of the nightmares?"

He tensed, jaw clenching even as he told himself to relax. "No. The *one* nightmare isn't a problem." Which wasn't a lie so much. Okay, maybe it fucking was, but so be it. "I just want you to know, the guys will give us crap for this. I can make sure they only give me—"

"I don't mind them teasing me over something I have no shame about. But if you feel weird about it, then, you know, we shouldn't. I don't want to make you do something you don't want to do out of some misplaced sense of...something."

"It is not that I don't want to do it," he repeated firmly. It was just all those other things he didn't want to discuss.

"Are you sure? Because it *seems* like you don't want to do it. It's not a big deal. Really. I just thought I'd ask."

Damn Becca Denton and how she was always

dragging these confessions out of him. But the last thing he wanted to do was make her feel like her request wasn't fair or that he was balking at something because of *her*.

Damn it all.

"Remember how I said I'd pretty much only done the relationship thing once?"

She nodded.

"It's not like in high school there were any sleepovers. Then I was almost always living on a military base or what have you, which isn't exactly conducive to a lot of spending the night places. So, you know…it's not that I don't want to. It's just that I've never done it." Fuck it all for embarrassing confessions.

"I am just your first in so many ways." She grinned at him, clearly pleased with herself, and how could he fight that? The way she seemed so happy about it made *him* happy.

He didn't know what the hell to do with all this joy, but he knew he wanted to give it all to her. So he had to go with it, no matter how uncomfortable it made him.

"I have no problem spending the night with you," he said firmly. "I'm just as clueless as you about the protocol of that whole thing."

"I don't actually think there is protocol on spending the night with someone. I think you just do it."

"There can be protocol for everything."

"Only for you, Alex," she said with a shake of her head. She pushed the truck door open. "Don't worry. I'll wear my goat pajamas just for you." She hopped out of the truck on that note, leaving him puzzled and far too charmed.

He got out of the truck and followed her toward the porch. "I'm sorry. Did you say *goat* pajamas?"

"Of course."

He met up with her at the bottom of the stairs. When she smiled up at him, he could only smile in return. This whole thing was crazy, completely out of his control, and when she smiled at him like that all he could think was, *Why not give in to that?*

*Because it isn't who you are*, a little voice in the back of his head said.

He ignored it. He ignored everything except the enticing curve of her mouth and pulled her to him. Not quite as at-his-wit's-end as he'd done in the past, but not exactly gentle. She fell into it easily though, smiling the entire way.

"I know you said I could enjoy them all, but I really do like the grabby kisses the best."

"And why is that?"

"Because it means you can't resist me. Who doesn't want to feel that?"

He didn't have an answer for her, so he kissed her instead. A grabby kiss to show her just how much he couldn't resist. Because he couldn't. She was trouble, most certainly. Complicated one hundred percent. And she was something akin to magic.

He never would've thought to believe in magic in the whole of his thirty-four years, but here under a Montana sky with the sweetest woman possibly on the face of the planet in his arms, how could he believe in anything else?

"Let's go to bed," he murmured against her mouth.

"That's code for sex, right?"

"You grabbed the box of condoms, didn't you?"

She patted her coat pocket. "What do you take me for? A fool?"

He laughed and pulled his keys out of his pocket to open the door. The house was dark, and he could only hope that meant Jack and Gabe would be tucked into their beds and far away from him and Becca.

It wouldn't stop them from giving him crap, but he could take it. He wouldn't stand for it if they made Becca feel awkward though.

They walked through the dark, quiet house hand in hand, and Alex tried to keep his thoughts from going too loud or too complicated.

"I sure as hell hope you have a bigger bed than I do," he whispered as they passed the door to his room.

"Well, probably not as big as you're hoping. It's only a full size mattress, but don't worry. I'll make plenty of room for you."

"As long as you wear those goat pajamas, how can I resist?"

She laughed and opened the door to her bedroom. It was dim, but she must have left her bathroom light on because a little light shone from the door. Her room reflected her exactly. Nothing frilly or fancy, and yet there was a definite feminine quality to it. Cluttered and colorful.

"Oh, I did forget to mention one thing."

"What's that?" he asked, stepping in and closing the door behind him.

"Hannibal gets pretty mad if I don't let him sleep with me."

"God help me, who is Hannibal?"

She gestured toward the corner, and in the dark, he

could make out the gleam of a cat's eyes. "He doesn't leave my room much. Hates people, dogs, and everything. Except me, I guess."

"Honestly, a cat is much better than any other possibility I thought of."

"What possibilities did you think of?"

"You have a goat you call Ron Swanson, a rooster named Rasputin, and you talk to the horses like they're people. I'm just glad it wasn't like a rabbit or a badger or something."

"A badger. Badgers aren't very good house pets, but then again, you never know. Different animals can have different personalities."

He stripped off his coat and flipped on the light. "Now, to talk of far more important things. Before you can get into those goat pajamas, I need to get you naked." He grinned and she grinned right back.

He pushed aside the uncomfortable realization he couldn't remember ever being this happy as she began to strip off her clothes. Because what did it matter if he'd never been this happy as long as he enjoyed it while it was here? As long as Becca was in his sight, he was going to hold on to that happiness.

The doubts would have to wait.

---

Becca woke with a start, not sure what had jerked her out of the deep sleep she'd fallen into. Alex was still there, and she was curled up next to him.

She didn't feel Hannibal at her feet, so maybe he'd squirmed out of bed and that had woken her up.

The bed shook though. She blinked, trying to

understand why the bed was moving. It felt like an earthquake, and then she realized it wasn't just the bed. It was Alex himself.

She gave his shoulder a little nudge, hoping to wake him up. He was shaking violently and he had one arm extended straight above him, as if pointing at the ceiling.

Clearly he was having a nightmare and Becca had to swallow down the emotion that assailed her. It broke her heart that he was plagued this way. Worse, that he didn't want to admit it or deal with it. He just thought he had to live with it.

Maybe he did. What did she know about it? She'd never been through anything like what Alex had not just experienced, but seen *routinely*.

He murmured something she couldn't make out, and she gave him another little nudge, harder this time.

"Alex. You're dreaming."

He rolled out of bed and she gasped and reached out for him, but he didn't land in a heap as she'd expected. He landed in a crouch, looking around the room, his breathing heavy and uneven. In the dark, she couldn't tell if his eyes were opened or closed, but he stood there in a ready-to-fight position.

Becca's heart hammered. She didn't know what to do to help him. How to comfort or soothe him. How to make him feel safe. She blinked at the tears in her eyes and tried to focus on finding some courage. After all, if spending the night was something she wanted to have happen again—which it was—she had to find a way to deal with this.

*So will he.*

She pushed the thought away for now. Once she got him awake and calm, they could talk about what he needed to do, but for right now, she needed to make him feel safe. She scooted to the edge of the bed.

"Alex. Wake up. You're home. In Montana. You're here and safe. Nothing bad can happen here."

Still he crouched, and still he shook. A tear slipped down Becca's cheek because she didn't want him to have to deal with this. It seemed wrong and cruel, after all he'd gone through as a SEAL, to have to still experience things in dreams.

"Alex." She slid off the bed and inched closer to him. "It's Becca. You need to wake up."

She reached out to touch him and he moved away. Something in that ready-to-fight posture slumped. She moved toward him again and tried to touch his shoulder, but he jerked away.

"Go back to sleep," he said roughly.

"Come back to bed," she returned, trying to keep her shaky emotions out of her voice.

"No. I need to go to my own room."

"Alex. It's all right. You had a nightmare and—"

"I know what I had. I'm going to my own room. And you're going to stay here."

"But—"

"No buts." He straightened, and even though it was dark, she knew he was still shaking. That he was shaken.

She followed him to the door, unwilling to let him walk away scared. He needed a hug and someone to comfort him.

She took his arm, but he jerked away. Violently.

"Do not touch me right now."

"Just let me hold you," she implored. Maybe it wouldn't fix anything, but it couldn't hurt him.

"No." He made a sound she didn't know how to classify. Certainly not anything remotely kind. "Give me space, Becca."

"I don't think that's what you need."

"I don't give a shit what you think I need," he returned, frustration and fury in his tone, but there was something underneath it all. Something she wondered about. Fear maybe?

"I know what I need and it's to be left the hell alone." He paused at the door and she knew him well enough to know he regretted those harsh words. He was not a man comfortable with lashing out at people. "I'm sorry for yelling, but trust me, you don't want any part of this."

"I *do* want part of it," she replied, heart aching. Yeah, it was sad and maybe a little scary, but it didn't mean she wanted to pretend it wasn't there. It was part of him, and *he* was who she wanted. "I want to help you."

"You don't."

She knew she shouldn't get mad. Not when he was upset from a nightmare, but the way he refused to take her words at face value was too much. "I want to comfort you and make you feel safe. If you can't take that, all right, that's fine," she said, her voice wavering. "But don't sit there and tell me it's for my own good or what I don't want when I know what I want. I know what I want from you, and I don't think you have a clue of what I'm capable of withstanding."

His back was still to her and he didn't move. She held her breath and hoped he would realize she wasn't stupid. She knew whatever he was dealing with wasn't easy. He hadn't led an easy life, and leaving the military didn't magically make all those things he'd seen and done go away.

"I'm going to sleep in my own bed so you can get some sleep. So I can…"

"You can what? Pretend it never happened? Tell me about it, Alex. Maybe if you talk—"

He whirled on her then, clearly at his wit's end. She shouldn't have been poking at him when he was dealing with so much, but…but what was she supposed to do? Just shut up and let him pretend like this wasn't happening? Pretend he was fine and not dealing with something hard and serious?

Doubt crept in as he advanced on her. Actually, maybe he knew exactly what he needed. He was the one who'd seen the awful things. Maybe she didn't know what the hell she was talking about.

"You want this to be something, right? Me and you?"

She lifted her chin even though she felt like cowering. She knew no matter what she ended up saying or agreeing to, she couldn't be defeated by it. She couldn't let him intimidate her. Even if he did.

"Yes, I do."

"Then you let me deal with this my own way. That is the beginning and the end of it. We don't discuss my nightmares. You don't worry about me because I have my shit handled."

She swallowed, because she wanted to argue, but at the same time, how was it her place to argue? She didn't know anything. Maybe…maybe she was wrong.

Except he clearly did *not* have his shit handled, and she didn't even care that he didn't. She just wanted…she wanted him to trust her with it. But maybe they had to build up to that, and maybe that was okay.

"Can I give you a hug good night?" she asked.

Having to ask that was…well, not what she might have expected. But she'd deal. She'd find a way to deal.

He gave a terse nod, and she moved forward and wrapped her arms around him, wishing she could soothe or fix or whatever it was he needed. But she couldn't. All she could do was offer hugs. All she could do was brush her mouth across his. "I had a really lovely night."

"Until now."

She looked up at him, his dark eyes tormented even in the low light. She brushed her fingertips across his jaw gently, thoughtfully. "It was the perfect night. Thank you." Because it didn't matter if he left now. Everything that came before *had* been perfect.

She heard him swallow and eventually he lowered his mouth to hers. "For me too. Thank you. I'll see you in the morning."

Then he stepped out of the circle of her arms and left her room. Leaving her feeling confused, alone, and restless.

Which wasn't exactly what she'd been hoping for, but life was never as perfect as a person wanted it to be. Tonight had been really great. If she deleted these last ten minutes, it really had been absolutely perfect.

She'd give him his space and she'd respect his wishes, and slowly he'd come to trust her. She had to believe this was building to something, which meant laying a foundation first.

She wanted them to *work*, and she would find a way to make it happen. *That* was life right there. Working toward good, no matter what blood, sweat, and tears you had to put into it. Burt had taught her that.

She wouldn't fail.

# Chapter 22

IT WAS NO SHOCK ALEX WOKE UP IN A DAMN FOUL MOOD. Sure, sex was supposed to lift a man's spirits, but when a perfectly wonderful night was ruined by the shadows and ghosts of his past...

"Fuck," he muttered, scrubbing his hands over his face, hard and unflinching. His behavior last night was all too clear in his head.

He didn't know how he could have done it differently. Not in the middle of a terrifying nightmare that was both memory and fiction. The smell of flowers and Becca. The smell of explosives and death.

It had all been too wrapped up together when he should have been able to sleep, or at least dream lightly enough he didn't wake her. Didn't stir up that damn pity.

He wanted *her* pity less than he wanted just about anyone's.

He just wished he'd had the presence of mind to handle it better. He just wished he'd been able to avoid the way she'd hugged him, kissed him, told him it was all perfect.

What a lot of patronizing bullshit. Someone waking you up with their fucked-up nightmare wasn't perfect. In any world.

But he could either lie here and dwell on it, beat himself up over it, or stand fast in his conviction that leaving her room had been the right thing to do. He'd gotten out of there so she could sleep, so she could do it without him thrashing around or whatever he'd been doing.

That was the problem. He didn't remember. None of it was clear until he'd been crouching on the ground and she'd been reaching out to him. Before that it was all a mist of explosions and blood and yelling, Mom's voice weak and shaken—none of it real.

At least, not real in this time.

But whatever. A nightmare was a nightmare, and maybe he'd keep having them and maybe he wouldn't. Sadly, he couldn't control his subconscious. But he could *try* to wear himself out so completely it didn't win.

He'd work out this morning, then this evening as well. He'd force his body to do things he hadn't done since his initial training days. Then surely, *surely*, he would sleep normally again.

Maybe if he did all that, he could fathom sharing a bed with Becca, but until he could get through a night without the plague of ghosts, he wasn't sharing a damn bed with her.

She had to give him the space to fix himself. He tried not to think about the disappointment he'd undoubtedly see on her face. Or worse, that pity. Oh, she wanted to disguise it in help and holding and *comfort*, but it all boiled down to pity that Alex Maguire wasn't half as tough as he should be.

He would not stand for it. He didn't have to. No rules, codes, missions. Just him and what he wanted. He did not want *that*.

He forced himself out of bed and pulled on clothes. He'd grab some coffee, maybe take a run around the ranch or something to get the blood pumping, and then he'd go to work. Because even if everything with Becca last night up to the nightmare had been damn near perfect, it didn't mean he got to ignore work.

There was a lot to do before winter. A whole hell of a lot. Once that work was done, things would fall into place. He was sure of it.

He trudged down the stairs and into the kitchen, stopping short when he realized the figure pouring water into the coffeemaker was Becca.

She looked at him over her shoulder. "Hi," she offered, smiling. Sort of. Not one of those full-wattage things, which made him feel like dirt.

"Hi. I mean, morning. I mean..." Seriously, what was wrong with him? He was not some tongue-tied teenager. "Neither of the guys up yet?"

She shook her head. "Not that I've seen."

Okay. So that was fine. The guys were still sleeping and Becca was making the coffee and he...

Needed to stop being a baby. He opened his mouth to ask something inane about breakfast, but she started speaking at the same time.

"Sorry," they said in unison.

Christ, this was like high school. When she didn't speak, just stood there looking flushed and fidgety, he took a few steps forward.

"Sleep okay?"

Her gaze met his for the first time, and those green eyes held all sorts of emotions that poked at all the reasons he should never have let last night happen. It seemed inevitable he would hurt her now, and that sucked.

*Except nothing is inevitable if you work hard enough.*

"Not really," she returned, clasping her hands

together, then letting them go, then clasping them again. "You? I mean…after?"

"All right." Which was mostly true. He'd managed a few hours of dreamless sleep. To his knowledge.

"Right."

She looked somehow bothered by that, or hurt, and he wouldn't stand for it. Awkwardly, far too awkwardly, he reached out and touched her cheek.

She looked up at him through her lashes, her mouth curving slightly. Pretty and tempting. Complicated. But her skin was soft and warm, and she still smelled like *flowers*.

Hell.

He lowered his mouth to hers, slowly, giving her a chance to back away if she wanted to. After last night, wouldn't she want to?

But she moved up onto her toes and met his mouth with hers. Soft and sweet and willing. It was so damn easy, to sink into it and her. To wrap his arms around her and pull her closer to him, to trace her lips with his tongue until she opened for him.

She tangled her fingers in his hair, and he smoothed his hand over the sweet curve of her ass. This…*this* was what he wanted.

They kissed until he'd pushed the dark tangle of emotion completely out of his mind. Until he didn't know where he was or what time it was or why she tasted like… Finally he managed to pull back an inch. "Why do you taste like cake?"

She gestured vaguely toward the sink where a few bowls were piled up. "I made muffins. Cake's sadder little brother."

"What kind of—no, let me guess." And then he took her mouth again, feeding off the laugh against his lips until every bad part of last night vanished from his head.

A loud groan sounded from somewhere, and Becca jerked away. Alex kept a firm hold of her though. Hell if he was letting someone interrupt this.

"Come on," Gabe said, stepping into the kitchen as Becca squirmed out of Alex's grasp. "That's the last thing a single man wants to see first thing in the morning."

"Then go away," Alex returned.

Gabe shook his head. "No make-out session shall keep me from my coffee. You could be going at it on the kitchen table and it wouldn't stop me."

Becca turned an all-too-appealing shade of pink as Gabe strode for the coffeemaker, which had finally finished making coffee.

"Okay, ground rules," he said as he poured his coffee and then turned to face them, all mock seriousness. "No kissing in common areas." He pointed to Alex, then Becca. "No groping. No sex talk, and for the love of God, no pet names."

"I was really committed to the idea of calling Alex shnookums," Becca returned deadpan.

Gabe laughed, either at Becca or the horrified look on Alex's face, or maybe both.

"That one I'll allow. But run it by Jack first and make sure I'm there so I can see his face."

"Well, anyway. Muffins are in the oven. Take them out when the timer goes off." Becca moved away from Alex and grabbed a thermos.

"You aren't staying to eat?" Alex asked.

She shook her head and poured the coffee. "I need to

check on the horses. If Knightly doesn't eat his breakfast, I need to call the vet again. But I'm on lunch duty,
unless something goes wrong."

"We can put Jack on it if you get waylaid."

She nodded, screwing the lid of the thermos on. "See
you later, shnookums," she offered sweetly. She walked
past the table and Gabe, giving him a pat on the shoulder. "Bye, sweet cheeks."

"I'm kind of in love with her," Gabe said on a laugh
after she'd exited the room. He must have noticed that
Alex found that humorous, oh, not at *all*, and cleared his
throat. "Platonically, of course."

"Damn straight platonically."

"Why, you already in love with her?"

"Why are you such a damn woman?" Alex muttered,
grabbing his mug.

"I find that a very intriguing nonanswer."

"Find this very intriguing," Alex returned, flipping
Gabe off as he went over to the oven where he could
now smell Becca's muffins baking.

Love? So not something he was even going to
contemplate. That was for people who had their shit
together. Not that he didn't have his shit together, but…

Okay, maybe not completely together. Mostly. Ish.
Whatever. Wasn't relevant, because *none* of this was
relevant. So, subconscious him wasn't as in control as
he'd prefer—once everything was in place, he would be.

He flicked a glance at Gabe. They'd been through
most everything together since BUD/S. A happenstance
of time and place, two kids from opposite sides of the
country, completely different childhoods, and they'd
landed in that same place.

And been friends ever since. From the navy to the SEALs, pushing each other to do better and to be better. Surviving close calls and then surviving the end together.

If there was *anyone* he could talk to, it would likely be Gabe.

"Something you want to say?" Gabe asked, sliding into the chair across from him.

It was tempting, momentarily, to spill his guts. But for what? What would it do? So he had some nightmares. So they were currently affecting his life. It wasn't exactly life-shattering stuff. Gabe had his own shit to deal with.

"Nope. Everything's fine." The refrain was starting to sound thin even to his ears.

---

Becca found that it was beyond weird to be 99.9 percent ecstatically happy and that 0.1 percent...worried or something.

It shouldn't matter, that 0.1 percent. Not when it was so small. Not when the happiness and excitement and *hey, guess what, not a virgin* giddiness was so big.

But it seemed no matter how hard she tried to push it down or away, drown it in memories of last night under the stars or this morning in the kitchen, that little percentage of a percent niggled. Poked.

She shook her head and focused on the work ahead of her.

Knightly had eaten, so she'd been able to forgo the follow-up call to the vet. She'd taken Pal through the therapeutic horsemanship course she'd been setting up for them. She'd been in periodic telephone contact with Monica regarding moving sooner rather than later, if only so Becca could get her mentorship hours underway.

The only thing currently holding them back on that front was housing for Monica and her son. And maybe, just maybe, Becca had concerns about what might happen when Monica finally did show up.

As much as she wanted it to happen and as important as she knew Monica's role would be to their foundation, she also knew that all three men had reservations about having a therapist on staff.

God knew they all needed it, but…what did she know about forcing people into a kind of healing she'd never had to dream about?

Her phone trilled for approximately the tenth time this morning. Becca knew she couldn't ignore it for much longer without risking Mom coming out to the ranch, but what did she say? She'd already told Mom she'd be working all day and couldn't text back. Did Mom want her to get more specific?

That she didn't want to talk? That she didn't want Mom to ruin the happiness Becca was feeling? Because as guilty as it made her feel, Becca was pretty darn certain her mom's reaction about her and Alex would not be a pleasant one.

*Well, it's never going to be, so maybe you should suck it up and deal with it.*

Damn that rational voice in her head.

She dug her phone out of her pocket as she led Pal back to the stables, but before she could read the text, a voice greeted her.

"Hey."

Becca glanced up to find Alex striding toward her from the bunkhouse, where she knew he and Gabe were working. Apparently Jack had been deemed unhandy and relegated to calf duty with Hick.

It was downright stupid how everything in her mind and body just…vanished because Alex was there. But when he was there, tall and strong and otherworldly hot, a damn marvel, it was hard to think of anything else.

Except that he'd kissed her and touched her and made her feel like she'd never felt before. Made her feel like she'd never believed an isolated, bumbling girl like her could.

He was magic, and of course that wasn't going to be perfect. Even magic wasn't perfect. She just had to deal with the slightly uncomfortable notion that he had nightmares he wouldn't address. The sneaking suspicion he might never want to share a bed or those troubled pieces of himself. That wasn't such a terrible price to pay for this beautiful man walking toward her, smiling at her, kissing her at breakfast, and all the other things.

"I think we're going to have to call in a professional for the plumbing issues in the bunkhouse. Do have the number for that guy you were talking about earlier?"

"Yeah, it should be on the fridge under the llama magnet."

"The…llama…magnet."

"Oh yeah. Felicity has this whole collection of adorable llama stuff for sale at the store ever since Dan Sharpe started his llama ranch. People are gaga over it. I bought some llama socks."

"Llama…magnet. Gaga. Llama…ranch and socks. No. I don't want you to explain to me. I want to pretend

I never heard those sentences." He shook his head in horror, adorably perplexed. "I'm going to go give him a call."

Becca tried not to look disappointed at the fact that this little stop by had been business related and nothing else. There would be times when they would have to discuss business-only things with each other, and there would be no touching or smiling or flirting during those times.

But Alex didn't turn away.

Her mouth curved. "Was there something else?"

"No. I'm going to go get that number." But the corners of his mouth twitched, and instead of walking toward the house, he took a step toward her. So she did the same thing, pulling Pal along with her as she took a step toward him.

"You've got a good horse there."

"He's been very good to me. Reliable. Calm. Patient. Sweet."

"Please tell me you aren't comparing me to a horse."

"Me? Compare someone to an animal? That's just downright silly."

"Ha."

Another step for him, and then another step for her. By this point they were both grinning and incrementally getting closer to each other.

"You know, I didn't come over here to make out with you," Alex said, failing to look serious.

"Well, that's a darn shame," she replied, not even trying for serious.

"And we have things to do. Work. Very important work," he continued.

"It is very important work."

But now they were standing nearly toe to toe and grinning like idiots. She couldn't think of anything she wouldn't overlook for moments like this. To have someone look at her like that and want to spend time with her. Not a mother or a stepfather, just a person. Just a guy. A guy who genuinely liked her. Goofy, fidgety, odd, little her. He didn't even make her feel goofy or odd. He made her feel smart and beautiful. Like every confident thought she'd ever had about herself was *right*.

Pal nickered and stamped, clearly irritated about the pause in their movement toward the stable.

"You know," Alex began, his voice a shade rough. "If you go inside to make lunch a little early, and I go inside to make the phone call to the plumber…it's possible we might end up in the same room. Preferably naked."

She burst out laughing even as she blushed a little. She loved that he would say something like that to her, but thinking about him naked…about sneaking inside to…

Well, yeah, she was a little warm.

"You have a very dirty mind. This inexperienced young woman finds it perplexing."

"Then I guess I'll just have to corrupt you a bit more than I have."

"I was really hoping you'd say that."

His mouth was a precious centimeter from her mouth, and she was ready to grab on to the thrill of going inside and making out while everyone else was working. It was awful. Terrible. Irresponsible and wrong. Possibly the most exciting thing she'd ever heard.

A loud, long honk interrupted the forward trajectory of both their mouths. Alex's brow furrowed and Becca looked over past the stables to the part of the lane that she could see.

Her mom's car was parked there. Which was odd considering that the end of the drive itself was a few more yards up.

"I'm guessing she didn't like what she saw," Alex offered.

Becca sighed, all the excitement of the moment flowing out of her like she was a popped balloon. "Oh, I can almost guarantee it."

Alex studied something. Whether it was Mom's car, the sky, the mountains, the ranch house itself, she couldn't tell. She could only tell he was deep in thought, and she wasn't sure she liked whatever he was thinking about.

"Did you tell your mother about what happened last night?" he asked, that dark, unreadable gaze finally turning to her.

"Yes, Alex. I texted my mother last night. Virginity finally shed. It was *fantastic*. You should probably bake me a celebratory sex cake."

"I don't know what women talk about with their mothers."

But she couldn't get over the idea this was more than that. "Do you...not want me to tell her?"

"I want you to do whatever you feel comfortable doing. And whatever you choose to do, I will stand by that."

"You don't want a say in it?"

He smiled a little at that. "No, sweetheart. I think whatever stand you're trying to make with your mom probably starts with deciding what to tell her about your life."

"That sounds reasonable and awful."

"Welcome to life: reasonable and awful."

Mom was swiftly approaching and Becca knew she had to make a decision. An adult decision. If she wanted her mom to treat her like one, she had to be one.

"Hi, Mom. What brings you out this way?"

"You weren't answering my text messages," Mom returned, though her glare was on Alex, who was standing there, as if he *would*, in fact, stand by whatever she said.

"I told you I'd be working in the stables, and I wouldn't have time to text back. It didn't necessitate a trip out."

"Yes. Clearly you're so busy *working*."

Becca took a deep breath. There was being an adult, and there was being a masochist. Alex being around for this conversation was more masochist than adult. She turned to him and smiled thinly. "Why don't you go call the plumber?"

"You sure?" he asked, searching her face.

God, she liked him. She nodded and gave his arm a squeeze. "Thanks."

He took a few steps forward, nodding at Mom. "Sandra. Good to see you."

Mom didn't say anything, though she was clearly livid, but Alex didn't say anything more. He walked toward the ranch, giving Becca one last look over his shoulder, and that bolstered her. Because if he were in this position, if he were standing here having to explain himself to his dad, she knew he would stand there with that soldier posture and *do* it. He'd be honest and certain, so that's all she needed to do.

"Why are you really here?" Becca asked Mom as gently as she could manage.

"Because I'm worried about you. I didn't like how

we ended our conversation last week, and I don't like how things have been. You weren't answering my texts. All you would say was you're busy, so I had to come out here. I am not a stupid woman, Becca Denton. I know what I saw."

"I know what you saw too."

"I told those boys to watch after you. I certainly didn't mean…"

"What? You didn't mean for them to like me? To be interested in me?" She'd never quite felt like this before. Like *she* was the rational one, arguing with her mother's irrational behavior. She'd always felt wrong or ungrateful for arguing with Mom, but…she was too old for this. She was too… She couldn't play the game anymore. She didn't want to.

"You don't have a clue what men are like," Mom said firmly, eyes flashing with a million hurts Becca would never understand.

It softened her. "You're right. I don't. But I know what Alex is like."

"After a few weeks?" Mom scoffed.

"Yes, actually. We've talked a lot, and we have a lot in common—a lot of shared people if not shared memories. I've never been afforded that—friendship. *Companionship*. No one has ever given me what he has."

She hadn't meant to hurt Mom, but she knew in the aftermath of those words, saying that someone else had given her something her mother never had was a cut. Which wasn't fair to either of them, but there it was.

She wanted to cry or apologize. She wanted to run away, but that wasn't what independent adults did. It wasn't who she wanted to be anymore.

"Shared people. Yes, you were raised by the same father, and that doesn't strike you as problematic?" Mom demanded.

It was such a grasp at straws. "No. No, it doesn't, and you know it doesn't. Alex was never here. He was never a son to you. My relationship with Burt never had anything to do with Alex. You were *there*. You know that as well as Alex and I do."

"I don't know a thing that Alex knows. Everything about this strikes me as a much older man taking advantage of a young, naive girl."

Becca tried to shake off the word *naive*. It wasn't meant to be an insult, so she focused on the point of Mom's argument. "The age difference is smaller than your age difference with Burt."

"That was different. I had a *child*. I was emotionally mature."

That one hurt. She wanted to be the rational adult, but it cut. Hard. "Do you think this little of me?"

"I think the *world* of you," Mom snapped.

"It doesn't feel like it." Becca swallowed at the emotion clogging her throat. She'd swallowed these emotions for so long now though. Maybe she needed to do what she wanted Alex to do. Open up. Explain. Talk about it. "It feels like you think I'm stupid and frail and can't handle myself. I know that's not what you mean, but I can't help but *feel* that."

Mom's lips pressed so tightly together they disappeared, and she was silent for the longest time. So Becca could only go further, give more.

"I really like being with Alex. He took me out on a date last night, and it was nice and fun. It was good. I know I don't have any experience dating guys, and I know most of your experience with men was not good, but, Mom, this was really, really good. I'm happy with him. You don't need to jump with joy that I'm growing up, that I am building something with a man, but I need... Mom, I *need* you to treat me like you trust me, like you believe in me."

"It's not you, Becca. It's him. I know you think you know him because he's Burt's son, but what do you know about a man who was a soldier overseas for so long? Who never visited his father? What do you know about what he did over there? What do you know about him really? Maybe you know about his childhood, and maybe you know the people he knew, but has he really opened up his heart to you and told you about the hard things he must've seen or done? Has he talked about the future? Or is he just telling you what you want to hear?"

Becca tried not to visibly react to that, because she didn't want Mom to see that it landed. Poking at that 0.1 percent of worry or dissatisfaction. No, Alex hadn't opened up about whatever gave him nightmares, but that was fine. He didn't need to. They hadn't talked about futures exactly, but she hadn't brought it up either.

"I, um, get what you're saying," Becca managed, because she couldn't lie to her mom and say he'd given her all those things. And yet...it was one date. It was a few moments. It was still so early.

They were building. It was fine. *And what if you're building without a foundation?*

"So you'll be careful and take things very, very slowly?" Mom prompted.

Becca assumed Mom was talking about sex, and

since that ship had sailed… Well. "I'm very careful. But what are you so afraid of happening?"

"That he will break your heart," Mom returned as if it were the only possibility. "That you will fall in love with him, head over heels, stupidly and irresponsibly, and then be devastated when he doesn't give you what you want him to give you. It's very easy to want something from a man and want it so hard and so badly you overlook everything else. But he won't ever give you what you're looking for. You can't make a man give you something."

Becca rubbed her hand over Pal's muzzle, trying to keep all reactions under the surface. She knew this stemmed from Mom's experiences with Becca's father and the ensuing fallout with her family. Becca knew this wasn't about her and Alex, but…

It hit that sore spot again. If Alex didn't want to talk about his nightmares, and he didn't want to address them, she'd never be able to *make* him. There would always be this thing standing between them. The things he kept locked away.

But did it matter when it was 99.9 percent good?

"Alex is a really good guy and he would never purposefully hurt me." She knew that deep in her bones. His conscience wouldn't stand for it. "But if I do get hurt, then that's life. I've never had my heart broken. Is it really such a bad thing to put myself in a position where it might happen?"

"Having had my heart broken, crushed, losing my entire family and everything I had because of it? Yes, it's that bad, Becca. I think you're bright and sweet and wonderful and *smart*, but all of those things are so easy for men to stomp on. I would never accept my child having to go through what I went through. I can trust you and still feel that."

Becca let go of Pal's reins, trusting him to stay put or not wander far. She took her mother by the shoulders, needing this conversation to be over as much as she needed Mom to understand. Really. Truly.

"Mom, in some insane pseudo-world where I get knocked up and Alex wants nothing to do with the baby—which would never happen, by the way—I know you would never let your pride or your skewed morals or whatever it was that your parents had to hold on to stand in the way of me. I know you would support me, and you would give me everything, the same way you always have. So maybe I'm not afraid to have my heart broken because I know without one tiny shadow of a doubt that I have a soft place to land. No matter what I do or say, I know, I *know,* you'll always be there for me. Won't you be?"

Mom sniffled, clearly blinking back tears. "I hate this place," she croaked, waving her arm to encompass the whole of the ranch. "I hate being here and remembering him and I hate that you're all grown up."

"I can't fix any of those things."

"No, you can't. And neither can I." She let out a long breath. "I keep thinking I can. If I work hard enough, pretend hard enough, I can make all the hurt go away." She stepped away from Becca's hands and rubbed her chest.

"Mom."

"No, you're right. I'm sorry. I want to protect you because that's *my* soft place to land. My comfort zone was always fighting for you." She stepped forward and rubbed Pal's nuzzle. "I would and will be here for you no matter what happens. I'll protect you."

"Just love me," Becca returned.

Mom looked over at her, still pained, but Becca thought maybe they'd had a good talk. She had to remember that even though it had been a year, her mother was still grieving and getting used to her new life. It wasn't an exciting new start like it was for Becca. Mom had to figure out who she was and what she wanted to be all over again.

"I do love you," Mom finally said. "More than I'd ever be able to…" She shook her head, still teary, still struggling. "Love is complicated, and I'm sorry if mine ever…hurt you."

"I love you too, and I'm sorry if mine ever hurt you."

Mom managed a wobbly smile. "I used to think love shouldn't hurt, but once you're a mom, you realize it always will."

Becca thought of Alex, of the pain in watching him struggle with that nightmare last night, and she understood that in a way she might not have not so long ago. Love did hurt, but she wanted to believe it could heal too. When you opened up like this.

She thought she understood her mother better, and that her mom understood *her* better.

"You could always help us. I know being on the ranch is hard, but there are things you could do for the foundation in town." Involve Mom instead of shut her out.

"There are?"

"Sure. In fact, I'm trying to find a place for the therapist I've hired. She has a son. He's nine. She said they don't need much, but something affordable, obviously. Something close to the ranch, but close to a bus stop for the school. You know people and talk to people in town. Maybe you could see if anyone's renting anything out or selling. We could use help from someone who's not drowning in ranch life. What do you say?"

Mom dropped her hand from Pal and stepped forward, taking Becca's hands in hers. "I say I have an unbelievably amazing daughter who humbles me daily."

"Who's everything she is because of you."

"And Burt."

Becca smiled. "And a few very good animal listeners."

Mom managed a laugh.

"Mom, I know you don't want to see my heart broken, and you have reservations about Alex, but I really, *really* like him and how I feel with him. He makes me feel strong and confident, and you know I've never felt either of those things."

"So, back off, Mom. Huh?" Mom said with a heavy sigh.

"Just a little."

"I'll do my best."

"Then come in and help me make lunch. Eat with us. I think if you spent some time…"

But Mom was looking at the ranch house, ghosts flashing through her eyes, painfully enough Becca didn't finish.

"Not today, sweetheart. I need to work up to going in there again. That dinner was one thing because I was protecting you, but being in there just to be in there? I can't. Not yet. I'm going to head back to town, and I will find you your affordable housing for your therapist. How does that sound?"

"Perfect."

Becca knew life was never perfect. In fact, every time it felt a little bit perfect, something drastic happened to upend everything. But she didn't want to think about the possibility of that right now.

Right now, she was going to enjoy the perfect while it lasted.

# Chapter 23

THERE WAS DUST AND SAND EVERYWHERE, CHOKING THE AIR, burning his eyes, his nose, his mouth. He couldn't see, he could barely breathe, but he knew he had to keep moving or his men would die.

They would die, and that would be on his head even if he died too. His legacy. A failure. The cause of so many deaths.

Mom's voice. No, not that car. Afghanistan. *That* car. A grenade. Had to get out or down or something.

So he pressed forward. Except he didn't have his pack or his gun. He didn't have anything to fight with. He was in this swirling mass of a desert, defenseless, with men to save, and he had *nothing*.

Something touched him and he whirled to fight it off with his bare hands, but he was knocked flat, and after a few disorienting moments, he realized he was...

Montana.

Home.

Not a soldier. Not a SEAL. Not anymore.

He blinked up at the figure before him. Jack.

"Hey," he offered, though the response came out scraped raw.

"Care to explain?" Jack asked in an even tone that failed to hide the myriad emotions in his expression.

"Nope." Alex swallowed, trying to coat his dry throat with something, anything. He realized then he was sitting on the floor of the bunkhouse, breathing heavily, heart pounding wildly, fictions mixing with truths in his brain.

"Did I…" He'd felt a touch and he'd tried to fight it, hadn't he? He tried to focus on his surroundings and clear the fog away. Tried to breathe and think and…

Fuck, this was so not good. Not with a bystander. Not in the middle of the day. In the bunkhouse.

"Did you go after me?" Jack supplied, still maddeningly even and so *Jack*. Cool and vaguely furious. "Kind of, but I knocked you down when you lunged at me, which is a reflex *I'm* not particularly happy about myself."

"I'm fine."

"No. No, that is increasingly not true. For any of us."

Alex couldn't believe that. Maybe it was true things weren't going quite the way he wanted them to be going. But that just meant he needed to try harder. Focus more. He had to be more aware of his surroundings and do better at noticing when things weren't quite copacetic.

That didn't mean things were getting worse. It just meant he needed to be more careful. He'd gotten lenient. He'd been enjoying things too much lately and letting his guard down. He needed to focus again and work on being in tune with everything.

He needed to finish this fucking bunkhouse. They needed to get men here. Once that mission was completed…

This didn't have to mean something, and it didn't have to be a big deal. He got up off the ground and brushed the dirt off his pants. They'd made good progress on the bunkhouse. That's what was important. If the whole idea of exercising himself into not having nightmares was making him have them during the day, well, then he would change what he was doing.

It wasn't getting worse. He refused to accept that.

"Alex. This is not good."

"It's fine," Alex returned, looking around and trying to remember what he'd been working on.

"Look. Nightmares are one thing. We all have them and probably always will, but the middle of the day? Anyone could've walked in here. Becca could have been the one to walk in here."

"What are you saying? I'm some kind of threat to Becca?" Alex demanded, a sick feeling he refused to name sinking into his gut.

"I don't know. All I know is I walk in here and you lunged at me. Maybe if I thought you took that seriously I wouldn't be concerned, but you refuse to accept that this isn't normal."

"It was nothing. I must've dozed off. I've been working really hard." He'd change that. He'd fix it.

"Alex, you were wide awake. You were moving through here like you were in some fucking war zone. Having, you know, been there with you when you've done that, I know."

Alex didn't say anything. He wasn't having this conversation. He wasn't...

"You want me to pretend that didn't happen?" Jack asked incredulously, not taking the fucking hint. "You want me to ignore you're having some sort of waking whatever?"

"Yeah. Because it was nothing. I'll fix it." And he would. He would keep making adjustments until this didn't happen anymore. If all of his adjustments so far hadn't worked, he'd adjust again until he found the trick. He just needed time to accomplish something, and it would be okay. He would make it okay. Because there were no other options here. He could live with it, or he could make it okay.

What else was there to do?

"Okay, it was nothing. You'll fix it. So you're going to tell Becca about it, right?"

Alex tried to stay relaxed or get relaxed. This was not a big deal, and he wouldn't let Jack turn it into one. But if he was going to maintain that there was nothing amiss here, then he had to remain calm himself.

"Why would I tell Becca anything?"

"Because you two morons are ridiculously happy and damn near inseparable outside of work hours. I don't want her to be surprised if you accidentally go after her because you're having some episode."

"Not happening."

"Why? Because you will it so?" Jack demanded.

Alex breathed through the anger rioting around inside of him. Jack was just being cautious. And protective. Which was good. It was good they would be protective of each other. Even if it was fucking annoying. "No, it's because she's not going to sneak up on me in the middle of the bunkhouse."

"I did not sneak. It's the middle of the day."

"Go find something useful to do and stop bugging me while I've still got an ounce of patience left."

"I'm going to tell her."

Alex had to fight his initial reaction, which was to punch Jack in the face and tell him this was none of his fucking business. But he was rational. He was calm. He was right. "I don't sleep with her."

Jack snorted. "Yeah, you two disappear behind closed doors to play Yahtzee."

"No, I mean I don't *sleep* with her. I'm not putting Becca in any kind of danger. Okay? You don't need to tell her, because it's not a factor. I don't sleep around her."

"You don't think it will be a factor eventually?"

"No, because I'm going to get my shit together before…"

"Before what?"

He didn't know. Before anything serious happened. Before he…whatever. Fuck if he knew, just *before*. It didn't matter because he wasn't going to let anything hurt her until…just until he figured this all out. And he was going to. He'd been figuring out his own shit for a long damn time, and he'd continue to do so.

"I'm handling it, Jack."

"By pretending it doesn't exist?"

"No, by trying to find a way to make it stop. I don't take this lightly, but I am going to fix it."

"And if you can't?"

Alex didn't like to lie. In fact, he thought it was damn cowardly to lie. But if he didn't get away from Jack soon, he was going to throw a punch.

*Because he's right on the money?*

Alex pushed that thought away without hesitation. "Look, that shrink will be here soon enough. Becca's mom found a place for her, so a few weeks, tops. If I actually do something that makes me think I would be a hazard to someone, I'll talk to her."

"You willing to promise that?"

Alex had to clench and unclench his fist to keep himself calm. He couldn't promise something and go back on it. Maybe he could fib a little, but he couldn't straight-out break a vow.

"I'm not leaving without your word. That's one thing I know you won't go back on," Jack pressed.

"Fine," Alex muttered. "You have my word." He'd just make sure he fixed this whole thing before the shrink got here. Before he had to do anything.

He was going to solve his own problems. He didn't need anyone's help and he didn't need anyone's pity. He hadn't expected to have a timeline on that, but that was fine. It was probably best. Because the sooner he got over all this crap, the sooner he could give Becca more. She deserved more.

"On one condition," Alex added, because hell if he was getting his shit poked into without giving it right back.

Jack tensed and that was when Alex knew he had, maybe not the upper hand, but at least an even hand.

"The same goes for you. You make the same deal with me."

"Last time I checked I haven't tried to lunge at you in some sort of waking fugue state."

"No, but I know you're not sleeping. At least not at night."

"Some of us are still in a lot of pain from our injuries," Jack returned in a growl. "And I'm not going to take those damn painkillers. Last fucking thing I need."

"That's fine. But if by the time the shrink gets here you're not sleeping better, then you need to talk to her or you go back to the doctor about your pain."

"I'm fucking done with hospitals."

"Is it a deal or what?"

Jack ran a hand over his hair. "I don't have a nice, sweet woman waiting for me to get my shit together, Alex."

"So find one."

Jack laughed a little bitterly. "Thought I had." He shook his head.

"It's been a long time." For the first time, Alex wondered if it would have been better for Jack to go home and deal with the aftermath of his cheating fiancée.

"Yeah, well, I loved her for a long fucking time. Whatever. You're right. Been a long time. You giving me your word?"

Alex held out a hand. "If you're giving me yours, it's a deal."

Jack reluctantly shook, which meant Alex had to make sure he worked hard enough not to have to regret it.

———∿∿∿———

"I have some great news," Becca said to the three men sitting around her dinner table. She placed the lasagna she'd made in the middle and could barely contain her excitement.

"If this is about the shrink, you're the only one who's excited," Gabe muttered.

"Well, you should be excited. You should be excited that we are building the kind of program you three dreamed up. The Shaws got the cabin on their property all fixed up to be rented out, and Monica should be moving in, in less than a week."

Jack opened his mouth to say something, likely to complain, so Becca steamrolled right over him. "Which means I can start doing my mentorship hours for the therapeutic horsemanship, and we can start building the program. And if we start building the program, it means we can figure out what your roles will be in terms of the cattle operation."

"We've still got a ways to go on the bunkhouse. We've got to get that done before we can bring anyone *into* the program," Jack said, clearly needing to get an argument in.

Becca wouldn't let that deter her excitement in the least. "Thank you, Debbie Downer," she said, sliding into her seat sandwiched between Alex and Jack. "I am aware of that. But if we get the bunkhouse done and the program done, because we're working on those two things simultaneously, there's no reason why we couldn't open in the fall."

"You that interested in rushing it?" Gabe asked before shoving a forkful of lasagna in his mouth.

"I'm interested in accomplishing a goal," Becca returned firmly.

"You two are perfect for each other," Jack muttered at Alex.

Alex didn't pay him any attention, so Becca followed suit.

"That's great news," Alex offered, smiling and clearly not thinking it was great.

But Becca wasn't going to dial down her enthusiasm just because these three men were afraid of a mental health professional. In fact, Monica being here was even more exciting because of that prospect. Maybe having a therapist around would…get a few balls rolling for these guys too.

*Preferably Alex.*

She shoved her own bite of lasagna into her mouth. Things were good, and she was going to keep believing that. So she chattered happily as they ate.

And because she had lucked into working with three really good men, they were mostly good sports about it. Definitely quiet and not excited, but they didn't tell her to be quiet. They didn't sigh heavily and roll their eyes. Well, mostly. She'd gotten a few heavy sighs from Gabe and one eye roll from Jack, but that was pretty good, considering.

Dish duty fell to Jack that night, so Becca, Alex, and Gabe retired to the living room. Except when Gabe tried to sit down, Alex jerked a thumb over his shoulder.

"Beat it."

"What?" Gabe demanded.

"Go find something else to do, somewhere else," Alex replied.

"You two want to have sex, you have bedrooms for that."

Becca still couldn't quite get through those blatant kinds of statements without blushing, no matter that it had been nearly a month. Still, it was better they treated it casually than making a big deal about it.

"Yeah, well, I want to sit on the couch, alone with my woman, and watch a movie. So get out."

"Your woman. You're going to put up with chauvinistic bullshit like that, Becca?"

Because she was a very simple creature, and because Alex was kind of superhot when he said *my woman*, Becca shrugged. "I think so."

"Un-fucking-believable," Gabe muttered as he grumbled off upstairs.

"It's probably not fair to evict him from the premises just because you want to watch a movie with me."

"Probably. But he was being a dick all afternoon. Had to get back at him somehow."

"So you don't want to watch a movie with me?"

"I absolutely will watch a movie with you." He stopped and turned to face her, grinning. "As long as movie is code for making out on the couch, which will lead to going upstairs."

"Men really do just have a one-track mind, don't they?"

"Absolutely. One hundred percent."

"So, what are we are going to pretend to watch? Oh, I know!" Becca tried to sidestep him and move for the drawer with the DVDs, but Alex blocked her.

"No. No chick flicks."

"What does it matter if we're only going to make out through it?" She smiled sweetly at him, batting her eyelashes.

"Nope. Uh-uh. You'll stop at certain parts and say, 'oh, isn't that romantic,' and then I'll have to pretend like I give a crap about a guy on his knees in the rain giving some lame-ass speech. There will be no rain-filled lame-ass speeches from me."

Since she could see the teasing glint in his eyes, and she wasn't particularly looking for any rain-soaked speeches, she took a step toward him. She touched her fingers to the lettering on his T-shirt.

"I thought I was your woman," she said, looking up at him through her eyelashes. It was amazing, still, all these weeks later, the way she never felt...shy or fidgety flirting with him. It was easy. He *made* it easy, because she trusted him to…well, not embarrass her or make her feel silly.

He tugged her into his hard chest in that way that she had yet to get tired of.

"You are my woman. You're not going to lecture me about all that possession crap are you?"

"No," she replied, winding her arms around his neck. "I quite like the idea of being your woman."

"Good." He dropped his mouth to hers, somehow both possessive and sweet at the same time.

"Can't we go upstairs and forgo the making out on the couch part?" she asked against his mouth.

He chuckled. "Oh, I do like you, Bec. But I have to piss off Jack first."

"Why do you have to piss anyone off?"

"Because that's what we do."

Which seemed silly enough to her, but what did it matter when his mouth was so close? When his arms were around her? When she had a blissful night of *him* ahead of her?

It didn't take long to forget. To lose herself in the kiss. She sighed and melted into it, beyond happy. She'd never expected love to be so easy.

And, oh crud. She *was* in love with him. Which she'd kind of suspected, maybe for this whole time, but she'd been able to keep those thoughts pushed away. The more she let them run free in her head, the more she was afraid she would blurt it out one day and scare Alex off irrevocably.

She knew Alex liked her, and maybe he even could love her. She wouldn't be surprised. He was not a man meant for a lot of superficial entanglements, and he certainly wouldn't get tangled up with her if it were only superficial. But she also knew he had a lot of…issues and reservations. If he admitted to love, he'd have to start facing some of those things he was so desperate to pretend didn't exist.

"What's wrong?" he murmured against her mouth.

"Nothing."

"You stopped kissing me back."

"Oh. Sorry. I got lost in thought."

He pulled back a little, frowning. "Ouch, my ego."

"That's not what I mea—"

"That's okay. I'll just up my game." His mouth devoured hers this time, kissing until she was boneless and nearly completely dead.

"Oh, come on," Jack's voice interrupted. "You guys suck." Jack stormed off upstairs and Alex laughed. And laughed.

"You're mean," Becca said, though she had to admit his laughter did perilous things to her already shaky heart.

"Only when they deserve it."

"Let's go to my room."

"Gladly."

It amazed her continuously how easy this all was. They went to her room, and they undressed each other, laughing and happy. She hadn't exactly lived a terrible life. After moving here, getting settled, getting healthy, she'd had a good few years before they'd lost Burt.

But it wasn't like this. The giddy delight in finding someone who seemed to delight in *her*, who made her feel like a million bucks all the time.

They fell onto her bed and came together on a matching groan of satisfaction. It was good. Always so good.

The coming together like this, having his rough hands on her, feeling the calluses scrape against her skin. His mouth all over her. Tasting her. Making her feel worshipped and perfect.

It never got old, the feel of him moving with her, of being joined together. Finding new ways to drive each other crazy and over that tumbling edge.

She was head over heels in love with him. Because every night was wonderful. Every night he found new ways to make her groan and laugh.

Every night she felt more like she'd found her life. She'd found the person she'd always wanted to be and the life she'd always wanted to live. It was so big and so great she couldn't even be scared.

He brought her to orgasm in a quick rush and then found his own in a leisurely exploration that had her losing herself all over again.

How could she not think this was perfect? How could she not want more of it? How could she not want to give all her love to him and not be afraid he wasn't ready for it?

If she could convince him to stay, then she could tell him. Say those words, and even if he wasn't ready, it might be a step. Because she dreaded this moment every night.

The aftermath of a good day, laughter, conversation, amazing sex. Together in bed, happily sated and realizing he was going to leave. That he wouldn't spend the night until he felt like he'd overcome this thing in his head.

She understood him, too well, and much like her relationship with her mother, it made everything more complicated. Because she understood where they were coming from, and she wanted to be able to give them that thing that they wanted from her, but it wasn't what *she* wanted.

"What's wrong?" he murmured, tracing a hand up and down her arm. "You got all tense again."

She leaned into him, curling around him, burrowing into him. This was her favorite place to be, and she got so little of it.

In the light of day, she always talked herself out of asking for more. She could tell herself to give him time, to give him space. She reminded herself that so much of this was wonderful and perfect, so why focus on the one little thing that wasn't?

Except the more she experienced, the more she understood that this wasn't…right. She was beginning to think it wasn't healthy. It was something broken. A kind of fracture, and it wasn't going to heal.

Not if she kept ignoring it.

"Alex…" She stayed pressed to him but tilted her head back so she could look into his eyes. "Stay."

There was a flash of pain in his eyes, and she hated putting it there, but Mom had said love could hurt. Love *did* hurt. "Please, I want you to." Because *talking* to Mom instead of sparing her feelings or avoiding conflict had been a positive. It could be the same here.

"Better not." He kissed her temple then slid out of bed.

"Alex—"

"I know, Bec. I know. I'm working on it."

"Working on what?"

He shrugged, pulling his clothes on carefully,

not looking at her. "Just...everything. It'll happen eventually."

She didn't know what to say to that. The word *eventually* was so bland. So meaningless. "You know the nightmares don't bother me, and I know they bother you. That doesn't mean you can't stay. It doesn't mean—"

"Please."

He stood so ramrod straight, so tense, but it was that *please* that broke her. How could she push when he sounded so...

"Don't push, okay? Give me time." When he did finally look at her, it was that stoic, blank soldier look.

It broke her heart, and something awful and heavy stuck in her gut. She tried not to think this was always the way it was going to be. He was working on it—him admitting to working on it rather than ignoring the nightmares existed was some kind of progress.

Wasn't it?

Fully dressed, Alex leaned over and brushed a kiss against her mouth. "Good night." But he didn't straighten right away. He stood, bent over her, studying her face, and for a moment...

She held her breath, willing him to say the words. Willing it to be a step.

But in the end, he said nothing. He just straightened and walked out of her bedroom, leaving her alone.

Hannibal meowed from the end of the bed where he'd resettled himself after Alex had gotten up. Becca sighed. "Sorry. You're not the company I want."

She wanted Alex's company, his trust, his full heart—and was starting to worry that was the one thing she'd never have.

# Chapter 24

THE CLOCK WAS TICKING DOWN. ALEX COULD FEEL IT IN his bones. There was a bomb waiting to go off. To change everything.

He scanned the horizon, trying to remind himself he knew what he was doing. He was in charge. He'd been born of these mountains. Surely that made him stronger than all the disparate parts clashing in his brain.

Exhaustion dogged him. It was hard to eat. Everything was normal, work and calving going well and in what amounted to the closest a ranch got to a routine, and yet he was dogged by this feeling everything was spiraling out of control. Including Becca.

Jack and Hick joked about something from their position on their horses behind him. Absently, Alex wondered if the horse riding made Jack's recovery worse. Maybe he should force him to go to the doctor for some kind of release or permission.

But that would only circle them back to that promise. The therapist would be here soon, and Alex wasn't stable yet.

He wouldn't let that panic him. Panic got you killed. *In Afghanistan. Not here.*

Alex forced himself to focus. Breathe. Everything was fine. Everything *would* be fine. The bunkhouse was close. The foundation was getting built. It was normal he'd feel a little jittery right on the cusp of all these new things.

They reached the stables, dismounted, and began unloading the tools they'd used to mend the fence. Hick and Jack continued to talk, and Alex tried to join in, but he couldn't muster the focus.

Hick offered goodbyes, as he'd put in an extra hour and was mumbling about his wife having his hide. Alex muttered a half-hearted goodbye as he stored the tools where they belonged.

Jack nudged him. "You hear me?"

Alex looked up. Weird, his head spun a little bit. Maybe he was getting sick. "What?"

Jack's expression changed, something like concern etching in his sharp, stoic features. "Something going on with you and Becca?"

"No. Why would you ask that?"

Jack shrugged. "You're out of it today. She seems quiet lately."

"We're fine. She's fine."

Jack raised an eyebrow. "Your kind of fine or actually fine?"

Alex wanted to snap, but Jack wasn't off base. At least about Becca. She had been quiet these past few days. When she smiled it wasn't that full-wattage thing.

But she *did* smile. And she didn't say anything off or act any different, exactly. Just more that everything about her was…muted.

Alex frowned over the fact that Jack had picked up on that and he hadn't until Jack had pointed it out to him.

"We've just been focused on the foundation lately is all. She wants to get it all together and so do I, but that's…stressful. Tiring." That was all it was. Surely.

Alex walked next to Jack toward the house, Star

prancing ahead of them. Gabe was on dinner duty, and
it was about time for it to be ready.

"I'm not big on poking my nose where it doesn't
belong, but take it from a guy who ignored a lot of
signs—whatever's going on in that head of Becca's...
it isn't good. I'd do something about it if you want her
to stick around."

"She's not going anywhere," Alex grumbled.

"She wouldn't leave the ranch or the foundation, no,
but that doesn't mean she wouldn't..." Jack shook his
head and increased his limping pace toward the house.
"Never mind."

"No. No, say it," Alex demanded, because he couldn't
understand what Jack thought he was getting at enough
to refute it.

Jack stopped at the bottom of the stairs and jammed
his hands into his pockets and turned to face Alex.
"Anyone can see she's head over heels for you, Alex,
God knows why. But...that isn't always enough."

"Enough what?"

"Christ," Jack muttered, clearly uncomfortable.
"Look at yourself. Look how much *worse* you're getting. If there's anything I've learned it's that women
don't stick around for this kind of shit."

"Becca would," Alex replied stubbornly.

"Yeah, but you wouldn't wish it on her, would you?"

Alex tried to push that icy ball of dread away. "I
appreciate the concern and all, but what happened to
you... Becca isn't like that. And I'm fine."

"Look at yourself, Alex. Really. Look." And with that,
Jack walked up the stairs, favoring his better leg. "And
for fuck's sake, talk to the therapist when she gets here."

Look at himself? He knew things weren't perfect, but that didn't mean he wasn't working on it. What would looking at himself do? The only thing that could fix anything was to keep moving forward and leave all that haunting past in the past, where it belonged. A therapist would only stir it all up.

He rubbed at the tightness in his chest that never seemed to loosen anymore. He'd get there. Soon. He just hadn't found the key yet, but he would. He would.

––––––

Becca didn't go down for dinner. She was too nervous to eat. The past few days had been…crappy, and she didn't know exactly how to explain why. Everything was the same. Everything was exactly as it had been before the other night when she'd asked Alex to spend the night with her.

Except, that was the problem. She couldn't take the same. She couldn't take lonely nights after he left, and she couldn't take the way the weight seemed to be dropping off him. She didn't think he was sleeping *at all*.

Something had to change, and she'd finally accepted that change had to come from her. Because she needed this, even if she shouldn't have. If she was thinking about a future, *their* future, she needed him to let her in. Not just to the parts he thought were healed or worthy, but all the parts.

She loved Alex. She wanted to be able to love him all the time. Not just in the select times he deemed it okay. She wanted to be able to feel like this was real, and she wanted to be able to feel like…

There was a future in it. Not just the present. She

couldn't imagine a reason things would go poorly, but she could imagine—all too clearly—living in this space forever. Stagnant. Pretending.

She didn't want that, and more, she couldn't take much more of it. Knowing things weren't changing. She needed to know there was a chance, a possibility that—

A knock sounded on the door and she took a deep breath. "All right, Hannibal. Now or never," she muttered, knowing it would be Alex wondering why she hadn't come down to dinner.

She was going to tell Alex what she needed, and she was not going to back down this time. She couldn't keep being too afraid to ask for what *she* needed because he was struggling.

Because what she needed wasn't for him to *stop* struggling. She needed for him to share that burden. To give her the opportunity to be there for him. Otherwise, this was nothing but...

Well, it wasn't a relationship and there wasn't a future in it if all this was going to be was sex and him trying to protect her from something.

Bolstered, she opened the door. Alex stood on the other side, holding a plate of food. All that drive faltered.

He was so sweet to her. Caring and good. What was wrong with her that she couldn't just enjoy it?

"You didn't come down for dinner, so I bought dinner to you." He smiled, but there were such awful shadows under his eyes.

"No, I..." She bit her lip and took the plate. She gestured him into the room and put the plate on her nightstand. The physical evidence of all that was plaguing him, and the fact that nothing was getting better, had to spur her to action.

This was about her and what she needed in a relationship, but it was also about him. She couldn't keep being complicit in whatever was slowly killing him.

"Alex, we need to talk." She hesitated for a moment, trying to figure out what to lead with. She wanted to start with "I love you," but she was afraid it would sound too much like an "I love you, but…"

"Something wrong?" he asked, easing onto the edge of her bed, glancing suspiciously at Hannibal, who stared right back.

"Maybe you should tell me."

She watched the tension creep into him, that hard, stoic soldier posture taking over. "I don't care for riddles, Bec."

She hated that tone of voice. Hated that blank look in his eyes. She wanted his smiles and his warmth and it seemed… She wanted to cry because it seemed like being together had only extinguished that part of him. Inch by inch.

"You aren't well," she said, her voice scratchy. "I'm starting to think I'm some sort of…cause of that."

He softened at that and took her hands in his, pulling her closer. Him sitting on the edge of her bed, her standing there, not that much above him.

"Why would you think that, Bec? I'm happy with us, what—"

"If this is you happy, happy is *killing* you," she interrupted. "I'm worried about you, and I've kept my mouth shut for days. More and more every day because I didn't want to rock the boat, but the boat is sinking."

"I'm not following."

"I've been reading up on PTSD."

He jerked like she'd punched him, got to his feet violently. "Hell no. You're not going to internet psychoanalyze me."

"That's not what I'm doing," she said, trying to stay calm. Being calm and rational would keep him that way too and maybe she could get through to him. "I just wanted to know what the key side effects were, so I—"

"I don't have PTSD. I don't have anything wrong with me. I went through all the military shrinks, Becca. Cleared to be a civilian. Mentally. Physically. My knee hasn't bugged me in weeks."

"I'm not worried about your damn knee. I'm worried about *you*."

"Well, I'm fine. There is nothing to worry about. Whatever little…issues are left over will be fine. I just need to finish the bunkhouse and—"

"Please tell me you don't actually think that."

"You're right. I don't," he said, folding his arms over his chest in that military leader position where he stared down at her like she was beneath him. "I *know* that. This is a transition. Leaving military life and moving back home and not having Dad here, it's a lot of stuff. But I'm not fucked up because of it."

"PTSD is not you being fucked up, Alex." Why was he so deliberately misunderstanding her? Why was he so deliberately being an ass? "It's a very natural and common—"

"It's bad enough you're bringing a shrink here, and maybe I'll have to take this kind of shit from her, but I will not take it from you."

"Well, I don't want to take *this* shit from you. I'm not going to sit here and pretend you're not hurting and that you don't need some help. All I want to do is stand by you, and I want you to be happy. And I damn well want to spend the night with the man I…"

He backed away, a flicker of fear, and she knew it was now or never.

"I love you," she said, keeping her gaze straight on his, letting all those things she felt vibrate in her words.

He turned away, then just stood there, still saying nothing.

Which pissed her right off, and maybe it shouldn't have. Maybe she shouldn't have been doing or saying any of this, but she was. She wasn't going to stop. She was going to be *honest*, and she was going to stand up for herself, and she was going to *demand* something out of him.

He might be great in a lot of ways, but she wasn't going to let him keep locking her out.

"I know you're not ready to hear that," she began. "That's okay. It is. But that is how I feel, and because it's how I feel, I don't like only getting parts of you. The parts you deem worthy to share. Because I have shared everything with you. I have been stupid and goofy and shy and all of the parts of me I used to be embarrassed of. I have shown them to you and you have made me feel like they aren't silly or foolish. You have always made me feel like they were part of me, and you liked all those parts of me, and I want to do the same for you."

"I don't need that," he said, his voice gruff and pained.

Which hurt. Because though he said *need*, it felt a hell of a lot like want. I don't *want* that. "Gotcha."

He still didn't turn to face her, and she didn't know what else to say. Actually, that wasn't true. She knew exactly what to say, but she was afraid to say it. She was afraid to tell him all the things she really felt, and she was afraid they would make him walk away.

But she was tired of living her life afraid. Afraid of people, afraid of germs, afraid of hurting Mom. Afraid of all the things that could go wrong.

She was afraid of losing him because this was wonderful, but it also made her feel like crap lately. It wasn't that she thought love was all roses and champagne all the time, but she did think that…it wasn't trying to make each other feel like crap. Which meant telling someone when she felt like crap because of what they were doing.

Even if they walked away. Even if it ruined everything.

"I'm not going to keep doing this," she said, her wavering voice undermining the words. But she was certain—God, she was certain that she needed more. Needed it. "I love you. And I'll be okay if you don't love me back yet, but there's no chance if you won't open up."

"I am plenty open." He turned to face her, confusion and irritation dug into the lines of his face. "This is a good thing. Why on earth are you trying to ruin it?"

"No, honey," she returned, something about his accusation giving her the strength to be steady and sure. "I'm trying to build a relationship, and it needs a foundation. We could fix up the bunkhouse, and we could start this whole business that we've got going on. But without you and me and Monica, without Jack and Gabe and Hick and the cattle and all of these buildings, it wouldn't make a difference. It would have no mooring. You have to have the tools, and you have to have the ground, and you have to have the heart."

He stared at her for the longest time, and for a second she thought maybe he was going to say that he loved her too. She almost hoped he wouldn't, because if he told her he loved her, she might be willing to overlook a lot more things than she should.

"I'm sorry," he finally said, such a blank expression on his face.

She could only stare at him as she tried to work that out. "Sorry for what?"

"I'm sorry I can't give you what you want, but I won't put you in danger."

"I'm not afraid of you, Alex." She could tell he was really struggling with something, but he did it all so internally. So under the surface. "Why don't you tell me what you're thinking?"

But he was quiet, clearly working it out on his own. "I'm sorry if you feel like I'm not giving you something."

"Stop apologizing!" she said, surprised when it came out on a yell. Surprised to find her breathing uneven and tears stinging her eyes. But he wasn't *getting* it. "I am not asking you to apologize."

"Then what are you asking me to do?" he yelled right back. "Tell you I love you? Sleep next to you? Those are things I cannot do right now. But I am working on it."

"How?"

He shook his head. "Just trust that I am."

"No. No. You can't even tell me what you're doing? How you're trying to 'fix it.' I don't want you *fixed*. I just want you to be willing to open up to me. To tell me what's going on. To sleep in my bed and let me hold you through a nightmare. I just want you to trust me with it, not think you have to put yourself in some kind of order for me to love you. You'll never be perfect, Alex. I don't expect you to be. I don't want you to be. I'm not perfect. I love you no matter what. But love means giving all of yourself to a person, even when you feel…whatever it is you're feeling. I don't even know! You won't tell me."

"I can't do that."

She closed her eyes against the pain. She'd known. Oh, she'd hoped love might change him, fool that she was, but she'd known all along. He couldn't let anyone see him as less. Not his friends, not himself. He'd essentially run away from home rather than let his father see him struggle with his father's new life, new family. He'd worked himself to the bone these past few months instead of giving himself any kind of break.

He thought he had to be perfect to be loved, and she didn't know how to fight that. She thought the answer had been love, but…maybe it wasn't *her* love.

"I think you should leave," she said, her voice breaking on that last word.

She got him, knew she got him down to his soul. She just couldn't convince him that opening up to her wasn't the worst thing in the world. She couldn't change him.

And he refused, *refused* to even try. For her. It wasn't worth it. If he couldn't love her back, and he couldn't open up to her, then why was she spending all her time and energy hoping for different? It was stupid. It was foolish. She couldn't force him to trust her.

She had a life to live. To build. If he wasn't going to give himself over to being part of that foundation, then she had to accept it and move on. Now. Before it got any harder.

# Chapter 25

ALEX COULDN'T BELIEVE WHAT HE WAS HEARING. OF ALL THE ways he had expected things to go wrong with Becca, this certainly wasn't one of them.

He had never expected her to push for more. Certainly not after almost a month. But here she was, standing up for more, and maybe he should've known this would happen all along.

Becca had learned to go after what she wanted. She'd grown into the kind of woman who'd not just ask for it, but demand it.

Why couldn't she give him more time? He could give these things to her. Soon even. He just had to finish a few projects, then things would get better.

Why wasn't she giving him the damn time? "So you love me, but this isn't going to work out because I can't be exactly what you want me to be right this second?"

Tears shimmered in her eyes. He had to look away from that.

"Alex, I'm not asking you to be anyone but yourself," she said in an even voice that grated along his skin. "You can be anal and a neat freak and plan as much as you need to. You can be Mr. Strong and In Charge. But I will not let you shut me out. Not because it hurts me so much, even though it does, but because it is hurting *you*. Because I love you, and I care about you, and I want you to be okay and happy, and you are not. You've gotten worse."

"I don't know what you're talking about."

"You don't think I've noticed how little you sleep and how hard you work? How you're trying to exhaust yourself, all so you don't have to deal with whatever's haunting you? You've lost weight. Your color is off. I haven't said anything because I didn't think it was my place."

"I have not lost weight."

"My ass. Look at your pants."

He glanced down at his buttoned pants, and yes, they hung a little low, but honestly weight loss was to be expected. He'd spent the past year visiting hospitals and driving around in Texas. He'd worked out, but his life hadn't been hard ranch work.

The weight loss made sense. It did.

"You are doing everything in your power to ignore this. But the one thing you have refused to accept is that maybe you can't ignore it. Maybe it is part of you. And maybe pushing it away and pretending like it's not there is making everything worse."

That was when he knew what this was really about. Because *something* had to be pushing her here and not just him being unwilling to share her bed at night.

"Jack told you, didn't he?"

Her eyebrows drew together. "Told me what?"

There was something clawing at him and he had to breathe through it, remain calm, form a battle plan to survive. It was what he did. Who he was.

"Alex, what do you think Jack told me?"

"Nothing."

Becca shook her head, some of those tears spilling over. "I can't do this. I can't...I can't be shut out of things. Secrets aren't fair. To me or to you."

"This is not love," he muttered. She wanted to act like she loved him? Love was… Well, it wasn't pissing on a person, that was for sure.

"Sometimes I wonder if you even know what love is. Maybe you're so bound to duty and responsibility, you wouldn't know it if it bit you in the ass. I don't want to fight with you. All I want to do is love you. And hold you. And help you. I want you to want the same for me. But it can't be one-sided."

"Why the hell not?" he blurted out. He would protect her. He would love her in his way. She just had to accept that there were some things to be…avoided.

She shook her head, those tears on her cheeks killing him slowly.

"I don't know," she croaked. "If I could make it one-sided, I would. If I could ignore this one thing for everything else, I would. But I don't know how. I have been trying for weeks. The other night, I let you go even though it broke my damn heart. I kept telling myself this is too good and too right to throw away for something so trivial."

She closed her eyes as more tears fell over and he had to look away again.

"But I knew. Deep down I knew you wouldn't… You're so married to this idea of yourself as the strong leader that you will not let your guard down for anything. All I'm asking is for you to let me in. I'm not asking for anything else. You just need to let me know what's going on."

But she was asking for him to change the very essence of who he was, who he'd been since he'd found that control after Mom's accident. She was asking him to admit things that weren't true. At all. So maybe things had felt a little worse lately, but he was fixing it. He was finding a way to recover before the shrink got here. Becca wasn't giving him time. With enough time, he would make it all right.

Without dragging her into it. Without making her cry because of the things he said or did. The thought of hurting her... He'd lunged at Jack, and the idea he might do the same to Becca... If he was in control of things, he knew he wouldn't, but when she was asking him for more? For *all*?

He couldn't do that. He needed more time.

So maybe they'd step away from each other right now, but once he managed to fix everything, he would tell her...but he couldn't tell her now.

"I should go."

She nodded, tears streaming down her cheeks, but that would be fine. He would fix it. He had to believe that even walking away with her crying and hurt, he would find a way to fix it.

That was what he did.

That was who he was.

And in all his life, it had never been so hard to believe.

---

Becca was glad that it was a busy workweek and she could throw herself into that instead of worrying about Alex. Anything was better than thinking about how lonely the last few days had been without him kissing her or making her laugh. Anything was better than missing making *him* laugh or the happy little thrill when he came by during the day to "check in on her."

She kept hoping every random time she caught a glimpse of him that he was coming over to talk. To apologize. To say he would open up to her if she'd just take him back.

It was awful, this wanting him and not wanting him at the same time. It was awful second-guessing herself every time she saw him. Wondering if she should have let it go. Wondering if she should have not demanded so much. Who was she to demand anything from him?

But that's what it always came back to. She knew he wasn't okay. She didn't think Jack and Gabe were particularly okay either, but she could only handle trying to fix one person at a time.

Which wasn't the right word because that was the word Alex was forever using. Fix. He didn't need to be fixed. He needed to let go. Not be so afraid of whatever it was he was afraid to find if he stayed in her bed or told her his fears.

She didn't understand why that was such a terrible prospect for him, except maybe she did.

How long had she avoided people even after being healthy? All because she hadn't known what to say or how to be normal or accepted. She hadn't known how to make conversation, so she just hadn't. Maybe Alex didn't know *how* to open up.

Unfortunately, her hard line of saying he had to do it kind of ruined her opportunity to show him how.

Except hadn't she shown him? Just by doing it herself with him? She had been so completely open. She blinked hard and focused on the mountains in the distance as she drove up to the Shaw ranch.

Monica should have arrived this morning, and Becca

had wanted to stop by and see if she could help unload the truck. The cabin was tucked away on the east side of the Shaw property, and as Becca curved around the tree line, the cabin and a moving truck came into view.

She parked next to a little car that must have been pulled by the moving truck.

Earlier in the month, she had been excited about Monica arriving, but she'd lost that excitement sometime this week. She didn't want the complex emotions that came with this.

It all seemed so hard and really, really painful. She should have lived and let live the whole damn time.

There was a young boy hefting a box out of the back of the moving truck as Monica stepped out of the front door.

Becca got out of her truck and forced a friendly smile. "I figured you'd need some help."

"Oh, you must've missed my phone call. I called up to the ranch just a few minutes ago. I can get most of the stuff in, but I'm going to have to call in some bigger muscle for a few items."

The little boy tried to scoot past her, but Monica stopped him with a very motherly hand to the shoulder. "Becca, this is my son, Colin. Colin, this is Ms. Denton."

"Call me Becca. I'm sure we'll be seeing a lot of each other."

The boy gave a half smile and then nodded toward the door. "Can I put this stuff inside?"

Monica nodded and the boy disappeared inside. "He's not too happy about living in the middle of nowhere."

"Does he like animals?"

"We'll find out. I think he's pretty set on hating everything for a while."

"I'm sorry."

Monica shrugged. "It's no big deal. Children are a constant trial," she said with a smile. "You get used to it."

"I'm feeling surprisingly familiar with constant trial," Becca muttered.

Monica put her to work, and Becca helped carry what boxes and bags she could. But Monica was right. They would need some stronger arms to get the furniture inside. Maybe she could go see if Caleb Shaw could help and tell the guys not to come.

But just as she stepped out of the little cabin, Burt's truck came into view.

"Please be anyone but Alex," Becca muttered.

"I think it's all of them," Monica said, making Becca jump since she hadn't realized Monica was *right* there. "Problems with Alex?"

"Not...professionally," Becca returned.

"Oh, personally? Now that I find very, very interesting."

"Well..."

"You don't have to tell me. I'm constantly, forever nosy. Ignore me, and feel free to tell me to shut up if you want me to. I won't be offended."

"It's just...well...we've been sort of...involved."

Monica smiled, something a little wistful. "Involved. Oh, I miss those days."

"You do? Fights and not understanding each other and wanting to throttle the other person?"

"Oh yeah," Monica said earnestly. "I didn't in the moment, but when you lose someone, you end up missing even the stupidest things."

"I'm sorry. I didn't—"

"No, don't be," Monica said, giving her arm a squeeze. "He's been gone a long time. I'm used to missing. So what did the lunk do? I figure since there's three of them and two of us, we have to stick together. I'm on your side, girl."

Becca smiled. "If we add your son, there's *four* of them to our two. Even more reason to stick together."

Monica laughed. "I think we're going to get along just fine, Becca. So spill the beans before he gets out of the truck."

"I'm worried about him. I don't think he's all right."

"Oh, honey." Monica let out a sigh. "That's a pain I know all too well."

Alex got out of the truck followed by Gabe. Jack must have stayed at the ranch with Hick.

Alex looked rough. She didn't know how he kept just looking…worse. Like he was still going through hell, except that denial must be hell in and of itself.

"Hi, Monica. Need some furniture moved?" Alex greeted.

"Thanks for coming, guys. I think we could have done the beds, but the couch is approximately three hundred tons."

"We'll get it."

Colin stepped out of the house. He eyed the two men before taking a little step back into the cabin.

"I see you brought us a grunt," Gabe offered, his voice loud enough to carry to the boy.

"Oh, I don't know. He's very disappointed about living here," Monica said, eyeing her son. "I'm not sure how much work you'll get out of him."

"He is a little tiny. Not sure what kind of work he can do."

"I'm pretty strong," Colin said. He took a few forward steps. "I bet I can do a lot."

"Good," Gabe said with a nod. "Man to man, we need the help."

Becca sat back and watched as Gabe easily maneuvered the young boy into conversation. She wasn't the only one who was surprised. Monica was watching wide-eyed as Gabe stepped inside with her son, so he could show him where to put the couch.

When Becca flicked a glance at Alex, he was staring after his friend a little wide-eyed as well.

"Does he have kids of his own?" Monica asked.

"I don't think so," Becca returned, looking at Alex for confirmation.

"No. I think he was the oldest of a big family though. Maybe that's it. Always had little kids around."

Monica nodded. "Excuse me. I better check on the instruction Colin's offering and make sure the couch placement makes real sense and not just video-games sense."

Monica stepped inside and that left Alex and Becca in the yard next to the moving truck. All by themselves.

Which was fine because they had been doing this all week. Pretending like they didn't love each other, weren't bleeding all over the place on the inside at being apart. Or maybe that was just her pretending those things.

Whatever. It was fine. She'd gotten quite good at pretending like she didn't want to cry every time she saw him. She turned to grab something from the truck, but Alex had moved to the same point and they ended up bumping in to each other.

"Sorry," she muttered.

"Yeah, me too."

"Thanks for coming. I know you're not jazzed about this, so the help is appreciated."

He shrugged, squinting into the truck. "It is what it is. It'll be good for the foundation."

The foundation. Right about now she wanted to say screw the damn foundation. And why shouldn't she? Why was she pretending like she wasn't hurt or *broken*?

Why should she curl up inside of herself to make *him* comfortable when he was the one who was refusing to help himself? What a waste to kill himself like this. All the hurt and sadness over the past few days crystallized inside of her into something a lot closer to anger.

Anger felt a hell of a lot more active than depression.

"Yes. That's what's most important. The foundation. Not your own mental health," she muttered under her breath, climbing into the truck.

"What was that?" he asked, climbing in after her.

"Nothing."

"If you think her being here is going to magically change things…"

She whirled to face him, hands on her hips. "If you think being an ass is going to magically change things…"

"I didn't come here to fight with you," he returned through gritted teeth.

But she *wanted* a fight. She wanted something to explode, because this was no better than when she'd been swallowing down all the I-love-yous and pretending like he wasn't withering away. "Then don't. You're Mr. Fine and In Control of Things, aren't you?"

"I don't need a shrink," he said resolutely, crossing his arms over his chest. "I was cleared. End of conversation."

She snorted. End? No. Definitely not. "Clearly they were so right about you. You're looking so good! Healthy. Well rested."

"I'm starting to think you're the one who needs therapy, Becca."

"Oh, fuck off," she returned, because if she didn't use nasty words, she was afraid she'd haul off and hit him.

"Mom," a little boy's voice called. "The short lady just said the f-word."

Becca closed her eyes and tried to bite back the groan of embarrassment. Until she opened her eyes and Alex was trying not to smile. Which was irritating. Not cute at all.

"I'm sorry. Poor word choice on my part," Becca said to Colin, but he was grinning.

He grabbed a box clearly marked *TOYS*. "Mom says that sometimes too," he offered, clearly pleased with himself. He hefted the box and walked out of the truck.

She sighed and looked back at Alex. He was staring at her, and it wasn't that irritated, baffled staring she was getting used to. It was the staring that broke her heart and made her wish everything were different.

She didn't want to fight anymore. It leaked right out of her. "Let's grab that chair, huh?" she said, gesturing toward a recliner.

"Yeah."

They moved together, accidentally brushing arms, and it was torture, this thing they were doing.

"I miss you, Bec," he said quietly, under his breath, clearly regretting it the minute he said it.

"I miss you too," she said, her heart aching in time with each beat. "But you made your choice, Alex." Because what was the point if he didn't get it? If he didn't *want* to get it? Mom had said all along you can't make a man do what he doesn't want to. So here they were.

When his mouth firmed and his face went blank, she knew here was exactly where they'd stay. One of these days, she'd stop hoping for different.

# Chapter 26

"Emergency."

Alex jerked at Jack's flat, hard voice. He looked around the bunkhouse, trying to remember what he'd been doing. But everything was dim, and he just... didn't know.

The flutter of panic at not knowing still existed, but it was so faint underneath all this exhaustion, this fog that had become something like a comfortable blanket he didn't even fight it anymore.

Somewhere below, a dog whined, and Alex realized with another start that Star had been sleeping on his feet. How long had he been standing here?

Best not to dwell on that. "What kind of emergency?" he asked.

"Just come on," Jack said. "Out in the north pasture."

Alex frowned, but he followed Jack. "What's the problem?"

"Hard to explain." Jack nodded toward the stables, where his and Alex's horses were saddled, reins tied to the post. "Follow me, yeah?"

He opened his mouth to say something about Jack riding, but it seemed such an effort to form those kinds of words, to press on what the emergency was. So, in the end, he simply got onto the horse and followed Jack on his up toward the north pasture.

Something eased inside of him, an odd tension he

wouldn't know how to name, wasn't even sure he'd known it was there.

Here, on the horse, he was in control. He felt some stirring of that rightness he'd felt when he'd first arrived—fresh air and mountains, a trustworthy horse beneath him taking him wherever he needed to go.

When they reached the north pasture, Gabe was already there. Alex frowned a little because the fence seemed fine and the cattle were all a good distance away.

He got off the horse and walked toward Gabe, Jack falling into step behind him.

"What's the emergency?" Alex demanded, something prickling at the back of his neck. An odd foreboding that reminded him too much of a desert road with these same two men. And one who was dead.

"Let's call it less of an emergency and more of an intervention."

Alex stopped walking, but Jack was behind him and gave him a little shove toward Gabe. Alex glared, but Jack only gave him another shove.

"Enough."

"You're right, Alex. It is enough," Gabe said, that obnoxious grin spread over his face. The kind of grin he lobbed at anyone who crossed him.

"I don't know what's gotten into you two—"

"Friendship, I guess," Jack said, still giving him little shoves.

"I'm warning you, Jack. Knock it off."

Jack resolutely shoved him again. "Or what? Hell, Alex, you can barely walk these days."

Alex stood to his full height, glaring as much down at

Jack as he could manage. "I'm fine. Your limp is worse than mine." Might be an unfair jab, but it was true.

"Fine." Gabe laughed, that hard, sarcastic edge filling up this little corner of the pasture. The breeze was cool as the sun set in the west, an occasional cow's moo breaking through the peaceful evening. Clouds billowed in the east, dark and angry.

"You haven't been fine since that grenade blew up, and in the past few weeks, you've withered away into nothing. I could take you with one hand tied behind my back."

"My ass."

"Then let's fight."

"What?" Alex scoffed as Gabe held his hands up in fists. "I'm not going to fight you."

"Scared?"

"You're not going to insult me into it. I'm not fighting you."

"Okay, how's this—you land a punch on either one of us, even a weak one, and we'll let this be."

"Let *what* be?"

"You, dipshit," Jack interrupted. "You. You're a zombie at best, killing yourself at worst. Ruining everything before it's even gotten off the ground."

"I haven't ruined anything. The bunkhouse is almost finished. We've had a good calving season, should leave our finances in the black, and—"

"And what about Becca?"

"Fine." They wanted to fight, then he'd punch the hell out of both of them. He swung at Jack, surprised to find himself stumbling when Jack easily sidestepped out of the way.

Alex found his footing and shook it off. Just needed

to clear his head. He knew Gabe's and Jack's weak spots. He could exploit them. He fake lunged at Jack, then went after Gabe again, but somehow it didn't work. He didn't connect with anyone. Just the hard ground.

He sprawled out there, nothing in his body responding the way it should. He felt shaken and weak, and that wasn't who he was. He struggled to get up, but it was too much, so he simply rolled over and looked up at the dark clouds encroaching on blue sky.

"You can't even get up, Alex. When is that going to sink in? You're *killing* yourself."

He had arguments, but he couldn't seem to verbalize them. Even in his mind, they seemed to simply turn to ash and blow away on the hard wind.

"I'll be fine. I can fix it." But even to his own ears it sounded like rote memorization and the words failed to feel right or make sense.

"No, man. You can't."

He couldn't be fixed.

He couldn't fix it.

It was Mom all over again. Driving into the embankment. Becca demanding more of him than he could safely give. He was not in control. He had no say.

He couldn't fix this.

Jack and Gabe each grabbed an arm and hauled him to his feet. Even once he was steady enough to stand on his own, they didn't let go of him.

"When we were discharged, what did the shrink tell us?" Jack asked softly.

"That we were fine." They had been *cleared*.

"But that if we stopped feeling fine, it was time to talk to someone," Jack said, and his voice sounded rough and pained. "I know you got the same talk I did, and I know…it sucks and I don't want to do it, but this is worse. Watching you do this to yourself is worse."

Alex swallowed, but his throat was too tight. "I just haven't figured it out yet."

"You don't have to figure it out by yourself. And I don't just mean the therapist, though I'd say that'd be a hell of a first step. All of us. All we've wanted is to help, but you have to let us."

Alex looked at Gabe. "I was supposed to…" He was supposed to lead. He was supposed to handle his own shit so everyone around him could handle theirs. He'd had to be strong for his dad, prove he hadn't been damaged by being in that car. Had to be strong for Jack and Gabe because he'd failed them already. Had to be strong for Becca because she deserved better than a broken soldier.

And he *couldn't* be.

He thought the admission would break him, turn him into dust where he stood, but something loosened inside of him. Something eased.

"You know that through that gate, a ways down the hill, is Shaw property. Colin's at school. Monica's there."

Alex stiffened, but Gabe's and Jack's grips on his arms didn't ease.

"You gotta make the choice," Jack said. "It has to be yours."

"And if you can't make it for yourself, make it for us. For Becca. For the people who love you and can't watch you kill yourself like this."

"She said she loved me," Alex offered, because even now he wasn't sure he could wrap his head around that. That she'd looked him in the eye and said she'd loved him.

"No shit, Sherlock, and even two bitter ex-SEALs aren't stupid enough to think you don't love her right back."

"You told Monica I was going to…"

"Becca just asked her to be there. *You* make the choice if you go, if you talk."

"Becca…" Something bitter and sharp poked at him. "So you three sat around and concocted this intervention. Forced my hand and—"

Jack and Gabe let him go. They stepped toward their horses. "We went to Becca. *We* asked her to set it up with Monica."

"And she jumped at the chance?"

Gabe and Jack exchanged a look. Alex glared at Jack then Gabe when they didn't answer. "Well?"

"She told us not to hold our breath," Gabe offered, raising his eyebrows in challenge. "She said you made your choice and she doesn't think you'll ever change it."

It didn't hurt. Why would it? He *had* made his choice, and she had made hers. She couldn't give him time to fix things. That was her deal, not his.

"We want the Alex we know and love back, not this shadow," Gabe said, softer now. "Whether Becca says it or not, that's what she wants too."

"But the next step is up to you. Not us. We just had to try and help. That's all we ever wanted to do. Not fix it for you. Not take away your control. Just lend a hand, a shoulder, help."

"Take it, Alex."

He didn't say anything, and Gabe and Jack both

shook their heads, Jack muttering something about Becca being right.

Fuck it. He'd prove them all wrong. He'd go right over to Monica and prove to them all some therapist could not fix what was wrong with him.

He angrily flung open the gate, led his horse through, and then got on. And then he rode, hard and fast and without a whole lot of thought to safety. Thunder rumbled somewhere in the distance as the sky darkened around him, and all he could think was he wanted to ride like this until he was far away.

He wanted to run until he had control again. He wanted to be far away from Blue Valley, where time always seemed to slip through his fingertips.

He was panting when he reached the old Shaw cabin Monica was renting. What was he doing here? He could handle this himself. It would happen. He just needed more time. He stood and stared at the house, trying to talk himself out of this whole thing.

But he thought of taking a swing at Gabe and Jack and falling flat on his face and…

Maybe he couldn't fix a damn thing. He didn't think Monica could either…but he was here, wasn't he? Becca thought he'd made a choice, and standing here, he could only think about all those times she'd stood up to him or the guys despite her nerves and her insecurities. She'd stood up to her mother.

And what she'd never once done was run away like he wanted to.

Whatever epiphany he'd been working toward with that was cut short when the front door opened. Monica smiled at him.

He hated shrink smiles.

"Why don't you come in? If you decide not to talk, that's fine, but you're giving me the creeps standing in my yard, doing nothing."

He felt compelled to move forward at that. "Sorry," he offered.

She gestured him inside and he paused at the threshold. "I'm not here to talk. I'm here to prove a point."

Her smile didn't falter, though it changed. "Sounds about right. Want anything to drink?"

"No."

"Want to have a seat?"

"No."

Still that pleasant smile didn't leave her face, even as she perched herself on the arm of the well-worn couch. "You didn't come to talk, but maybe you'd be okay with listening for a little bit?"

Alex shrugged. He was here to prove a point after all—that he didn't need this. Why not listen?

"See that picture?" she said, pointing to the fireplace mantel and a picture of a man in an air force uniform.

"My father," Monica said conversationally. "You remind me of him."

"All us military guys alike?"

"Not by a long shot. But he was a leader, much like you."

Alex didn't know what to say to that, especially since he remembered all too well her saying her father had come back from Desert Storm a changed man.

"It took me a long time to understand him. A lot of years, a lot of maturity, and a lot of studying and working as a therapist. It's a strange thing to help people because of the person you couldn't help, and a stranger thing to finally understand him through other people."

Which didn't make any sense to him. He'd always understood his father. A good man. An uncomplicated man. Said what he meant or said nothing at all.

It hurt a little, because even in this mental fog Alex knew he wasn't being honest. Not with the people around him, and not with himself.

He was a mess. He was broken. He was unfixable.

"My dad, and a lot of men like him, survive the military thinking everything is under their control. The good things were because of him, and bad things were really because of him. Because if he had to admit that shit happened because of bad timing or being in the wrong place at the wrong time, he'd have to admit and accept he had no control out there, and that's fatal to a soldier, isn't it?"

Each word hit with startling accuracy, like bullets. Piercing through the skin and the heart. Alex stood completely still, staring at the picture of a stranger, but he felt every blow.

"He held on to his control even when he was retired, because it was his comfort zone. His safety blanket. Because thinking we have control, for those of us who want it, is safe. It's easy. It's a hell of a lot harder to realize it doesn't matter what we do or decide or want, the universe doesn't give a shit."

It was that damn same realization again. That it didn't matter. That he couldn't fix anything. That Monica was absolutely right. The universe around him definitely did not give a shit what he wanted, what he was trying to do.

"So you've got this all coiled inside you," she continued, curling her fingers into a fist and tapping it to her stomach, dark-blue eyes making unerring contact. And it didn't escape Alex's notice she'd gone from using *my father* or *they* to *you*.

Still, he didn't stop her. He didn't know how.

"And you push it down, and you control it, but see, your brain isn't under your control. Not completely. Not when you sleep, so that's when it kicks your ass. And it will. It just will—until you stop trying to control it into submission."

*How?* he wanted to ask, and yet the word wouldn't form.

"It's hard to convince a man who survived that way that it isn't your world to shape," she said, and maybe it was the emotion in her voice that kept Alex from stopping her. "That you can't keep everyone safe, and you can't always be fine. I tried to convince him he was not worthless without a mission. You are not pointless. I think that is the hardest thing for men in your position to understand and accept."

Alex felt a lump in his throat, and when he swallowed, it didn't dissolve. With no mission, he was pointless. Hell, it felt like *with* a mission, he was worthless. He didn't know what to do if he wasn't saving people. If he wasn't fixing the bunkhouse or building this foundation. If he was doing that, he wasn't this broken thing.

This broken thing that seemed to envelop him deeper and deeper, stronger and stronger, until he could barely function in his denial. Because he wasn't a stupid man, even if he was a stubborn one.

Things weren't right. He wasn't right, and he didn't

know *how* to change that. He'd run into gunfire and hell, but he'd always, *always* run from all this emotion inside of him.

"So that's all it takes to fix a person?" he asked hoarsely. "Accept you're not pointless without a mission?" How the hell would he ever do that?

"I can't make you who you were before, Alex. No therapist could," she said gently. "But none of us are what we were before war touched our lives. I can't fix you. You can't fix you in the military sense of solving a problem. You are not a problem. You are not defective, and believe it or not, therapy isn't here to fix you. It's here to give you the tools to deal with the way you've changed. This, here, is you."

Thunder rumbled in the distance, lightning flashing in the windows, but the rain hadn't started yet. He had time.

"There are so many things you have to offer. You don't have to be perfect, or feel in control, to offer them. It's a tough lesson, and you can't expect it to happen overnight."

It was those words more than all of the rest that cracked something open inside of him that had been locked tight for a long time. Maybe since before his navy days. Maybe since his mom had died. To consider his father hadn't wanted him to be *in control* after Mom died, he'd just wanted him there. To consider Gabe and Jack didn't need him to be the perfect leader anymore, they might just need him to be a friend. To consider Becca might…mean what she said. That she didn't need him to be all right, she just needed him to let her in.

"I know you're no stranger to hard work, Alex.

Healing is hard work. It will take time, but if you allow yourself to open up to the conflict you're feeling instead of shutting it all down, some of that healing is going to happen."

Then Monica smiled a real smile, none of the fake-pleasantry stuff. "Love is also a great help in that department. The giving of it and the receiving of it. You have a lot of people who love you."

People he'd given his love to but he hadn't exactly opened to receiving. No, he'd run away from that. "I need to go."

"Well, whenever you're ready to make another appointment, you let me know."

Even in the midst of all this *feeling*, that rankled. "Was that what this was? An appointment?"

"It was whatever you want it to be."

Whatever he wanted it to be.

He wanted it to be a start.

———⁓———

It was raining. Becca watched it pour in sheets against the window, a worried frown frozen on her face. She knew Jack and Gabe were worried too, but they were dealing with it by drinking and playing cards at the kitchen table while the dogs snoozed underneath.

Becca hadn't been able to stomach it. Maybe if it hadn't been storming she could have pretended like she didn't care if he didn't come home. She wouldn't even be remotely tempted to call Monica and see if he was there and safe.

"I'm going to go check on the horses," she called in a rush, and was sure neither Jack nor Gabe believed her.

"You know he was a Navy SEAL, right?" Gabe called. "Pretty sure he can survive a thunderstorm."

She wasn't so certain Alex could survive *anything* right now. She wasn't going to go looking for him though. She was just going to…check on the horses. Like she said.

She went over to the line of boots and shoved hers on, pulled on a coat, and flicked the hood up. She sloshed through the mud and rain toward the stables. The air was cool, the rain itself colder, but the heat of the day lingered enough to make it bearable.

The animals were still her refuge, and maybe if she talked to them, she could figure out how to cope with all this hope inside of her. No matter how hard she tried, she couldn't quash it. She loved him, and she wanted him to be happy and smile again and…

*Ugh.*

She made it to the stable and pulled open the door, practically stumbling inside. Alex looked up from where he was standing next to Pal. He gave the horse an absent pat and then stepped out of the stall.

"Everything all right?" he asked in that awful empty tone he'd been using all week.

She bit back the *Where have you been? I've been worried half to death.* "That was going to be my line for you."

"You're soaked."

"Yes. It's raining quite hard."

He blinked, looked out the door behind her, and then he started walking into it. Without another word, just stepped out into the downpour.

"Alex, what are you doing?"

Because he wasn't walking back to the house, he was just *standing* there. Face upturned to the sky, getting absolutely soaked. She stayed inside the building, though stray drops of rain blew into the doorway where she was standing.

"I'd say I finally found some perfect timing." He turned to face her, eyes locking on hers even through the rain. "Remember when I said no rain-soaked speeches?"

Becca swallowed, her heart tripping over itself. "Yeah."

"Maybe I lied. Maybe I lied about a lot of things. Lies are cowardly. I always thought that, but it's funny when you can lie enough to yourself that you're downright convinced you're not telling any lies at all."

She stepped forward. As much as she wanted him to keep talking, they couldn't have a real conversation in the rain. "Let's go inside."

"No. You deserve rain-soaked speeches and far better than me."

She took another step toward him in the squelching mud. "We deserve each other. There's nothing *better* than that. What could be better than the man I love?" Because she wasn't going to shout nonsense at him over the rain. If he wanted to talk, they would get straight to the heart of the matter.

Rain poured down his face, but he didn't blink. "You don't still love me," he said, something like flat certainty in his voice.

"Like hell I don't."

He stepped toward her, and there was so little between them now all she wanted to do was close it.

Eviscerate that space between them. This was too much, being apart, fighting, trying to give up and failing.

She wanted him. She loved him.

"I'm broken," he said, his voice raspy and barely audible over the steadily pounding rain.

"Aren't we all?" she returned, her voice a little broken itself. She knew it was a thing for him to admit that. Big. Important. "You think I don't have a few screwed-up pieces inside of me? It's called being human, Alex. You're the only one who's holding yourself to an impossible standard of righteous perfection."

"A lot of people have been saying that. About the perfect thing. I didn't think I was trying to be perfect. I was just trying to be…"

"Perfect. So nothing could ever go wrong again."

"You know, my mom was killed by a drunk driver."

Becca nodded, because she did. Burt had told both her and her mom, though he'd never been much on sharing the details.

"I was in the car."

It hit her hard, so hard the word *what* whooshed out of her on a gasp.

"I was in the car. But I was on the opposite side and in the back, so I was fine. Barely a scratch. I was eight, and I just… For a long time, I'd just go through the day, over and over again, trying to find a way to change it. To find what I could have done to fix it."

"Alex."

"Eventually, I…moved on, or whatever. I decided I couldn't fix that, but I could fix other things. I could help people. I could save people. With the right skills. Because fixing it, finding the right skills, it means you don't ever actually have to deal with the grief or the loss or the pain. You keep doing, and you don't have to feel. That's been so much of my life, and I don't know how to let it go."

He tried to wipe the rain off his face, and she couldn't help but wonder if there were tears mixed in, because she was definitely crying herself. Crying for that little boy and for the man who thought he could fix anything.

"Maybe you don't have to let it go so much as... accept you're going to save people in a much different way now. Because you will still be helping people. This thing we're building is going to help people."

"I think, maybe, I might need to let it help me a little too."

"I would agree, and I would also suggest maybe you could let *me* help you a little bit. Especially with the emotion part of things. I'm not afraid of them. I'll hold your hand through them."

He reached out, pushing wet strands of hair off her forehead. "I don't know how, but maybe it's a skill that you learn like any other. You think?"

She nodded.

"I can't promise to make everything right. I can't even promise that I...I'll always know what to do. I don't know how... I..." He took a deep breath and let it out, the rain pelting them at an even steadier pace. "This is a really shitty rain-soaked speech."

"You're touching me, so it's going pretty good." She'd remember this moment always. The moment he didn't try to make promises or fix anything, the moment he admitted he didn't know *how*. It was everything.

He kept brushing his fingers across her temples, down her cheeks. "I don't know how to be a man who isn't in control of everything, but I guess I have to learn. No, not I guess. I *have* to learn. Maybe you could help out with that?"

Everything inside of her soared, and she didn't care that she was drenched or cold. Not with Alex asking for help, opening himself up. "I could help, and I want to."

"Okay, good. Good." He visibly swallowed, running a hand over her wet hair, cupping the back of her head, and bringing her mouth to his. But before he kissed her or let her kiss him, he pressed his wet forehead to hers.

"I love you, Becca."

She tried to choke back a sob, but he probably heard it even over the din of the rain. She leaned into him, clutching his shirt. "I love you too," she managed to squeak.

"I won't always be perfect or even very good at this whole thing, but—"

"You just have to love me, Alex. That's all. Love me. Talk to me. Let me in. It's not so hard, I don't think. Not if we both want it and are willing to work for it."

"I'm more than willing. More than. Hard work isn't what scares me, but I don't want to disappoint you, and I don't want to hurt you."

"You'll probably do both. I think it's okay if we tell each other when we do and work to do better. I think that's...that's love, when it's working. When you can tell each other what you want, what you need. And you know what I need right now?"

"What?"

"To get the hell inside. It's *pouring*."

He laughed against her cheek, pulling her in tight against him. "Thank you," he whispered into her ear.

"For what?"

"For loving me. And telling me when it didn't work and not stopping loving me when I was an ass."

She linked hands with him, pulling him toward the ranch. "As rain-soaked speeches go, it wasn't half-bad, but I'd like to be dry now. And possibly naked."

"And you think men have one-track minds."

"Turns out women do too. Or at least this woman." She kept tugging him toward the house, wanting to be inside and dry and warm and, yes, naked.

But mostly she wanted to curl up with him in bed, knowing he'd stay. Knowing he loved her, and knowing that even if things were hard again, they'd tell each other. They'd give, and they'd hurt, and they'd probably get mad.

But together.

# Epilogue

SUMMER STRETCHED OUT, A MOUNTAIN OF WORK AND SUN. While Becca and Monica worked on Becca's therapeutic horsemanship hours and the foundation programs, Alex and Gabe focused on the bunkhouse, Jack on the cattle with Hick.

Things weren't perfect, but they were clicking. Alex wouldn't say any of the guys were quite comfortable around Monica yet, but it had only been a few weeks. Her kid, Colin, was a riot, and all three of the guys got a kick out of teaching him about things around the ranch.

They'd all decided by way of unanimous vote to put off bringing men in. They still had a lot of work to do, not just with the ranch, but with themselves. They had decided to give themselves time, and with time, all of the foundation's goals seemed infinitely possible.

"Are you going to get out of bed anytime soon?" Becca demanded, finishing braiding her hair by fastening a bright-yellow band around the end.

He had no idea why, but it never failed to arouse him, the deft way she spiraled her hair together. Not that much about her failed to arouse him.

"I like watching you get ready in the morning," he replied from where he was still sprawled out on her bed. "Now come here."

She rolled her eyes. "I am *not* falling for that. I have work to do, and you have your appointment to get to."

He grimaced, because though the therapy sessions with Monica were…well, helpful, he didn't particularly enjoy them.

"You've been doing better," Becca said gently, smoothing over that annoying observation by scooting onto the edge of the bed next to him.

Which was true. He still had nightmares far more than he was comfortable with, but he felt himself regaining his footing. It was hard, like learning a new skill, to try to not control everything, but he could actually feel the progress he'd made, in his bones.

That progress had some to do with therapy, but it also had some to do with the beautiful woman sitting next to him. "Maybe it's just all the sex," he replied, tugging the band out of her hair to her shriek of outrage.

"Damn it, Maguire."

But her mouth was curved, and when he rolled her under him, she did nothing but ineffectively give him a little push…that quickly turned into her arms around his neck.

"You know the bunkhouse is mostly done. The guys can move out whenever we want to kick them out."

She cocked her head at that, studying him in that way he was learning to appreciate rather than fear.

"*The guys* as in…you won't be going with them?"

"I've been thinking."

She smiled, ruffling his hair with her hands, toying with that lock that never would stay all the way down. "You've been thinking, huh?"

"I don't know what point there is to me moving out there when I'm planning to spend every night in your bed."

Her smile softened, and she brushed a kiss against his jaw. "I like that line of thinking."

"Good."

"That's probably something I'm going to have to break to my mother at dinner tonight."

"You sure you want me there for that?"

"Oh, you'll be there," she returned, trying to squirm free of him. "Now let me get to work."

"Hold on a sec."

"We do not have time for sex!"

"I bet I could change your mind," he returned with a grin, nuzzling into her neck in a way that made her go boneless. "But that's not why I was asking you to hold on."

"Then why?" she asked on a sigh, melting into him.

He considered it, the timing, the way it would ruin the whole plan he'd been making, but then he figured that was kind of symbolic. Tossing out a plan in lieu of a better opportunity, one that would make her happy.

He hoped.

He rolled off of her and off the bed. "Stay put," he ordered, striding out of the room. Nerves threatened, but he wouldn't have gotten to this point, wouldn't have started a plan if he wasn't sure. Even now, he wasn't a man who did things without being sure.

He went to his bedroom and opened the top drawer with a jerk. Okay, so he was a little nervous. Didn't mean he was wrong—just meant he was an idiot.

He grabbed the item and stalked right back to her room, propelled by…something. Those nerves, irritation at himself, whatever.

But she was sitting on her bed, braiding the hair he'd messed up, and that smoothed it all away. The fears or jitters or whatever else, because how could he not want this?

Every day. Always.

"So what am I screwing up my day's schedule for?" she asked him with an arched brow, pushing to her feet.

He could have said a great many things, but he found his throat too tight to get any of them out. So he held out what he'd brought instead.

She fell right back into a sitting position on her bed. "That's a ring," she said on a shaky exhale.

"My mother's engagement ring, actually," he returned, twisting the ring in the light dappling the room. "She was buried with her wedding ring, but Dad thought I should have this."

"Alex." She fisted a hand to her heart.

"Don't cry," he said, walking toward her. "Just say yes. Please."

She blinked profusely, clearly trying to keep the tears at bay. "You didn't ask me a question."

"Always so difficult," he muttered with the shake of his head. Then he figured he might as well go whole hog, because he would, without a shadow of a doubt, do anything to make her happy.

He got down on one knee, wincing a little when he remembered it was his bad knee. "Hold on."

"Oh, get up here," she said, pulling him onto the bed before he could switch to the other knee, covering his face with sloppy kisses, wet with tears.

"I love you, Bec. I don't know that the nightmares will ever completely go away, but—"

"Shut up," she managed, her voice rough. "Like I care about that." She kissed him on the mouth. "I love you. As you are, however you are," she murmured into him, where it reached into his soul, his bones.

"Becca?" It was Jack's voice echoing through the hallway.

"Go away," Alex returned, because he was not going to be interrupted.

But Alex and Becca both grinned when they could hear Jack's groan all the way through the door.

"Your damn goat is on the roof again, and I don't care what you're doing in there, but I am not touching that rooster."

"Goat duty calls," Becca said with a sigh, still touching his face, a few stray tears dotting hers.

"This first," Alex said, slipping the ring onto her finger. "Proposal trumps goat."

"Every now and again," she returned, her grin wide and pretty and sure.

She'd healed him, in some ways, and he was still healing in others, but he knew he'd found where he belonged, and he was ready to take that leap of faith. Forever.

# About the Author

Nicole Helm writes down-to-earth contemporary romance specializing in people who don't live close enough to neighbors for them to be a problem. When she's not writing or taking care of her two rambunctious boys, she spends her time dreaming about someday owning a barn. Visit her at nicolehelm.com.

## Also by Nicole Helm